AN IMPRINT OF WHAT BOOKS PRESS | LOS ANGELES

ALSO BY CHUCK ROSENTHAL

Loop's Progress

Experiments with Life and Deaf

Loop's End

Elena of the Stars

Jack Kerouac's Avatar Angel: His Last Novel

Never Let Me Go, a memoir

My Mistress, Humanity

The Heart of Mars

Are We Not There Yet? Travels in Nepal, North India, and Bhutan

Coyote O'Donohughe's History of Texas

West of Eden: A Life in 21st Century Los Angeles

Ten Thousand Heavens

Tomorrow You'll Be One of Us (sci-fi poems with Gail Wronsky & Gronk)

The Shortest Farewells Are the Best (flash noir with Gail Wronsky)

The Legend of La Diosa

You Can Fly: A Sequel to the Peter Pan Tales

How the Animals Around You Think: The Semiotics of Animal Cognition

The Hammer, the Sickle and the Heart: Trotsky and Kahlo in Mexico

LET'S FACE THE MUSIC AND DANCE

LET'S FACE THE MUSIC AND DANCE

Chuck Rosenthal

Publisher's Cataloging-In-Publication Data

Names: Rosenthal, Chuck, 1951- author.
Title: Let's face the music and dance / Chuck Rosenthal.
Description: Topanga, CA : Giant Claw, an imprint of What Books Press, [2022]
Identifiers: ISBN 9781733378949 (paperback)
Subjects: LCSH: Novelists--California--Topanga--Fiction. | Aging--Fiction. | Love--Fiction. |
    Ontology--Fiction. | Horses--Fiction.
Classification: LCC PS3568.O8368 L48 2022 | DDC 813/.6--dc23

Cover art: Gronk, *untitled*, 2021
Book design by Ash Good, www.ashgood.com

Giant Claw
363 South Topanga Canyon Boulevard
Topanga, CA 90290

GIANTCLAWPRESS.COM

In memory of my brother,
Wil Rosenthal 1945-2021

"There may be trouble ahead
But while there's moonlight
And music and love and romance
Let's face the music and dance . . ."

—Irving Berlin

PREFACE

LET'S FACE THE MUSIC AND DANCE combines several narrative forms. The first is a third person contemporary literary novel following the lives of two characters, a novelist, Path, and a poet, Carla. That story folds around a first person philosophical essay by the novel's narrator on the ontology of desire. Amid those narrative lines emerges an historical novel by Path set in New Orleans and Vicksburg leading up to Grant's 1863 siege, a novel that borrows freely from the film *Casablanca*.

NEXILE
COME ALL YE FAITHLESS

PATH WAS LIVING ON THE EDGE of something. What? Not so many nights ago he sat across a round glass table from his lover, Carla, whom he'd now known and loved for over half his life, now a relatively long life, sixty-six years and ticking. She was six years younger. A shaded ceiling light glowed above them. There was a dog, Nadine, twelve years old, diabetic, going blind, a big brown hound. She lay at Carla's feet. A noise outside and she lifted her head. Her throat rumbled. She was yet on watch. She would never give it up. Not until she died. What would Path hold onto with that kind of tenacity? The table was tall, a bar table, and they sat on stools made of Mexican leather and wood. The house around them, built on the side of a hill, was a summer cabin as early as 1923. Historical placement: In the last two years the idols of their worlds, for that's what it was, worlds, at least two of them, if not more, those idols began to die: William Gass, Larry Levis, David Bowie, Leonard Cohen, Galway Kinnel, Adrienne Rich, C.D. Wright, Jean Valentine. What did that say. It said, Don't ask. Just get in line. Nothing lay in front of Path but inevitability. Eight years ago he'd contracted cancer and he thought his future had been stripped. Then he didn't die and the future fell in front of him again, blank, as if he'd closed every door, in and out, and nothing surrounded him but nothingness. His lover raised her glass of tonic on ice, a slice of lime. Only weeks ago they'd stopped drinking liquor because it was killing her liver. He joined the bash of abstinence. He'd been drinking hard since he was thirteen. As someone said to him, that's a good long run. They touched tonics. She sipped. She said, I want a glass of wine. He said, I can taste the bourbon on the tip of my tongue. A couple of nihilists suffering to save their lives.

He bought a bicycle. Once he'd been an athlete. It was hard to tell how good. Explaining would be complicated. And narcissistic. He hated that about the arts, the amount of narcissism it took to survive. Now, with the ubiquitous internet, his computer screen was lambasted by poets and painters, photographs of kids and pets, lunches and dinners, breakfasts, bees, and birds, photographs of paintings, dogs, cats, and horses, unabashed selfies, photographs of photographs, flattening the flat world flatter, flat as a pancake, fat self flattery even flatter than flat, what's wrong with that; that's what's wrong, lives streamed out on Instagram, titter, twitter, tweeter, fee-fi-fo, you wish. It was only 2017. Kobe Bryant wasn't dead yet. We had yet to fall to the Covid Plague.

And yet, we're here to simplify. Complicated task enough.

The new bike had seven speeds. In 1975 he'd bought a ten speed Sekia. It was light as a feather. He rode it everywhere wherever he lived. Even in the winter, if the pavement was free of snow, he rode. Finally, he bought a motorcycle. Then a bigger one. It was 1982. He drove that bike from Davis, up the California coast, Oregon, Washington; in the wooded forests of Washington it rained and rained. You must brake very evenly in the rain, front and back. In Port Angeles, he ferried to Victoria Island, drove about, then ferried to Vancouver. He crossed Canada. Something should have happened then. Maybe something did. All that time alone, three hundred bucks and a sleeping bag, each night a fire and a bottle of cheap, Yugoslav red wine. He camped, waiting for the devil. Turned out to be a good way to avoid the devil. But the devil doesn't tell you, here I am; once, you slept with him, Path, you loved him; he bought you tea and oranges that came all the way from China, steaks and booze; look at your beautiful body, said the devil, and you stared down, Is this what you want, is this what you want, and the devil said, Yes.

He never liked the image of the black hole, he didn't like holes, but this was a multiverse where things were disappearing and he wanted to be in one where things emerged, the debris of other realities exploding anew, but he wasn't even the god of his own imagination and he wants to live a life that isn't about himself. Who am I, his lover said to him, who are you, and he said, St. George, raise a sword against the dragon of my ambition; he remembered a summer evening in the backyard of his childhood home in a city spread on the shore of a Great Lake where the nights were gray and the days were gray and everything was under a blue shadow, dusk fell holy and leaden, his father had just come down an extension ladder that he'd scaled, twenty feet into limbs and leaves, to gather Bartlett pears the size of your fist; Path stood below with a fielder's mitt as his father threw them down, the pears pushed through the leaves, phoosh- phoosh, then smack into the mitt, as the light fell away, fireflies blinked in the air, gnats and mosquitos thickened, and the swallows swept in, diving through the clouds of insects, the shoulders of their wings ripping at the air as they descended, rdr-rdr-rdr; his father, who fought in the Pacific, said, Listen, that's the sound the Zeros made when they dove.

Path was discovering gravity.

Carla drew a hit of mild Indica from the waterpipe, after that she lit a cigarette, a long Parliament, he fidgeted, he wasn't a smoker, not much of one, and pot exploded inside his head, Have a drink, Carla said to him, Don't suffer; he went to the refrigerator to get ice, in Australia when he asked a hotel keeper for an ice bucket the manager looked up from where he was playing cards with another man and two women and said, I forgot, an American; Americans used ice; in India you couldn't find it, in Mexico you couldn't drink it, the French drank wine, the British drank their booze stiff, he thought of these things every time he fetched ice; here in his kitchen he puts three cubes in a small glass and pours a shot of rye. It tastes very good.

Here, Path is determined to be neither author, narrator, nor character in this story. Charlie Parker called be-bop a story, each note could be a story; Parker hated the term be-bop, but you didn't get to name your terms, name your names. Path is living in the center of a vacuum. An Existential one. Not in the terms of common parlance, but in the Sartrean sense. Meaning pouring out of him into meaninglessness, meaninglessness pouring back in. He said to Carla, Everything I touch turns into nothing, she said, Like Midas, only the opposite, he said, Did I touch you once, Once, she said, once you did. He wished she'd been wistful, but she wasn't wistful, as she let parts of herself fall away, her heart rent like the Temple curtain in Jerusalem the moment Christ expired.

Lecture to No One:

Aristotle said that stories had three parts: a beginning, a middle, and an end. The beginning was where you began, nothing comes before the beginning, the end was where you ended, nothing came after, Path wanted to begin at the end. If he were writing a novel he would give the impression that he was at the beginning of something or in the middle of something that the beginning led up to, a result, the end of the dilemma or dilemmas, or at the very least write a narrative, a story, that explained, through psychology and scenes, how he ended up in the dilemmas that he's in at the end. But here we shall begin at what is currently an end, if every day the end stretches out, a constant present that is constantly the end; Path once wrote a book, or rather worked on a book, that went on and on, it wasn't a journal (and neither is this), he left that book about 800 pages in. Some days now he looks at it. Kerouac invented a kind of constant present in his work, at least the work about his adulthood, and maintained it by the impression that it was about the NOW, or as Cassidy called it, the IT, by saying that he never rewrote, never edited. A ruse, of course, even unto himself. He was writing about what had already happened, if it happened at all; he was a very smart man, well read, at least in terms of literature and Buddhism, but his understanding of narrative was peculiarly naïve, once anything is written, it becomes the past, immediately, even if you never touch it again, even in the present tense. It's part of the absurdity of the *first person present*, which, even as it is being written, is neither written nor conceived in the present tense and only read in the present tense if you're blind enough to believe you're reading something that's happening as you read, which, of course, we all often do, for the most part, even when something is written in the past, or future for that matter, because that is where we live, in our present moments; narrative, narrative fiction, is a hall of mirrors and the author, via the narrator, is the magician twisting and sliding them, with enough craft and art to hold us in sympathy, if not empathy, with the language constructs called characters; how committed we are emotionally to those constructs is an inexact dance; that's why there are literary schools. For example: What is *stream of consciousness*? Stated most simply, it's the recapitulation of the consciousness of some *character*, though that character doesn't exist, is not a person; the character is a deduced construct based on the fact that we are apparently reading their thoughts, and someone, the narrator, is a singularly omniscient *teller*, capable of offering us the purported access to the character's thoughts, to the consciousness that isn't consciousness at all, but words, words written, and not even by the narrator, but by an author; we read a construction of what we are pretending, that a character thinks, that we read what she thinks, even if we choose to re-read it again and again. Once, when Path had colleagues, so to speak, they taught stream of consciousness, Joyce, Woolf, Faulkner, just like that, naively, as first person present, even with their Ph.D.'s plastered on their foreheads, though often they confused stream of consciousness with free indirect discourse, another lecture for another time, if at all; regardless, this is neither, though it's the folk psychology of literature teachers to describe any running discourse that appears to arise spontaneously, like Kerouac's, rather than lean on the structures of plot or story, to be deemed stream of consciousness, i.e. that the author is using it as a technique for exposition, and so too, then, for the first person present; at the very least, if narration is some kind of magic trick of rhetoric (thank you Wayne Booth), then how sophisticated is the audience, how sophisticated is the magician; for my part, I want to see all the cards and yet be surprised, a line, if we want to continue this way, between author as magician and author as wizard.

Right now we're going to pretend to follow Path as he leaves his home to go see his horse, his mare, Nikki, La Femme Nikkita, for the last time, though it isn't necessarily the last time this time, whenever he thinks it might be, it's hard to describe all of the circumstances, though eventually I might, he touches his horse on the neck, pets her gently and weeps, When it finally is the last time he will weep for days, he will cry so hard his chest aches, his preparation will have meant nothing. You can't prepare for death either. But right now he's going to his horse for one of the hundreds of goodbye's that he'll tell her, though it will be meaningless to her and none of it will suffice at the moment when he must, in fact, give her up, He gathers his water bottle, a bag of carrots, an apple, hitches his trail watch to his belt loop, puts his sunglasses in one vest packet and his wallet in another, puts his open-blade hunting knife, sheathed, on his belt, puts on his straw hat with feathers that he's gathered from the trail stuck in its brim, He turns and spies a magazine on his kitchen counter, It's a magazine he often gets in the mail and immediately throws away without looking at it, an alumnae magazine from his undergraduate school, Allegheny College. At the top it says, in capitals, **ALLEGHENY**, with SRING 2018 in the right corner. On the cover, the tip of a football, and an ALLEGHENY banner laid over a blue-black sweatshirt with a golden **A** on it. There's some Polaroid-like photos, cheerleader here, graduation gown there—enough—Carla must have mistakenly brought it in with a pile of fashion catalogues. Before casting it into the recycling he casually flips the magazine open and it falls onto page 38, a list of years and names, and he sees a year close to his own graduation, this one the year before his, it says:

'72

Thomas Miller on December 1, 2017. As an all-star basketball player, he played the sport he loved at Allegheny. He served in the U.S. Army as a dental technician and from there attended Temple Dental School in Philadelphia. He returned to the Army Dental corps as an officer and served three more years. In 1985, he purchased a small dental practice in downtown Washington, D.C., where he worked for the next 25 years. He is survived by his wife, Margaret Ann Miller; two sons, Jeffrey S. Miller and Brian D. Miller; his sister, Dorothy Konjancic; and his brother, David Miller.

In 1970-71, Path was the other starting point guard. They shared the backcourt. Miller was a year older and must have died at age 67, though it would seem, if he kept his practice for 25 years that he retired at 60, I hesitate to go further on the basketball, Path himself could go on forever, a man's athletic biography runs deep and, as Shunryu Suzuki says, gets more exaggerated with each telling; one might ask, well, if there is no audience for this writing, what does it matter, but where is the aesthetic in indulging in one's history, an aesthetic of harmony more important than truth, even for an audience of the self. Path is about to sell his horse, a deep and life changing admission to old age, to a life that failed to produce economic security for Carla and himself (though it was a joint failure), but the failure implied that if he grew old he would not be able to afford his horse and if she grew old he wouldn't be able to sell her, an acknowledgement of death; by age 21 he could no longer dunk a basketball, by 66, Rabbit, he could no longer run, now he sees that his partner in the backcourt at Allegheny College has died and Path wonders if Tommy, he went by Tommy back then, was overweight, a chubby dentist; dead at 67, he had two sons, a wife, he didn't seem like the kind of guy who would divorce; a dentist, he was likely a good provider, better than Path who'd chosen to be an educator; well, he didn't choose, it happened to him, if inevitably, Path supposed that dentistry happened to Tommy Miller that way too; he was picked number one in the first military draft lottery in 1972, Path's was the next birthday picked but it was matched with number 270, Path saw Tommy that day at the gym, Path heading in for a workout and Tommy leaving, though by then Path had given up college basketball and Tommy had finished out his senior season coming off the bench, Path went to a game or two back then and he felt embarrassed for Tommy when he went into the game, he missed a long range jump-set, was pulled, they were losing to Hiram or somebody like that; only two years before Path and Tommy led Allegheny to a tie for the league championship after seventeen losing seasons in a row, what had happened, Path wasn't paying attention, somehow Tommy wasn't starting anymore, newer, younger talent, but Tommy Miller hung on to the bitter end, stoically entering lost games for a few minutes only to be pulled; Path would have walked away before he let that happen, one of the reasons he walked away, to walk away before that could happen; it might have happened and it might not have happened but we're not going to let Path re-enter that world and the spiral of infinities of memories, though now he's going to do the same thing, walk away from one of the centers of his life and he wouldn't have thought of it like that had he not seen Tommy Miller's obituary; the afternoon after the draft lottery was announced, they faced each other in the narrow hallway outside the locker room, each holding gym bags; Path knew Tommy was chosen number one, everyone did, it spread like wildfire, and Tommy Miller, with the news in his shirt pocket, a month after the end of his last (dismal?) basketball season, went to the gym to play basketball, stepping outside the team locker room from which Path had been exiled after quitting, another nexile, a place between nothing and nowhere, though he was young, twenty years old and couldn't contemplate nexile, unless now, looking back and realizing he was facing it is a way of realizing it then, too, decades ago standing in a vortex of unresolvable crises that could at best end in quivering dissolution, then, there, Tommy Miller stood in front of Path, and didn't they have a world of things to say to each other about the choices they'd made and the choices they were going to make, however true it might be that the choices didn't matter or, if they did, were not choices but fate, or something else, something already written by God's left hand, fate management, now he remembers standing there in front of Tommy and neither of them said a word. It might have been their last encounter.

Now, forty-six years later, Tommy was dead and marked by a scant paragraph in the Allegheny College Alumni Magazine, Now, forty-six years later, Path reads it, Where are those years, Path wonders now, if it had been his own obituary and Tommy Miller read it, what would Tommy have thought, his life of dentistry behind him, his sons and daughters grown, his wife extant, what future were they planning; now there is neither future nor past, there is but a headstone, Path once wrote a book, a manuscript anyway, that no one has ever seen, where every week he wrote himself a different headstone; it was meant to be funny, darkly, now he can't remember a single epithet, now he doesn't want a single epithet, maybe not even a name.

This is wandering where the usual meditations on death go and Path wants to go deeper, no, not deeper, but somewhere other than non-existence, though not to any kind of suchness either. Did Tommy Miller's sons stay in Washington D.C.; Path's daughter moved to Australia, got on a plane at age 23 and left, oddly, he and Carla saw her as she crossed in front of a window in a line that led to baggage inspection, she turned and spied them on the walkway where they stood, grinned at them and raised her right hand, splitting it between the middle and ring fingers, Spock, Live long and prosper; they'd recently seen her again, she and her Australian husband, an acrobat, flew back to LA for a couple weeks, half of the time spent in the desert, above, below, and inside Joshua Tree, his daughter, now almost eight years since her departure, made a living producing cabarets in Sydney, she started out as a stripper on a tourist pirate boat show on Sydney Bay, now she's a famous Drag King, Trans Kafka; Path is about to throw away the Allegheny Alumnae Magazine and when he tries to flip it closed he sees the inside of the back cover, a young woman twisting above a diving board in front of a blue tile wall with a big gold **A** behind her, beneath her a quote form Mohammad Ali, If my mind can conceive it, and my heart believe it—then I can achieve it, the dash grammatically misused, here he wonders how the unlikely becomes maxim and then sold, if it is just in America, or inside the guts of corporate capitalism, or sports, Herbert Marcuse wags a finger, what is failure, after all, but the loss of what the mind conceived and the heart believed, Tommy Miller, did you achieve what your heart believed?

Be reminded, this is not a novel, this is not stream of consciousness, Path's younger brother, in the labyrinth of a nervous breakdown, used to say to him, Ph.Duh; learning to break down the obvious with underbelly intellectualities, Derri-duh; Path actually liked reading Derrida, once rubbed shoulders with him, with Leonard Cohen, too, there are mazes of stories there but he is practicing not going to those places, he gets his thermos and fills it with filtered water from a container inside the refrigerator, reminds himself that he lives by folklore, myth, and voodoo remedies, nutritional supplements, though at present he's apparently survived cancer, an event his oncologist called beyond medical explanation, now the word survival haunts him like a ghost, though really not like a ghost because his house is full of ghosts and they persist inside none of his memories, they are but fuzzy images, inexplicable knocking sounds, smells, Carla smells them, Path was born without the sense of smell, a gift like survival, an emptiness that blessedly or horribly can't be filled, now what; he fills the thermos, it keeps the water cold, checks his body for his watch, his knife, his wallet, his sunglasses, his cell phone, which is something he now thinks he should always bring because what if something happened to him on the trail, what if Nikki spun and dumped him on his titanium hip, his surgically repaired back, no one on either side of his families has ever had a stroke or a heart attack, if he lay there in the dirt or over the side of a ravine, immobilized, he would pull out his cellphone and be out of range of everything; out the window the other side of the canyon rises in clusters of manzanita, scrub oak, sagebrush, ponderosa pine, he yells upstairs to Carla, I think I'm trying to leave, his most recent cat, Frida, jumps onto the counter and moves under his hand, at the door, another cat, Mr. Scott, kept outside for the time being because he tried to kill Frida five times, cries for food, Path fetched kibble and brought it to his bowl atop the split system unit, Mr. Scott purrs and rubs his back against Path's palm, Path will descend some thirty winding steps down to his carport, an open space in front of his fenced yard off the side of the road, he'll skip checking the mail, he looks at the hills and thinks fire, has lived here thirty years under the threat of fire, been evacuated a half-dozen times, and opening the truck door he thinks of his horse, he will meet a man or a woman, he couldn't tell from their voice on the phone, their ambiguous name, Alex, a German who wants an American breed to ride Western on in Germany, and now, if this were a novel or a story I wouldn't make this leap, but he thinks of endings, loss, death, though less so now than when he actually sells her and other losses pile on him like blankets of void, who could have thought that nothingness would have such weight; I am stepping in now to contemplate God, to tell you that I am re-reading *The Tunnel* on my toilet, Mohammed forgive, but I've read the Koran there, too, twice, and the Bible, Old Testament and New, in my Indian bathroom in Gangtok, Sikkim, where I had eight faucets and no water, the *Mahabharata* (the *Bhagavagītā* is in there, in the middle, the big battle, oh Krishna, Path prays, let me be your Arjuna), the *Ramayana, The Puranas, The Diamond Sutra, The Lotus Sutra*, but what need do I have to continue this list for myself; I'm reading a fifth novel by José Saramago who inspired Ursula LeGuin—recently dead like Bill Gass—to begin blogging, Gass, who was my last connection to the pantheon of the literary, he was not a path, Path, and I am not a path for you, this mash of syntax, this cul de sac of void, my friend; Path, is wondering if Nikki thinks of him when he isn't there while Baltasar, in *Baltasar and Blimunda*, lies on a pallet recalling his father's story that on this very day he saw the Holy Ghost fly over him in the sky when Baltasar knows that what his father witnessed was a flying machine that he and Blimunda helped build, the science fantasy of a Franciscan monk.

Last Memorial Day, the fortieth anniversary of his mother's death, Path felt the "disastrous curtain of nothingness" fall; he told Carla, he took a bite of dark chocolate filled with Sativa, smoked some Indica, poured a touch of gin over his iced glass of tonic, What day it is doesn't matter, she said; their daughter had just left them, left them again after visiting from Oz, and he remembered again the first time she left, his heartache at the airport, during the drive home, and for a month after she was gone, he wouldn't have believed that his chest would actually ache; this time, the night before she left, he lay awake in bed and thought of the book he'd spent researching for five years and two years in writing and now couldn't find anyone to read it, he'd published sixteen books by hook or by crook and the more he published the harder it became; his mother's death, he was at her side, her eyes gray as glass, staring into the nothing, he knelt at her bedside and whispered in her ear, I love you, I will always love you, twenty-five years later his father would die with his wife's name, Eleanor, on his lips, but what Path remembers now is a photo in the newspaper of American sailors stopping and boarding a Russian ship on its way to Cuba, inspecting it for nuclear missiles; his mother looks at the picture over his shoulder and says, we should have never dropped the bomb, though when that bomb was dropped his father waited on board an aircraft carrier poised to invade Japan, and Path said to his mother, if we hadn't dropped the bomb I might not have been born, and she said, that's right, but eyes wide now, lying awake next to Carla, he thinks of a phone call from a reporter from his hometown, Erie, Pennsylvania; ten years ago he was the lead witness to a newspaper investigation into his former basketball coach who fucked him a thousand times, a grand jury in Pennsylvania has re-opened the case, fifty years old, hundreds of boys raped in the diocese, it's coming apart inside him, will he need to go back home and open that casket again; he thinks of his horse, his book, his daughter, his mother, his rape, he tries to get up but he falls to his knees and cries, his chest heaves, he has never cried so long and so hard, Carla holds him and doesn't have to say, one of us will die and leave the other alone, each of these things open like a lotus, inside Vishnu opens his eyes and they are gray as glass, Vishnu whispers, you know that I am nothing, Carla, the next night, her daughter flying 9,000 miles across the Pacific, says with her eyes, the suffering of privilege, the sufferings of a white man, he is not starving, his house is warm when it's cold and cool when it's warm; he has a house, he had a horse, you can't start your story here, you can't end your story here, Gass published *The Tunnel* in 1995 after working on it for twenty years, he was never in Nexile, he was, in fact, a happy man in the heart of the heart of the country, he said to Path, there's always some achievement unrecognized, an award you didn't get, a bad review, he raised his glass and said, life is meaningless; get in your truck, Path, drive through the canyon to where the hills become golden, go to the ranch, at the corral your horse will raise her head and recognize your truck, leave the others and come to you, lower her head for you to place her halter over her nose, place her soft lips on your ear and fluffle your cheek for a carrot; what gift is that, how long before he is too old to ride, she too old to sell, how did he ever have the money to keep a horse, how many things did Carla give up so he could pretend to be a horseman, Path, one year younger than Thomas Miller, but you Path, advance on the old German, a rich being of unidentifiable gender, a soft face and Adam's Apple-less neck, a blue denim shirt and jeans, a handkerchief tied around his neck in the style of Gene Autry; Path knew Autry's maid who brought his clothes for his cross dressing, Those cowboys, Path said to Carla who had forgiven Wayne for his Vietnam hawk years, though Path had not, now he's dead, not that it mattered but that it was a life lived in false duplicities, the Times published excerpts of a 1970's interview, he hated blacks, Indians and queers, Path, whose daughter in Australia calls herself queer, has achieved Sydney celebrity as a drag king, has married a man, an acrobat, has told Path, if I weren't queer I'd have no career, if John Wayne were straight or gay he'd be dead anyway; meanwhile, back on the toilet, Gass's protagonist, Bill Kohler, is recalling Sunday drives with his family, eating five cent ice cream cones, butter pecan, black walnut, Bergson is meditating on Nothingness, contemplating that it is the impossibility upon which everything resides, and Saramago narrates the death of thousands of men enslaved to build a convent under a mountain at the whim of King and Catholicism; Path has worked for thirty years under the subtle yoke of the Society of Jesus and looking back sees that they have wasted his life; at the ranch, the German, neither a he nor she, tells Path that they've had two knees replaced, two hips replaced, back surgery, Path shares that he himself has had back surgery and one resurfaced hip, so the German, saying they're purchasing the horse for their wife, won't even be able to mount Path's mare and his young assistant, a woman, tries to mount Nikki who begins to buck, the assistant jumps down, no sale today, they drive their million dollar horse trailer back to Paso Robles, what were they thinking, Nikki puts her nose on Path's cheek, but even so, Path won't have a thousand dollars a month to keep a pet horse when he retires, go cry about it white man, on the border of Mexico, Guatemalan mothers are being separated from their babies, that oughtta stop 'em from trying to get in, yessiree, and seventeen rednecks drown when a riverboat capsizes and sinks eighty feet to the bottom of Table Rock Lake outside Branson, Missouri, a hurricane sized wave, says the captain who survived, though he's also a Presbyterian minister, thus a determinist by faith if not implication; Path who was brought up on Lake Erie asks, a hurricane sized wave on a lake in Missouri, what information is missing here, yet each life as valuable as a Jew in Germany, a German in Dresden, a black slave in Vicksburg, death is timeless and

Bergson is saying that trying to perceive reality is like a child clapping at smoke.

Path looks at his hands and wonders if he has been made in the image and likeness of God. There was a time when it seemed plausible that God fashioned the world, back when God was He and made the world for Man, meaning Men; Eve out of Adam's rib, it seemed to Path that the shepherd religions, as he called them, the ones that grew out of the Middle Eastern sheep cultures and ruled, tribally, by patriarchs, were built on the shepherding model, Abraham, for Jews and Islamists alike, and Jesus, a Jewish reformer, offered himself as the Good Shepherd, and as the Koran repeats again and again, the fruits of the earth were made for Man's picking, it was just fucking obvious, pun intended, though this is wandering away from Path's intent, he doesn't want this to be a critique, he'd read Bertrand Russell's *Why I Am Not a Christian* but much of it was so obvious, likewise Joyce's in *Portrait*; there was once a time when you could imagine a God who shaped the world with His hands, a world ruled and named by Man, literally, Adam, and not Eve, though you can bet your boots she helped, a lot, like Mrs. Hammurabi and Eleanor Roosevelt, and however much the Society of Jesus might wish to argue that Man means humanity, that is, that it is inclusive of women, quite clearly Man includes women only peripherally, there are no women priests, and in the times in which we now live, it gets harder and harder to separate patriarchy from misogyny; Carla would point out that I'm proceeding in language far too packed to communicate and though Carla is of my own construction, William Gass would argue me God-like, her opinion counts, but I am reminding myself here, step by step, hopelessly, moment by moment, that there is no audience here, no actual reader, no implied reader, no future reader, not even me, like the turtles, it's audience-less all the way down, like Bergson's metaphor, it's both held up and contained by an impossible nothingness, all process, though I tip my hat to both Heraclitus and Buddha; so, creation myths more than imply, they cry out for a creator, west of the Ganges, a creator filled with intentionality and purpose, east of the Ganges the process is more inexplicable with multiple creators and sub-creators, multiple motives and stories thereof, and backing away from that further, the palms up shrug of Gautama Buddha who, even he, had to be convinced to allow women to be bodhisattvas, as long as they stayed away from the men; religion, it seemed to Path, was profoundly patriarchal, god the great Greek touching fingers with Adam on the ceiling of the Sistine Chapel; but the logic of that, as Freud pointed out, is in reverse, that is the God that Man, that men, created in their likeness, an ideal likeness, most of us don't resemble the statue of David even if once, for a brief moment, we might have, though let's not quite yet move on to aging and death; it's hard to say how many of us the Old Testament God envisioned when He created Adam and Eve as perfect, Saramago declares that God doesn't know the future though no argument is proffered, child birth and procreation, painfully so for Eve and all who followed her, having followed the expulsion from Eden; things have not changed dramatically, despite the rise of philosophy, science, and technology, since that moment; Protagoras yet called Man the measure of all things and science has inherited the legacy of Adam's task, to protect and rule the animals, the plants, the earth, even each other, even if by love or faith or hope, even if we've been doing a bad job of it; so if we're such fuck-ups, why blame God, well, if we're made in His image and likeness by means of his omniscient all powerful omnipresence, who else to blame, anyway, procreating a bunch of each other seems to have been another bane of Original Sin, so take a look at your hands, Path, they can't paint or play the guitar, your brain can't fly you to the moon or build a computer or barely use one, you can't see yourself as a little god, not even if you're half an angel, though let's not go there yet, you can't even see yourself as the best of humanity, as Sartre has said, you didn't write a symphony, you don't get credit for someone else having done it, are you to blame for the Holocaust, more so, times have changed drastically, the creator hides somewhere beyond the event horizon of the universe, or multiverses, or among them, or somehow in each of us or each and every thing; so it's hard to envision this crumbling body as made in God's image and likeness, what image, where's the likeness, what about the mind; yet it's too easy to take pot shots at God, like shooting ducks in a barrel, if that's where one ever shoots ducks, God never answers, yet why create all those multi-verses just to have this tiny steaming turd earth of cruelty and sin, love and greed and hope, maybe you need all that other creation to get this, maybe it was the only way; Carla says the whole thing is just a work of art, God made it and left it, moved on, but for his part, Path wants God, and this, let me remind myself, and Path as well, is what this painstaking effort is all about.

If this story, if I may call it that, takes place in the hours before Path sells his horse, it's surrounded by much that happened before and much that happens after, because Nexile, like Nirvana, is neither a place nor a state of being, neither process nor thing; Path wonders if, when he finishes Bergson's *Creative Evolution* he should pick up Sartre's *Being and Nothingness* or, to be conscientious, Heidegger's *Being and Time*; he'd recently picked up Spinoza and Kant but they were old hat, Carla, catching wind of it all, fetched some copies of Baudrillard and threw them on Path's reading chair; you want French, she said, that's French, and just when Path had contemplated going back to Bachelard, we'll see, but the whorl of Nexile has gripped Carla, too, as she contemplates making Blacklabel her middle name and changing her last name to Beer, her college roommate has skyrocketed to the top of the poetry world, worse than your college back court mate dying; her mother, now eighty-seven, is building a barn of psychological pathology and wants company in there, wants a barn building party; Path has written about Carla's mother, Jin-Jin, a couple of times, briefly, in humor, thank the gods that no one reads his books, particularly Jin-Jin or her friends, but now, with his own molestation re-arising like a monster sea turtle, yes, turtles all the way down, I know it's currently a pop cultural anthropological cliché, but that will pass, too, Path imagines standing in front of a classroom of nineteen year-olds saying it and none of them having a clue, in fact 95% of what Path thinks or says, including what they're supposed to be learning, means anything to them, but for the one or two who think they're there to learn something but think knowledge can be poured into their heads like so much unleaded gasoline, ding-ding, as the price per gallon goes up daily, he'd like to blame the Society of Jesus and maybe he'd not be far off, maybe Aristotle and St. Thomas Aquinas are the root of the problem, Ignatius Loyola aside, so much so that once, in a class on sci-fi that Path spirited into the curriculum by offering it under the title Introduction to Fiction, while decrying the plot gimmicks employed by stories dealing with time travel, he said he wished he could go back in time and keep Aristotle's parents from mating, which was only a rhetorical joke because Path came closer to believing that history would have invented Aristotle if he hadn't invented himself, though he didn't quite believe that either, nonetheless it almost got him fired, the only thing preventing it at that time, because Path was almost fired many times in his thirty year association with the Society, was that none of the students knew what he was talking about so nobody complained, how then did the Society of Jesus find out, well, Path figured it was the bugged crucifixes that adorned every classroom, which was another thing he pointed out in class that almost got him fired but once again, but nobody really complained; the Society of Jesus was subtly and notoriously tolerant, which Path pointed out was a form of Marcuse's repressive tolerance, he loved the Frankfurt School, so he slipped by on that one, too, he didn't really almost get fired until he quoted *Blazing Saddles*, that got noticed, ironically by a woman he'd deeply befriended, not sexually, but intimates are always your most grievous traitors, as his sexual molester always said, and Path, in his clutches for seven years and maybe more, depending on what one might mean by dependence, eventually betrayed him, of course, to no avail, even here in Nexile, even, as I have noted earlier, unto this day, but here comes another turtle upon which the world rests; Carla's mother, a ne'er-do-well floating Protestant who'd believed that she was to be the mother of the Second Coming, some new idea, and lay that onus on both of her sons, one after the other, with Carla falling in between; one might imagine how ontologically and logically complicated that is, but let's not, in the end that kind of stuff is boring, no matter how well written, at least to Path, who had a personal relationship with God until he met his sexual molester, okay, let's call him by his real name, Garvey, got hold of him, old God, God, new God, Garvey, it was that simple, no it wasn't, of course not, but I have all the time in the world here, at least as long as I live, though there is Path's memoir that was written to be read, and was not, not by many, though I'm informing no one here, I'm simply explaining to me why I'm not bothering to explain; yet the monster turtle that is Jin-Jin heard voices, holy voices, and how did she know they were holy, not insidious, how anyone knows, a clear and distinct idea, via Augustine and Descartes, by the way, whom she's never read, though Sartre, there he is again, later asked, what if God appeared in front of you, how would you know it was God, how could the visage prove itself, by miracles, can't the devil do that, Path is going to see some miracles soon, but he'll have to wait; so the holy voices told Jin-Jin she was the reincarnation of Joan of Arc and the Mother of the Second Coming too, why not, and she dictated those messages to the captive pre-adolescent Carla, thousands of pages, thousands, between arbitrary imprisonments in Carla's bedroom, what, said Path, you had your own bedroom, yes, cruelty knows no class boundaries, or bouts of locking her in the closet or garage, You had two cars, you had a garage, says Path, if Path's family had owned a second car, a garage, he might have run from his giant angry father and hidden there, instead he ran away to friends' houses or, later, into the arms of his molester, and on trips to the grocery store Jin-Jin, the Saint Jin of Arc, locked the car doors and beat Carla and screamed at Carla for not being an obedient daughter, wily abusers never leave a mark, and why didn't she tell her father, well, though I posit this question rhetorically from or for the non-existent audience, because if you can ask that then you know nothing about abuse, besides, one day, as a young teenager, she did tell her father and the Jin denied it all and her parents put her in an asylum, the old adage being that if you recount the exploits of a nut you sound like a nut; how about some home schooling, Saint Jin suggested, I'll give high school a try, Carla said, with lots of extra-curricular activities, but tormentors never give up, you can run but you can't hide; when Path and Carla had a child, their daughter, she got thrown out of daycare for believing she was a cat, exposing the owners as Jews for Jesus, then thrown out of elementary school for changing her name to Luke Skywalker, your daughter is a lesbian said the fourth grade teacher, so what, she entered middle school and changed her name to Jesus, well, that nipped Saint Jin's proselytizing, kind of like a backfire, but she lived in Florida then so with the help of three thousand miles and a couple decades she became a mere nuisance; Jesus quit high school when she was sixteen and spent several more years as Jesus in college, then became infamous on the Sunset Strip performing as a mermaid, then with her python as the Snake Girl at the Freak Show on Venice Beach, then got on a plane for Australia, Live long and prosper; Carla's father died, the Jin moved to a leisure community in Laguna, Laguna Woods, suffered some mini strokes, lived through a huge benign tumor in her intestines and moved to a care facility named, without irony, Freedom Village, that controlled every moment of its constituents' lives; Jin-Jin tried to escape but fell off a curb in a mall parking lot in front of the WalMart, broke her neck in three places and against bad odds didn't die; thus re-arose the rhythm of the saints; Carla and Path sat across from her in her Prison Village studio apartment, Let me show you what they told me today, No thank you, No I'll just show you, Thank you. no, Okay I'll read it, God loves you and God loves me, that makes us a trinity, a holy trinity of love, a gift from God our God above, now you read it Carla, well no, because Carla wasn't fifteen anymore, Carla was sixty, Let's get out of here said Path, but no, Saint Jin had cardboard boxes full of pages of this stuff, thousands and thousands of pages, okay, harmless enough you say, but the Jin was the self proclaimed, if not Voices proclaimed, Pen of God, and this the new gospel of love that would change the world and she was giving it to Carla to edit and Path to publish, he was so well connected, and after the imminent apocalypse—the global warnings were everywhere—Carla's younger brother would become president of the world and use Saint Jin's teachings to create the New Eden of Love; maybe she was like William Blake, maybe she was just nuts, maybe William Blake was just nuts though he was a way better writer; when Path and Carla taught at the Queen's College in London it was right after Path's forty days of radiation, forty days and forty nights, were the radio- oncologists reading the Bible? every night he woke up in the middle of the night, poured himself a glass of port and took an Ativan, watched the double decker busses roll by his window in the pre-dawn and read William Blake; daytimes he wandered in Victorian cemeteries and in Kensington Park where he found every single spot where Peter Pan frolicked; meanwhile, back in Prison Village, Jin-Jin tells Carla that she must take the writings and hold onto them until the apocalypse, Path can wait that long, so he lugs the boxes out of the apartment and down the hallway to the elevator, out the elevator and through the entry lounge where old folks stare into the air over their walkers, through the parking lot and into the car, out of the car at home and up forty steps, throws them into his Spider World basement and two weeks later Jin-Jin wants the Writings back to show her Christian best friend; Path lugs the Writings out of Spider World and down to the car, drives them to Prison Village, he and Carla lug them to the elevator, down the hall and back to Saint Jin; I am the Pen of God, the Jin once again declares, but God is not her co-pilot, her Christian friend suddenly professes that she's lost her eyesight and can't read the stuff, in two weeks the Jin wants to give the Writings to Carla again; do you see what she's doing to you, Path says to Carla, she's controlling you with her writings again, but who is she hurting, really, responds Carla, my back asks Path, and Carla drives the two hours down the 405 to Prison Village and gets the boxes of doggerel prophesy herself, at least as far as the driveway, whereupon Path puts them back in Spider World, but in a week the Jin is on the answering machine screaming, You stole my Writings, my Writings, they're not you're Writings, they're *my* Writings, God gave them to me, not you, and you've stolen them and if you don't return them in two days I'm calling the police; Path helps Carla consolidate the boxes and mail them back to Prison Village and when the Jin gets them she calls and says, Please take them back; this could have been dramatized, of course, or told more briefly, but I wanted to communicate the madness and exhaustion, the repetition, if only unto myself who, like Path, like Saint Jin, has no audience whatsoever; anyway, Carla changes her last name to Beer and finally says, No, the Jin recoils into a pile of gooey stories about her father and her sons that she's told hundreds of times and Carla worries, because on top of everything else, Jin-Jin can't remember anything and sometimes doesn't seem to be able to see or hear, depending on the context, Carla worries that if Saint Jin goes public then Prison Village might make the move to put her away; Path shudders, Didn't Carl Jung say self realization at sixty-five, You've been there and back already says Carla, and what better time than this, Path ruminates, to look into his retirement, whereupon the financial advisor in the Society's HR department notifies him that he can retire but he'll have to retire on skid row; I thought I was paying attention, said Path, and my life partner, he asks, You have a wife? Does it matter what you call it, We have no record of her, No record after thirty years he says, Why start now says the financial officer, Angela, who looks like she's sixteen going on twelve, Try making riskier investments, try envisioning success; Path's older sister, Aubrey, presciently phones him from Pittsburgh and tells him, Work till you die, that's my motto, don't let those bastards off the hook.

When Path got cancer he started praying, kind of, sort of, shit, it was hard to admit that he was a fool and a coward and afraid of dying, but he didn't pray for a cure, he just asked for help dealing with his cancer, he'd contemplate, meditate, wait, he figured much like the Vajrayana Tibetans explained encounters in the Bardo, that the images which came to him would be the images he'd been indoctrinated into, before Garvey obliterated them, Catholic images, angels, saints, and devils, and he even started with an experiment, like this, when he lost his keys he waited for an image and the image of St. Anthony came to him, not that he knew what St. Anthony looked like or what he was good at, did he have a beard, robes, a crucifix tied around his waist like a nun, well, regardless, he said, St. Anthony help me find my keys, then he remembered that he'd left them in the pocket of his hooded sweatshirt and that's where he found them; this could be a very long story if I recounted every time Path lost something then prayed to St. Anthony and found it, not that Jose Saramago or A.W. DeAnnuntis wouldn't tell it and do a very fine job of it, neither Path nor I have that kind of patience, but Path lost and found sunglasses, pens, lead pencils, books, hard drives, cell phones, keys, keys, keys, and not simply by retracing his steps, because that was a really good device for finding things he'd misplaced, but sometimes by simply saying, St. Anthony, help me find this and, often, within a day or so, the thing would show up; anyway, he didn't want to make a big deal over it, but as he went on the pantheon spread, St. Andrew to help him deal with writing, why St. Andrew, he didn't know, why not one or all of the Evangelists, St. Monica, who he thought might have wiped the face of Christ on the way to Golgotha only to have the image of his face reproduced on the rag, and though it wasn't St. Monica who did it, he asked her to let him see the gentle facets of God whether God existed or not, in fact, whether or not, because now he's remembering afternoons on the trail on the back of his first horse, Jackie O, riding in the warm day and pretending, just pretending, okay, for the next five minutes let's pretend that's there is a providential deity who looks out for me, let's just believe that for five minutes, or for the next five minutes let me be an incarnation of Shiva, or Kali, or Sita or Rama, Vishnu, let's take a few minutes and talk to the oak tree, he didn't have to believe any of it, and he didn't have to not believe it; it was around this time that he picked up William James' *Varieties of Religious Experience*; now, given, it would be hard to find a religious text Path hadn't read, right on down to Mircea Eliade and Ken Wilber, Luther, John Wesley, Nāgārjuna, Śaṅkara's commentary on *The Vedānta Sūtras of Bādarāyana*, go ahead, he'd even tip toed into the *Book of Mormon*, though Scientology, no, he couldn't do it, though his friend the psychoanalyst, Andre Paulson, tried to seduce him with stories from Edgar Cayce's autobiography and Path found them anecdotal at best, so, well, Path was a big fan of William James, had read most everything, even *Psychology*, he'd read a whole bunch, I mean a whole bunch, of the man who first inspired James, Charles Sanders Peirce, as well, including and especially his phenomenological categories and semiotics, another story, but one of the arguments of *Varieties* went like this, look at this person's religious experiences, written testimonies, then this other person's, and now this person's, on and on, and aside from the fact that there were some interesting similarities, and whether they could be said to be objectively true, true or not, these were experiences, and they were experiences that we could call religious, and whatever else you might want to deny, you couldn't deny that those people had them, they were experiences and thus, at least subjectively, absolutely true; James used this kind of argumentation a lot, he did it with the human Will, as well, i.e. let's ask ourselves, what is the Will? however much we might want to downgrade its ontological status to biology and impulse, it's hard to deny experiencing it, or seeing it operate in others, even other animals; now Path is thinking he should have read more Schiller, well, for now, he might have the time, maybe soon, unfortunately his *Encyclopedia of Philosophy*, where he'd start, is not here with him, it's in his office at the Society, maybe he'll try Wikipedia; so, if Saint Jin of Arc, by the way, said she heard voices, one thing we can't deny is that she says she hears voices whether they exist or not, in fact, at least subjectively, they exist, the difference being that in the cases William James sites the experiences are Transformational, the subject's life is changed significantly for quite some time, into a constant awareness of one's unity with God, God's love, God's providence, God's presence, though sometimes forever and sometimes not; Path's own path in this regard, his meditational prayers aside, is a little different and interesting enough but, for now, let's return to his prayers and, to conclude this current digression into Jin-Jin's voices, those weren't Transformational, they changed nothing; so now that a perfectly good story about the path to Path's poly-agnosticism has been hammered by this digression, let's continue with James a bit more; in the last chapter of *Varieties* James makes an interesting suggestion that possibly monotheism is the wrong way to think about religious experience, maybe polytheism makes more sense, lest we not forget that William James was a Pluralist, that is, not a Monist like say, Leibniz, not a dualist like Descartes or a Parallelist like Spinoza, not an Atomist either, from Leucippus to Bertrand Russell, no, James believed that there were multiple fundamental realities, many of them experiential, that crisscrossed the world as we discovered it before us, so he'd feel the same way about deities and religious experiences, if we cared to speculate about it; so now, back to Path's meditations, which is closer to what they were, or are, than prayers, if there is a difference, he meditated on St. Jude and asked for help to curtail his drinking, he'd visited Mother Theresa's hospital in the slums of Kolkata, saw her grave, so contemplated her help for the sick and dying, including himself, of St. Teresa of Avila, who according to witnesses, levitated during prayer, he asked for her help in opening his heart to God and help with having God open Her heart to him, though he read St. Teresa's memoirs and nowhere does she speak of levitation, only of ecstatic meditations where she felt herself lifted into God's presence, that is, metaphorically; Path asked St. Francis of Assisi, a favorite meditational figure for Arthur Schopenhauer, by the way, nihilist though he might have been, Path asked Francis to help open his heart to the natural world, to find peace in simplicity and help take care of his animals, let's not go into the labyrinth of Path's animals now, though he once, in his 800 page unfinished book, *The Last Book of Everything*, began a history of his pets that he never finished, as well; Path contemplated St. George slaying a dragon from horseback and asked for help being brave and kind, for help slaying his own dragon, his ambition, and he meditated on St. Michael the Arch Angel, often portrayed as wielding a great sword raised in one hand while offering the scales of justice with the other, Path asked for justice, which would take me down a long and circuitous route, so Path, we're not going there now, yes, justice, something Path held to be insane, seeking it, that is, but as Leonard Cohen once said, why not ask for more; Path contemplated Dionysius for creativity, Rumi for divine joy, and as to his cancer, he reasonlessly dwelt on St. Ann, St. Elizabeth, and Holy Mary, a genealogical triad he speculated, though he could be wrong, he asked them to help him deal with it, his cancer; Path meditated on Vishnu seated on his lotus for help understanding his mortality, and possibly his immortality, whatever that might be, and envisioned his and Carla's love on a lotus before Avidya's castle in paradise, Avidya being a Buddhist avatar of Vishnu, another long story, though Path found it on the toilet when reading *The Tale of Genji*; he envisioned a descent of Brahman where the God showed him his creativity and bounty, Path danced with Shiva and incarnated charisma, fire, destruction, and creativity, he danced with White Tara and Green Tara, Vajrayana Goddesses of health, envisioned the sitar playing daughter of Shiva, Sarasvati, to abide in his daughter, now non-binary child, Trans Kafka, and asked Sita, consort of Rama, and Kali, consort of Shiva, to abide in their sister, Carla; he contemplated Ganesh, of whom he owned a beautiful statue that he and Carla bought in Varanasi and placed near their kitchen, to Ganesh he gave up the wellbeing of his household; Path begins these medi-prayers by thinking of St. Veronica, at the time having no idea who she was, but he puts out his hand, his actual hand or a hand in his mind, and asks her to take it and just help him to get through the day, or night, or morning, sometimes at night booze and pot work, too, and then he thanks everyone, sometimes he just thanks everybody and that's all, just says thanks, finally he capped this litany of the absurd by contemplating Buddha, to achieve sympathy and detachment, however momentary, however brief; in the end, and continuing, he's come to the conclusion, as James might, that however ridiculous it might be, it might have helped. Dear William James, does belief make a difference?

How could it matter if it were true?

They are at the Glass Table. The moon has come over the eastern mountainside after the sun went down in the west; it happens slowly here because the sun sets early behind the western hills, much earlier than it would on the horizon, in fact their home is too deep into the side of the hill it's built on and the sky too obscured by homes and trees to even see the sunset, and the moon, though it has arisen on the horizon to the east, is late to rise above the hill (and contrary to popular consciousness, the moon only rises opposite the sunset when it's full, every 28 days or so, waning to a new moon in two weeks, rising a half-hour later each day), but when the full moon rises it is huge and golden and they can watch it from their living room or their kitchen window, and now, tonight, it has come up over the mountainside, and Carla takes a long look at Path and says, I don't know, I just don't know how much more I can take, Of your mother? says Path, Of anything, of all of it, my mother, my job, my sad career, she pauses, then gets out a cigarette, Of life, of death, she says, she lights, smokes, Of you, she says, I miss my daughter, I miss shadows, ambience, dark, light, revelation, And Path says, You have the moon, But I don't have the moon, says Carla, I don't have anything and nothing lasts, and Path says Nothing is the only thing that lasts, You won't last, says Carla, I'll be alone and old like my mother, she pauses, smokes, she says, We should have had another child, I'll have no one to take care of me, Could you, says Path, could you have? and Carla says, Probably not, you didn't want it, our daughter didn't, did I? I don't know; Path gets up, he goes to the freezer to fetch ice, but the bin is empty, so he pulls out three pale blue, plastic ice cube trays and empties them into the bin, refills the trays and puts them back in the freezer, they don't have an automatic icemaker because he believes that moving parts are the first thing to break down, especially small plastic ones in big machines, machines manufactured by robots or workers who don't care, he no longer buys things that are delivered in pieces and have to be put together, pieces which have never been together before, he doesn't want to be the first person to put them together, and often enough there are pieces missing, his old friend, J.D. (Path's last and only hometown friend who, in fact, Path hasn't spoken to in over a year, J.D. doesn't call or email, Path seldom texts anyone but Carla—his fingertips are too big) J.D. says that anyone who spends time with Path falls into his entropy, I just made ice, Path says, Because you drink, she says, Would you like some ice, says Path, I dream of making love to other men, Carla says, Are you married to me when that happens, asks Path, am I in the dream? I don't know, says Carla, Path doesn't need the details, where does it happen, is she naked, is the sex good, she says, if I dream of fire, do I want it or fear it, or both, he says, or neither, she says, Who's bigger, says Path, Mr. Bigger or Mr. Bigger's baby? Mr. Bigger's baby, says Carla Blacklabel, because he's a little Bigger.

DESIRE
THIS WORLD IS PRERECORDED

NOT LONG BEFORE MY LIFE PARTNER and I stopped watching television we were given a gift of a video recorder. This particular little miracle was called Tivo. I doubt I need to explain its skills, the majority of American households likely own one or something like it, though I assume its capabilities have been usurped by iphones or droids or clouds or streams, i.e. no one really needs to record anything at all, everything is available everywhere or anywhere all the time, streamed into/onto our screens, sight and sound, that world, those worlds, needn't be remembered at all, by neither human nor machine, they can simply be plucked from the sky, the air, and those of us who want to hold onto the mind and the heart, those two hyperbolic anachronisms, are living as strangers in our own strange land, we don't need to look *inside*, for anything, besides, if we did, what would we hope to find? though hope, now there's a mysterious word, hope might be exactly what we might hope to find, something we can't pluck from the cloud and put on a screen.

What is shadow and what is real? Of course, a shadow is as real as anything. Only metaphorically is it less real than the body that castes it. Like consciousness, I can't leave it, nor can it leave me. That there is some entity that thinks our thoughts, some thought-like, thought-making entity, the mind, has been disputed, ironically and thoughtfully enough from Gautama Buddha to William James, yet if we think metaphorically and not critically, if thought is not a thing but a process, it is nonetheless observable, if not physically, then, well, in thought, given that this me, this I, is as ineffable as mind, what is it to feel the flow of consciousness, even to feel, blankly, softly, aware. Loosely, I might say *I* am aware, or awareness is aware, or simply, moment to moment, *awareness is*, though like a shadow, like hope, it seems to insist, stubbornly, on attaching itself, like moonlight to the moon, the shadow to my body between them. This is how thought thinks. I want to ascribe the solidity of the chair in front of me, its size, its shape, to its chairness, but that kind of thinking falls back upon an old and dubious debate of whether the chair arises from its qualities or whether the qualities inhere in the chair, or is that simply how thinking began, riveted inside dialectic, in dualist patter, addicted to its hope for perpetuity, for immortality, as if we go on thinking or thinking goes on thinking after death.

Whatever idle doubt I had about the Cartesian ego, the most devastating case for denying it was my mother's consciousness as it waned during her decline and death by a glio brain tumor. There seemed no doubt then that the soul, the mind, the self, died with the body. All of those clinging mysteries, metaphors, or are they miracles, dissolved in death, the nihilist's house of dreams, but, you see, with the twist of a few words, I give death substance and hope to make it more than nothingness, afraid to accept that nothingness, emptiness, is nothing too.

The idea that the world in front of us, the so-called material world, lies on the back, or maybe lies on its back, upon a more fundamental, if more immaterial or invisible reality, is quite old, Brahman, Pythagoras' geometry, Plato's forms, the thoughts of God (Plotinus or Augustine), though the problems reconciling those realities with this one plague us still, e.g. Whitehead and Russell struggling to reconcile the phenomenal world of our sense experience with the buzzing subatomic quantum world. How do we get here from there and why isn't there something else in between? I've stated that too loosely in order to make a rhetorical point, that it's common for us to explain our visible world with invisible causes, if not a single, invisible cause, God for example, though any materialist will quickly and easily argue that we can measure electrons, we can't measure God or Gods.

Of the philosophers who seemed to have best understood the problem, Spinoza stands out. One of the earliest thinkers to take on the mind-body problem created by Descartes, he reasoned that mind and body, thought and extension, were but two of the infinite modes of existence expressed in God's infinite substance. Mind and body were but two parallel sides of God's infinitely sided coin. There is really but one substance, God Itself, filling all existence with Itself. Among the infinite modes of God's expression, we humans experience only two, thought, i.e. mind, and extension, matter. That's logic! However unsatisfying that might be to a Cartesian thinker, it solved the problem of how an immaterial being could create and sustain a material universe, that problem existing as a synecdoche in every human being, that is, how is it possible for an immaterial mind and the material body to interact? Monisms, including any form of atomism, from Democritus to Leibniz to Russell, whether ancient or contemporary, solve that problem the same way, quality arising in the proliferate combinations of quantity, witness the emergent characteristics of chemical combinations, classically, H2O. Why that would happen is nurtured deep in the structure, impulse, creativity, laws of our cosmos, for Plato, the forms, for Whitehead the eternal entities, but if law or laws are more than derived possibilities induced from repetitious observation, ala Hume, if they are, somehow, an existent part of the universe (be there others, whether sequential as in Hindu cosmology, Buddhist simultaneous co-arising, or Whitehead's co-terminus universes each with its own set of governing principles) the *why-ness* still remains mysterious. Spinoza diverts that ontological gap by exchanging why-ness for such-ness, though much of the infinite such-ness can't be known because the only modes we humans can experience are consciousness and extension. There is only one God and God is everything, everything we experience and everything else. Why couldn't one of those modes, or more, be spiritual? And if so, why would that spirituality be reduced to monotheism? As William James suggests, given the varieties of religious experience, doesn't pluralism in the form of polytheism make as much, if not more, sense?

The need to explain what seems to exist right in front of us inevitably creates an epistemological gap and there are those, like Kant, who attempted to close it by removing the impulse or plausibility of closing it. The world, as it can be known, must always be a combination of what the world is and the mind that tries to comprehend it. He called that 'phenomena,' and phenomena is all we can ever know; whatever the world *really* is, this we can never know; he called this noumena. His phenomenological categories attempted to systematize that meeting of mind and world, though like a lot of innovative solutions it created as many, if not more, problems than it solved, and in its wake created that poetic philosophical field called phenomenology. Since, and now, we have stepped away from metaphysics and turned our attention to epistemology if we haven't, like Buddha or Bachelard, simply stepped away from all of it; the issues of God, soul, self, the world, what they really are, or might be, are all so much noumena and best expressed in metaphor.

There are directions on this spider web I haven't followed, the radical idealism of Berkeley, Hegel, Royce, because I think they spin back to the problems of a monism like Spinoza's or, for that matter, materialist determinisms, which include psychoanalysis, like Freud or even Jung; there's always something ad hoc about anything that explains everything, like sitting in front of a tarot reader or an astrologer, not to compare them to serious philosophy, only to point out the gap between an explanation and the underlying why-ness of what the explanation depends on. More pointedly, the flightless bird of monism is yet a bird, even flightless nihilism requires a dance with negation, whether it's Buddha, Gass, Nietzsche, or Derrida. The problem with perfection is that it's impossible to live in nihilism or nominalism, in the end we must live in the inexplicable real.

NEXISTENTIALISM

PATH IMAGINES THAT THE WAY most people use the word 'existential,' hardly anybody knows what it means, or at least what Sartre meant by it, that might or might not matter; in common parlance today it simply means the current existing circumstance or current reality, or at most imply a crisis involving life or death choices; Path fell upon the Nexistential the other night across the table from Carla while trying to distance himself from nexile, a night after a day when he decided to take a walk, not that unusual, he'd been taking walks in the hills for almost thirty years, though the other day, August 1, was the 27th anniversary of his and Carla's moving to their house in Topanga Canyon and it was his dad's birthday, too, he thinks his dad would be 97, July 31 was his parents' wedding anniversary, did they marry in 1942 or '43, just before his father, Red, went to war in the Pacific, Path's older brother, Wil, was conceived then and then Red went off to war; on the wall to Path's right, above his desk, there's a portrait of his mom, Eleanor, on their wedding day, Carla and Path got married in the Eighties but they don't quite remember what day, that's an interesting phenomenon but not that interesting, and on Tuesday last week Path finally went to the dentist after more than two years, dentist horror, but anybody can go there on their own, it doesn't need a digression, in fact, almost every line here could spark some digression, some story, but why, why not, why choose one story over another, there might be reasons based on what kind of narrative one chooses to write, though it's self evident here that no particular kind of narrative has been chosen, or as the philosophers of the late Nineteenth Century asked, why is there something and not nothing? here's Path, on the cusp of falling apart, he's living on that cusp, August 3 was his daughter's birthday, she turned 31, a day ahead of time in Australia, and Path's new dentist is Japanese, when his father came to visit him in LA after Trans Kafka's birth some thirty-one years ago, he and Path encountered a Japanese cashier in the grocery store and his father sweated and shook with anger, when they left the store he said, I can't help it, I hate the Japanese, I was trained to kill them; his dentist, Path's age, and born in Japan, likely had a father Red's age and fought for Japan, then there's the Japanese internment; Path's not going to bring any of that up; now Path parks his truck at the foot of a trail in Santa Maria Canyon, the earth is red, the flora is green-brown, mesquite, manzanita, sage, huge oaks spread and sprawl ahead and into the valley on his left, on his right, above him, a hill rises that separates the trail from the ranch where he kept Jackie O, there's a trail up and down that hill where he once rode Jackie though he never took Nikki on it, different horse, different problems, and Path regrets that he didn't solve that one with Nikki, but Path got old, his back ached, his hips hurt, it wasn't hard to make him fear, Path locks his truck, puts his camp watch in one pocket of his black sweats and his keys in the other, his t-shirt is burgundy and his sneakers black, he wears a Pittsburgh Pirate baseball cap, no, we're not going to tell a story about the hat, Path, not now, maybe not ever, but who knows, he once ran his dogs on this path, H.D. and Piccolo, and Nadine before she became blind, those are pet stories, but now he walks alone, it's quiet right now and he can hear the shuffle of his feet in the dusty red dirt, he walks a dozen steps or so, thinks of St. Veronica, begins to contemplate the movement of his body, his self, when the shadow of a flying bird passes over his head, front to back; he turns to try and see the bird, but he sees nothing, so he turns back up the path and spots him again, he thinks him, not her, but he really can't tell which, the bird is black, not too big, he's seen much bigger vultures here with wing spans of four feet or more, this one has maybe a wing span of a little over a foot, and as she flies in front of him, let's call her she, about twenty feet above, she crosses the path and he spies a red marking on her throat; she's dipping in the current, not flapping her wings, but adjusting them and shifting them, she isn't a crow or a raven, by the way she seems to peruse the earth below her as she glides, wingtips like fingers, Path guesses a small vulture; she sweeps to his left and then rises in the air behind him; he turns around again to watch her and then she does the most unusual thing, she circles back toward Path and begins to fly toward him following the trail, she flies right at him, dips to descend about ten feet off the ground as she draws near, she's not attacking, her talons are tucked, she tips slightly, right, then left, then flies just over his head; he turns to watch her as she circles behind him again, rises, then drops to the trail again, flies toward him, and this time, as she approaches, as she drops almost level to his face, he can swear that their eyes meet only a few feet away, her eyes are red, she flies over him and then she ascends, now she rises up and circles him once, twice, and as he begins to walk she circles in front of him as if leading him down the trail until he reaches an archway of overhanging scrub trees and enters it; when he comes out the other side she's gone; it's hard to know how many times Path has taken this walk, over twenty-five years or more, probably thousands, he saw a puma once, puma tracks a few times, Nadine once left the trail, ventured into a gully and brought back two deer skulls, Carla said why didn't you bring them home, well, he didn't think to bring them home, seen tons of coyotes, he'd never seen a bobcat here, maybe too dry, there was a small mule-eared deer herd one year that sometimes followed him and Jackie O on the trail, ungulates for ungulates Path figured, or follow a horse and you'll probably end up in front of some grass or hay, they probably didn't even notice him, hundreds of ground snakes and fence lizards, skinks, one king snake, a couple horny toads, lots of rattlers, some babies, some five feet long, he had a bunch of rattle snake stories, a rattle snake rattle can chill you to the bone with its frightful beauty, but only twice did a snake ever coil up and raise her head, the females are bigger, like T-Rexes, twice he'd seen rattle snakes mating, they crawl up each other into the air, H.D. got bit by one through her ear, tough dog, he saw hawks, mostly red shouldered or red tailed, crows, hawks hunted snakes, even rattlers, flying down and pinning them behind the neck and then flying to a branch to peck their heads, what was the learning curve there, he'd seen plenty of crows and small birds, jays, and blue birds as blue as a Renaissance painting, as Carla might quote, Della Robbia Blue, but Path was no bird painting expert or bird expert, why did that bird do that, as he walked he thought about what the bird had just done, why would she do it, he was too big to eat, he'd seen swallows swoop at cats, but this behavior wasn't aggressive, at the moment they were the only two animals out there, maybe she was just curious, but of course it felt like more than that, something happened between him and the vulture and it was something that couldn't be explained and best left unexplained, it made him think of angels, well, maybe it didn't make him think of angels, maybe he just thought of angels right now, St. Michael was an angel, an archangel, he remembered reading a book by a priest about angels, he didn't read it upstairs on his throne toilet next to the bedroom but on the toilet downstairs near the kitchen, he read the *Roman Martyrology* there too, as well as the Penguin *Dictionary of the Saints*, how odd, he didn't remember spending that kind of time down there in the kitchen bathroom and he didn't remember much about the books either, though maybe they influenced his meditations, maybe something stayed in him after all, like shadows of ghosts out the corner of your eye, and he remembered that there were seven different kinds of angels with different jobs, though he could only remember four kinds of angels and he didn't quite remember their jobs, Michael a warrior, Gabriel a messenger, to Mary, if he recalled correctly, for the Annunciation, and to Muhammad, to narrate the Koran; the angel book author seemed to indicate that there were hosts of each kind, how many, Path wondered, and wasn't there a Medieval dispute about that, that if angels were pure form then there could only be one of each kind, though millions of them, matter-less, could fit on the head of a pin, like neutrinos on a thumbnail, though neutrinos, being matter, might fit a billion of themselves there, the number would necessarily be finite, so if there were subtle differences among the kinds of forms the angels might be, if they were matter-less, than an infinite number of them could sit on a pinhead, though that would become troublesome for what one might mean by kinds of angels, meaning there would have to be infinitely possible forms within each kind and, then, what would 'kind of angel' mean, what would differentiate them in kind; wherever one might end up in this controversy, heaven must tolerate matter somehow, Jesus ascended in his body, as did his mother, Mary, those were confusing times for heaven, no doubt, and theoretically yet so, because though an all-powerful God could accommodate a miracle, God can't do the logically impossible, that is, say, create a stone so heavy S/He can't lift it, so it would seem that God, having created the division between spirit and matter, would only violate that division with great exception, meaning God can transcend his own natural and spiritual laws, the questions being why, how, when, and where, well, God doesn't have to tell us, best to just accept things and say your prayers; but the question, as A.W. DeAnnuntis might put it, is just like why is there something and not nothing at all, a question that isn't answered by Descartes who kind of invented the problem and said that humans have a special gland, the penial I think, that allows the spiritual mind to interact with the material body, but yet how is that done, how can two fundamentally different kinds of existence, mind and body, spirit and material, penial gland and soul, interact; the Mormons just say that it's all material, so do Buddhists, though for Buddha the issue was metaphysical and thus not worth discussing, i.e. there is only the world we can observe, no talk of God, heaven, or soul, and the Mormons just go on as if the problem were solved by a twist of rhetoric, their celestial and telestial realms play by the same rules as the spiritual realms of Judaism, Islam, and Christianity; well just because something is a big problem doesn't mean we can't go forward by ignoring it, for example, evil; so, Path, Michael was a warrior who led God's angels, how many and what kind unknown to us, against the hordes of Lucifer, who were his recruits, presumably of the same ilk, Path read the Bible and that story wasn't in there, he read about the war in Heaven in *Paradise Lost*; later he read somewhere that it was in *The Apocalypse*, but leaving all that aside, now Path is thinking about Lucifer, what did the angels have to do before creation, if only to bathe in the Beatific Vision, that's where Aquinas would have us all end up, though people don't start there, our souls are created ex nihilo, by God, at conception, don't ask why, different religions have different views on that but right now we're talking about Path's dealing with St. Michael the Archangel, that's the ballpark, so given Lucifer, Light, God's number one, no equality in heaven, heaven purportedly beyond equality, in the perfect world, inequality doesn't result in jealousy or resentment, so what was it about God and heaven that Lucifer couldn't stand, how could he organize a revolt if God was omniscient, did God hide his omniscience, could S/He, or had Lucifer revolted knowing he'd be kicked out, if not already kicked out the moment he was created, that we're free to do God's absolute will is a tough one for anybody, well at least it was for Calvin, and Muhammad, so what to do but serve, what's the matter with that, but something was so wrong with that, so wrong that Lucifer couldn't do it, better to rule in hell, if rule or serve were the only choices, what were Lucifer's minions choosing then, what of any devil's free will, so who created evil, Lucifer, God, evil, that which Augustine says is the absence of good, rejecting his own Manicheism, then evil is nothing, a big, bad, mean nothing sometimes, it sure puts up a fight, if Good is so good and evil nothing, ah, Judas, poor Judas, Path thought as a child, poor Eve, doomed to freely choose the wrong road, and that made all the difference, and miles to drive, says Leonard Cohen, before I sleep, yet if Path was one of billions of inheritors of humanity's creation, made in God's image and likeness, then too Lucifer; Oh, said Eve to Adam, their backs to the Garden's gate, what angel cast them out, was it Gabriel, why is there anything instead of nothing, what was wrong with wanting to know stuff, maybe that was Lucifer's bitch, if he'd known his fate was sealed would he have chosen his fate, so he posed the question to Eve, what's wrong with wanting to know stuff, and Adam patting her bulging belly said, That's what's wrong with it; Path stops on a ledge that overlooks a broad swath of the Canyon, lowers his hands to his sides, remembers Bergson quoting Plato in the *Timeous*, Path has read all of Plato, God, unable to make the world eternal, gave it Time, a moving image of eternity; there are many, many paths to God, Path, whether God is waiting at the end of any of them or not; when Path wrote and failed to finish *The Last Book of Everything*, faltering somewhere after 800 pages, somewhere, he thinks, during his "History of Pets," back then Path was a free man, but instead of dwelling in Paradise, Satan appeared to him in the form of a publisher, yes, publication, the forbidden fruit, were either Path or I thinking about an audience we might have avoided such a cheap allusion, but to whom does that matter, as Gass might say, somebody, some person greater than me or Path is God here; then Path got cancer, he confronted mortality, would have to face painful births, abortions, lies, ambition, drinking himself to death; there's a bar in LA somewhere on Wilshire named the Barkowski, pictures of Charles Bukowski with quotes under them line the walls, Path only remembers Find what you love and let it kill you, but ironically, with more irony than Bukowski himself seemed capable, the place only serves wine and beer, no hard liquor; they love Bukowski here in LA, the movie Barfly, who played Bukowski, somebody O'Rourke, Mickey O'Rourke, maybe, Path's not so good with movie stars, he couldn't tell you who pitched for the Dodgers now (well, Kershaw, sometimes, when he feels okay enough) and that's even with reading the sports page and listening, sometimes, to the radio, Path doesn't care who plays in the games, sometimes he wishes he didn't know who wrote the books, the marketing of authors, dead or alive, even better dead, one of whom, Saramago, now dead and over-hyped like Rushdie, Kundera, Bolaño, let's stop there for now, Path just finished *Balthasar and Blimunda*, Path's fifth Saramago novel, and he hesitated to start another, but he had *The Tunnel* on the toilet, the narrator, Kohler, is audience to the crazy genius history professor, Tabor, or MAD MEG, his death rant, taken with appreciation, fear, and cynicism, though Tabor's rants sound an awful lot like Gass's if you've read him; Path went puttering back to *Omensetter's Luck*, Path himself once wrote a novel dedicated to Gass and Omensetter, it started out as *Moon Run* where it was set, a small town northwest of Pittsburgh, became *Tyrone's Luck*, then just *Luck*, set in the mid-Seventies, a man and a woman keep journals in which each accuses the other of having murdered their lover, the ubermensch hippie Tyrone Kismet, unreliable narration like crazy, but Path started the novel when he was twenty-seven, rewrote it, once from scratch, a dozen times, in his forties gave it to Carla who took on the pseudonym Taylor Moon and found an agent for it, but still couldn't find a publisher; I'll only give titles here of books Path failed to publish; Path stands on the ledge, living in heaven and hell at the same time, every second inhabiting Paradise and then the next second walking away, there it is, there it is now, but there is no now, or there is only now with its terrible rattling, his thoughts inescapably banging inside his head, the clash of symbols, would that be excuse enough to kill yourself, Path, maybe, if there were some horrible and incurable suffering thrown in; by the way, I looked up Schiller in the *Stanford Encyclopedia of Philosophy*, there didn't seem to be much connection with William James at all, Schiller was a buddy of Goethe's, and for Schopenhauer the Will is a non-rational, uncontrollable force that, when it confronts the world, creates the madness that is reality, kind of an ontological entity if there ever was one; James is quite more circumspect, for instance, in what circumstances might we imagine the will operating, and if it did, could it make a difference, can belief help create the fact, there are the train robber and cliff jumping examples, everybody knows them, right; Reinhold Niebuhr, in an odd Introduction to *Varieties*, accuses James, due to his historical circumstance of writing before the First and Second World Wars, the Holocaust, the atomic bomb, of being naïve, but as Path stands upon his ledge contemplating the inhabitants of the realms between earth and heaven, California is burning, there are fires in the Arctic Circle, glaciers are melting and flooding the earth, some say ice, some say fire, but for what I know of desire, Path remembers stumbling to a flight in JFK and passing a man who, holding a credit card above his head, is screaming, St. Anthony, St. Anthony found my lost credit card, high interest rates aside, and what happened to Path's cancer, that they tried to cut it out, that they bombarded it with proton rays, no luck, and then, after three more years of dallying inside him, it went away, his radiologist said, Impossible, his surgeon said, No conceivable medical explanation, his oncologist said, Boy, I seldom see anything like this, Seldom, said Path, Okay, never, but this makes me think it could happen again, we'll open a special file and keep an eye on you, It's not gone, Well, for now it's gone, An X-File says Path. Nexile. Why did that bird circle Path and swoop down to take a look at him, Path is thinking it's senseless to try to explain it, yet it happened, he's thinking about guardian angels, is it Zoroastrianism or Islam where you have two, two devil companions as well as two guardian angels, is Bergson's Naught like Zen Nothingness, are there only two words, Arthur Schopenhauer, that mean anything, yes = existence, no = nothing, do you see me, God, does God have eyes, what image, what likeness, Path wonders if he should take a look at Deepak Chopra and remembers an interview he saw on TV, way back when he was watching TV, and Chopra said we needn't worry about our children, why, his own son seemed to be wasting his life, spending hours preoccupied with video games, doing nothing else, but one day, after he turned thirty, he got serious and became a video game mogul, so don't worry, things always work out, but Deepak, what if I can't afford a video game for my son, shall we start there, maybe Path was missing the larger point, he would be the first to admit that he held a tenuous relationship with the world, the larger points in front of his face; that morning, at his desk, he turned and spied a copy of Salman Rushdie's *Midnight's Children*, a book he never made it through, it should be on a pile of books Path couldn't make it through, a list of authors, Rushdie, Pynchon, Grass, Eggers, Chabon, Cormac McCarthy, Bukowski, Proust (in the future he will pick up *Swann* again, on the throne, and begin to like it) others who he forced himself to read and hated, well, if not hated then disliked, Henry Miller, Kundera, David Foster Wallace, Solzhenitsyn, even Joyce, though he didn't make it through *Finnegan's Wake* and he tried several times (in 2021 he'll pick it up again), as his friend, the inimitable Mary Mammarella said, Pin the Penis on the Genius, but there were far too many of them, not even enough penises to go around, put'em in a bag and shake'm up, any day now Path will read in the newspaper that V.S. Naipaul has died, another one, as Carla says, here today then gone, back in Davis, California Path had a housemate named Buzz who read all of V.S. Naipaul, Naipaul who said that the novel died in the Nineteenth Century, as Path's mother used to say, consider the source, when Path picked up Naipaul he felt like he was reading a Nineteenth Century writer, though in fact Path was a big fan of the Nineteenth Century, Do I contradict myself, then I contradict myself, I am large, I contain multitudes, and, I tell Path, too implicit, For whom, says Path, where is the bottom of It Doesn't Matter, it doesn't matter all the way down; how about Flannery O'Connor, Path liked George Eliot a lot, too, at least, like Tolstoy, she confronted religion, and the infrastructure of social injustice, because often the thing that bugged Path about the geniuses with penises was their politics, reach into that bag we're shaking here and pull out a book, likely you'll find a social reactionary or at least a world that is deeply bourgeoise, but Path, Oh Path, once an owner and lover of horses; some years back a writer contacted Path about sitting on a panel at the Associated Writing Programs, that year meeting in Pittsburgh, a panel about what it meant to be a working class writer, in his precis Path talked about the drug of mass cultural entertainment ala

Huxley and market censorship as implicit corporate mind control, he was thrown off the panel and replaced by Phil Levine, They feed they lion, who talked about wine and jazz, but Path knew plenty about wine and jazz, if only it were a wine and jazz panel; says Baudrillard, The real, moreover, has never interested anyone, It is a place of disenchantment a simulacrum of accumulation against death, And there is nothing more tiresome, What sometimes renders the real fascinating— and the truth as well—is the imaginary catastrophe that lies behind it, Do you think that power, sex, economics—all these real, really big things—would have held up for a single moment unless sustained by fascination, a fascination that comes precisely from the mirror image in which they are reflected, from their continuous reversion , the palpable pleasure borne of their immanent catastrophe; lots of puns on the word real here, Thanatos, reality principle = pleasure principle = death drive, give me liberty or give me what, Path, he thinks of his vulture, birds, give them liberty and give them nests; Path read all of Virginia Woolf but couldn't get through Charles Bukowski who, after a reading in Davis attended a reception at Karl Shapiro's home and proceeded to write on his walls and art with a Magic Marker, Written anything since V-Day, Karl, writes Bukowski on Shapiro's walls, Shapiro was stoic, beyond praise or blame, but the writing director then, Jack Hicks, declared Bukowski a hero, was Lucifer ever so cruel, later, in Salt Lake City, it became fashionable among the fiction writers there to proclaim, ala Henry Miller, that all writing was shit, why bother, though he bothered, didn't he, and Bukowski's line that no writing was more pleasurable than a good beer shit, So could you get me an agent? Path is leaning forward, his hands on the trunk of a dying oak tree, but the tree has been dying for thirty years, trees think and move very slowly, live slowly, die slowly, once, in another book, Path gave a chronology of the things he'd read, lots of stuff, so he wants to leave this desert of the unread geniuses, this bitter rant; in the morning now, since his nexile, as he wanders between the semi-conscious and sleep, he sees his corpse, gazes at his own cold forehead, it comes to this, what have you done today to ease or abate it, if all is wasted time (Suzuki Roshi, quoting the 6th century B.C.E. Chinese master Sekito, Do not pass your days and nights in vain) then what, he's hanging from the bottom of nadir by his fingertips, Jimmy Dale Gilmore, I'd kill myself but what's the sense, committing suicide in self defense; Path's sitting in front of Saint Jin with Carla, Jin on the couch holds a piece of paper, this is what they told me today, they being them, her voices, let me read it to you, she says, then oh, I can't read it, my eyes are too bad, Use your glasses, says Path, she puts them on, I still can't read it, would you read it for me, honey, she says to Carla, and Path is thinking that she wrote it and can't remember what she wrote, can't read it, as the Jin holds out the piece of paper to Carla, just read it, honey, but it doesn't matter how harmless or nuts her intentions are, that piece of paper puts Carla at Jin-Jin's knees again, and Carla, you are a real poet, more real than 99.9% of the people out there calling themselves poets, Path sees Carla bleeding humiliation, and though it is the life of the artist to bleed humiliation, we are not that humiliation, not that car, that house, that job, that horse, that editor that doesn't know the difference between his shit and his ass, that man who fucked Path a thousand times and who got away with it, died a civic hero, not even the love you have for this mother in front of you, Carla, your mother who holds this doggerel from the saints in front of your face, because when you touch it you will be locked in that garage again, locked in that room again, that closet again, and no matter how much you love her, Carla, don't read it, don't touch it.

Did I tell you that Path was on the spectrum? Anyway, we never talked about what happened that night at the Glass Table, did we.

DELUSION VS. IRREALITY

LOTS OF THINGS THAT PEOPLE THINK ARE THE SAME are really different, and the other way around. People think, at least the few people who might think about it, that Charles Bukowski and Henry Miller were Beats, but the Beats preceded them and were Romantic writers, Bukowski and Miller were not; compare Kerouac's Tristessa or Mardou with any of Miller's nameless whores, male or female; Bukowski wore his inebriation like a merit badge, Kerouac drank and wept and lived with his mother, but Path is not a fan of writers' lives, though he has read all of Kerouac and, in this rare case, biographies, seven of them; Path wrote the only book about Kerouac that isn't sold at City Lights, an episode he wrote about and published, so the title is excluded here; I'm asking no one to remember here that Path is not me and I am not the author and that this narrative, if it can be described as such, because the narrative elements here have long since escaped—a book mark in time—last night Path's sister Aubrey called, on the news in Pittsburgh they'd announced that the Attorney General of Pennsylvania would release an 830 pp. Grand Jury investigation into sexual molestation in six Pennsylvania diocese, earlier in the year the A.G. released a list of 51 people, predominantly bishops, priests, and others, of whom there was credible evidence that they molested boys, Dr. William P. Garvey, President of Mercyhurst College, Path's molester, and his brothers' molester, was on that list, now, decades later; on the day that list was released Path's younger brother, Simon, called on the phone and wept, the Arch Bishop in Erie, Pennsylvania, Path's hometown, expressed his sympathy to the victims and asked them to forgive, Yeah, said Simon, and what's he going to do about it; Garvey was buried in December 2017 under a marble gazebo engraved with quotes from Thomas Jefferson (a slave owning hypocrite?) Path knows that Garvey's Board of Trustees, who'd hired and then fired an investigator after Path and his brothers interviewed with the Erie Times News and named Garvey as their molester; the investigator came to the same conclusion about Garvey's activities so when the trustees fired him they knew about the molestations and did nothing, all this in 2005; then in April, 2018, when the new news just broke, the Erie Times News contacted Path again, because he was the leading witness when the paper did the exposé on Garvey's activity, that was fifteen years ago when nothing came of it but a lot of nasty letters to the Times condemning Path; last April Path simply said, first justice, then forgiveness; then came talk of opening a two year window on the Pennsylvania statute of limitations on sexual molestation; the current bishop has leaked to the reporter who stays in touch with Path that if this breaks out, Path could bankrupt the diocese; that's right, Path, your failing to forgive the molesters would ruin thousands of innocent lives; the Grand Jury investigation, supposed to be released at the end of April is held up by the Supreme Court, purportedly because some people named on the list want to be redacted, how can they do that ahead of the game; Path, fearing that the same trustees who smothered the case for fifteen years are now trying to cover up their cover up, contacted the lawyers in Philadelphia who conducted the lawsuits against Penn State in the Sandusky molestations, the lawyer he spoke to said, There's yet a lot of money stacked against you and the Catholic Church is very powerful in Pennsylvania; like Path really wants to go back to it, though he must, if you can wait till dark, Path, have a bourbon on the rocks; Garvey handed him his first drink when he was thirteen; so put down that bourbon, Path, be bigger than all of it, save your life; this is not you; drink rye instead; now Path doesn't want to think about Kerouac and Bukowski, and what the hell does Baudrillard mean by seduction anyway, how many little boys did Allen Ginsberg, a member of NAMBLA, fuck, how many Bill Burroughs, how many Foucault while knowing he had AIDS; Path has read each of them and even liked their work, but he doesn't forgive them, has stopped reading them, never liked Michael Jackson, just separate the man from the work, why don't you, and why not separate the man from his penis first; but in the next twenty-four hours the Pennsylvania Grand Jury releases its 1,300 page report that names 301 priests and over 1,000 victims of child sexual abuse in Pennsylvania, the Bishop of Erie releases a new list, Garvey isn't mentioned on either of them. And Pennsylvania never drops the statute of limitations.

No one is going to publish your book on Trotsky, Path, your horse will be sold, your life will be mold, in two weeks you go back to work and you are too old, your tooth is gold, you have a bird you like to hold; one day, when his father was dying, Path sat with him on his porch; it was summer 2002, barely a year since 9/11, Path had driven across the country with Marlena, now named Jesus, taking only highways across the southwest, then following the Mississippi River from Vicksburg to St. Louis where they spent two days with Bill and Mary Gass; Path has written about it in other places; they stayed overnight in Memphis on the way to St. Louis, Jesus pushing hard to get Path out of the Vicksburg War Memorial park and on to Graceland; along the highways, outside small towns, billboards of the other Jesus and eagles marshalling the souls up from the twin towers into the arms of heaven, now, over fifteen years later, Path is reading histories and firsthand accounts of the Vicksburg siege, researching for another doomed novel, but after five years of research on Leon Trotsky and two years writing a novel about Trotsky's time in Mexico, 1937-1940, his first Realist novel, devotedly and stupidly putting his heart and soul into that book, it's been sitting for months with a publisher in Berkeley and an agent in New York, cuddled in the new rejection protocol, that is, no response at all, you don't ripen on the vine anymore, you rot; Carla loved the book, particularly the portrayal of Trotsky's lover, Natalia Sedova, as well as several other women, including Frida Kahlo and Jacqueline Lamba, Andre Breton's lover, and Rivera's second wife, Lupe, as well as a poem written by Trotsky's warrior-lover on the armored train, Path's best poem, given he's a lousy poet, a lousy photographer, a recreational bicyclist, a peripheral horseman, I mention those avocations here because they're the kinds of things that almost everybody thinks they can do immediately after they pick up a pen, buy a camera or a bicycle or a horse, or skis, unlike say, the piano or guitar or slack rope walking or high diving, well, Path isn't that stupid, it took him five years riding every day to be able to sit on a horse, keep his butt in contact with the saddle no matter what the horse did, when you can do that, then you're a beginner, Path might be a fool but he wasn't that kind of fool, so Maria Sizskaya's poem in the novel is pretty good, even Carla thought so, but she thought he didn't have a chance in hell of publishing his Trotsky book because he was a white North American man and Frida Kahlo was owned by the Latinx, though half German like Kahlo, he still he would not be permitted to write about Frida, or Mexico for that matter, such is identity politics today, for good or ill, such is Nexile, the few people who know who Trotsky is hate him, so Path has set his sight on another novel that will be impossible to publish, the siege of Vicksburg, because as a white man born in the North he certainly won't be permitted to set a novel in a Southern slave-owning city during the Civil War, he ain't Black enough nor white enough, can't touch it Path, so let's go Roland Barthes, Audience Degree Zero; Path and Jesus drove through western Kentucky where they got gas at a station with metallic pumps, the numbers rolling, little boys in overhauls rode sting ray bicycles beneath the dike that held back the Mississippi, in Arkansas, while Path searched for a Confederate cemetery, they saw boys playing basketball on dirt with a bushel basket, the bottom cut away, hanging from a tree, Path once did that, too, but that's what I like about the South, still on the river they had lunch at a small diner in Cairo, Illinois overlooking the Mississippi's green water, Path seldom ate lunch, but in Carla's white Forerunner with California plates they were a hit everywhere, though at the Canadian border on the way to Niagara Falls they were strip searched and the car vacuumed, it was the summer after 9/11, Jesus had black, red, purple, and blonde hair, Path in his straw cowboy hat stacked with the feathers of wild birds that he found on the trail while riding Jackie O, but the Mounted Police were taking no shit from Americans at the border, and meanwhile, back in LA, Path's absence had helped Carla realize that his presence had been suffocating her, she had the house painted red, stopped picking up his phone calls home, quit stalking me, she'd said to him, he said, From a continent away? So she's throwing out his mail, going out to bars, tempting pick-ups, does she consummate them, Path doesn't want to know, he can't pull enough out of his guts to even hate her and she hates that about him, she sorts through pictures of herself, eyes herself in the mirror, realizes, is she realizing it for the first time, that she is beautiful, gorgeous, why has she wasted her life inside Path's self-absorption, Path could feel it from 2,000 miles away, his heart was coming apart; his nothingness was too much for Carla to bear, his absence more oppressive than his presence, at night, before sleep he keeps a journal—she's given him everything, she owes him nothing, he writes every night, preparing to return to an empty house, when does it happen, when did he fail to notice he was crushing her (like her mother?) now, his child asleep in the motel room, he won't tell her of this travail, they shall travel together, this vacuum around them and between them, in his heart he says goodbye to Carla every night, Why don 't you call Momma, I'm calling Momma, he says, she's not picking up, Where do you think she is, says his child, in a bar? Yes, he says, maybe at a party or in a bar—in the Toyota, Jesus was teaching him the history of David Bowie; Disney had taken over Graceland and turned it into Gift Store Village, hubba-hubba, Jesus, not quite fifteen, bathes her feet in the Mississippi while the truckers honk from the road, They love you, said Path, I hate them, said Jesus, But Jesus loves everybody, Not this Jesus, You'd rather they hate you, I'm going to be an artist, she said, I'd rather be crucified, Metaphorically, said Path, Do you want the last word on me, Father, said Jesus, and Path realized that he would never have the last word, on anything; they spent two days with Gass in St. Luis, a night in Cincinnati with Carla's brother and his family, fundamentalist Christians, two days with Chuck Kinder and Diane Cecily in Pittsburgh, the East, towns and cities like a Johnny Cash song, on to New York where his brothers lived on East 93rd, one of whom barely survived Garvey's molesting, but it's 2002, we're yet on the cusp of much of that and New York City is yet sullen under the shadow of quietude of 9/11, working back to Erie, PA where Path's great powerful father is dying the death of all his strength, super nuclear palsy, death so ironic, twenty-five years earlier his cerebral mother died of a brain tumor, and Path, your heart breaking now, you know your heart won't kill you; but right now, on the bathroom throne, Kohler is at Mad Meg's deathbed, Gass mentions the *Nibelungenlied*, yes, Path, you read that on the toilet, too, next to his reading chair, two Civil War histories bookmarked at Vicksburg, he's already finished some anthologies of Vicksburg journals, he's got new short stories in a manuscript by A.W. DeAnnuntis, another 400 page novel in manuscript by Ron Alexander, he's finished Bergson's *Creative Evolution* and begun Saramago's *The History of the Siege of Lisbon*—Carla's reading *Blindness* which she'll finish in a blink, she swallows books one at a time while Path reads seven or eight at a snail's pace, he doesn't think he can read *Blindness* because he's read H.G. Wells' *Island of the Blind*, where can you go with that conceit, though you don't have to go anywhere, certainly if you're Saramago; on Path's reading pile stool next to his reading chair he's gone back to *Omensetter's Luck*, Baudrillard's *Seduction*, he's started Bachelard's *The Psychoanalysis of Fire* that he notices is inscribed by his sister, Aubrey, on Christmas 1978 and published in 1938, and Sartre's, yes, finally Sartre, *Being and Nothingness*; and here's the Nexistentiality, Path is being visited by his best friend of and during the summer of 1965, Alex, who lived one block south of him on 25th Street, one block north on 23rd was the black ghetto, Alex first contacted him forty years later in 2005 while the Garvey molestation thing was breaking out, don 't worry, Path, time is meaningless and no one will ever read this, but Path swirls, I swirl, into the vortex of writing for no one at all, holding the lie over our heads like Atlas holding the world, our unreliability descending like the backs of turtles; still, let us remember that Path is on his way to sell his horse and what might seem to happen before or after that in some ways does and some ways doesn't; when he wrote *The Last Book of Everything* he planned to destroy Time, narrative time, he wanted anyone to be able to pick up the book and open it anywhere and begin reading or end reading or keep reading all the way around to where they picked it up, though he also aimed for a spot where the pages stopped, when he returned home from his Road Trip with Jesus and Carla had left him, end there, start there, start or end anywhere, on the road trip he and Jesus circled back to Erie, his father, Red, almost died that day from heat stroke, Path is racing back from New York City, across Upstate New York on Route 17 to meet his brother, Wil, and install an air conditioner, his father doesn't want it, he wanted to die there in his home, I ain't dyin' in a hospital, he tells Path, I'm dyin' here, I'm goin' out feet first, and the next day, sitting on the porch on one of his metal chairs, chairs that go back before Path's memories, pale green with white lattice backs, iron covered with a thin raiment of porcelain enamel, Red sold porcelain enamel for a company Path thinks was named Erveen, he has an old bowling team shirt, once his father's, that says Erveen on the back, Red over the left breast, the front is short, your bare stomach shows, Red wore it and Path did too when their stomachs were hard and flat, Red bowled semi-professionally in an industrial league, sometimes went on long trips with the team, once storefronts and gas stations were covered with porcelain enamel, not lights, not neon, porcelain, Path thinks of the porcelain red Pegasus hanging at the corner of a brick Mobil station on the northeast corner of 26th & Parade, now there is barely any porcelain anywhere; what about your mother, Path, well, he's written about her a lot, but it's published, though more to come, he feels the pressure, the need to give her narrative weight here in this Bardo labyrinth on the back of nothing, his father stares out at his blighted neighborhood, half the homes burned down, the rest blown out, windowless, upper porches held up by stilts, pimps and crack dealers work the streets and his father says, I just want to sit here, I just want to sit here, To want so little is too much; he'll be dead in less than a year, dying almost twenty-five years to the day of his wife's death with her name on his lips, Eleanor, Eleanor, and Jesus says she's going crazy here but before Path can leave a reporter from the Erie Times calls and says he's investigating Garvey for child molestation and what can Path tell him and Path is thinking maybe nothing, maybe nothing, and he can't reach Carla, fifteen years after that it's the 40th anniversary of Eleanor's death, the 15th of his father's, his daughter is leaving again for Australia and when she leaves his heart inexplicably turns to ashes like Shelley's heart, it aches and aches and Carla weeps, the Diocese of Erie releases its molester list and his brother Simon calls him and weeps, Where is Garvey, some men, Path knew them, killed themselves, other's lives lay wasted by drugs, jail, homelessness; Path tells the reporter everything and when it's published in the newspaper Path is reviled, hundreds of letters to the editor call him a lascivious creep, a fame monger, a money sucking asshole, so foolishly, though only so because all action is foolish and inaction worse, Path flies back to Erie fifteen years later, I don't want to follow him, I don 't want him to go, his brother, Wil, lives in a house twenty miles outside of town, half put together to accommodate his crippled wife and half taken back apart to accommodate her evacuation to a rest home, Wil is 71 and very overweight, unemployed, used and trashed when GE evacuated Erie for Texas like a Tsunami escape route, a born again Catholic he's living off handouts from Protestant church food banks, his younger daughter who lives with him, is Path's niece, they watch 1950's Westerns 24/7, Aubrey shows up from Pittsburgh complaining that Path hasn't come for long enough and that she only has two hours to give him, Give me nothing, says Path, Or give you death, Aubrey replies, or nests, thinks Path, which makes him think of Ornette Coleman, did he have a concert by the sea at Carmel, Monterrey, in 1958, or was it '53, and maybe it wasn't him, maybe it was Erroll Garner, the family stays up late drinking, Wil bought a fifth of Jim Beam, which Path would never drink, having gone beyond even Jack Daniels, he drinks single barrel batch bourbon now, but tonight he's happy to drink Jim Beam, they talk about Garvey, their poor parents, their poor, poor parents, near dawn Aubrey claims the couch and Path sleeps on a mattress on the kitchen floor, in the morning they'll go to the graves after they visit the rest home to see Joan, Wil's wife, palsied by multiple sclerosis, can no longer walk, she has a computer, a TV, a sewing machine, as she says, What more could you want, Wil's other daughter, Laura, shows up, the younger one, Claire, never goes to see her mother anymore, Laura has a real job and a jobless boyfriend, they sit in the hospital lobby with Joan who displays her rather remarkable self-made quilts, then they leave Joan and go to the cemetery in Winter Green Gorge, Path has written about the Gorge and the cemetery a lot, but it's in stuff that he published, Eleanor had always threatened Red that if he died without converting to Catholicism he couldn't be buried in a Catholic cemetery where she'd get herself buried separately, but she died first and he put her here amidst the heathens, but next to him, next to him now, yet Path envisioned this moment differently, saw himself kneeling before the two graves and weeping, and now he feels nothing at all, Aubrey complains that the gravestones are unkempt, Wil says, So clean them, and she says, I haven't got the time I have to get home, and Wil kneels and rubs a stain on Eleanor's grave with his thumb, he lets out a deep heave of breath and finally, unfeeling, Path kneels, but like Camus' stranger he has no tears, nothing to say; did he kill them with his need to escape, his mother's dogmatism, his father's violence, escape the Church and God's quiet and hidden omniscience, escape their miracle love, They were so innocent, Aubrey whispers, and back home, on the scatological throne, Mad Meg, from his deathbed, lectures Koehler, Death makes life meaningless, something Gass himself said to Path on that long road trip, they sat at a table overlooking the backyard where Mary Gass and Jesus are swimming in the pool and Bill Gass, a sigh of fondness crossing his brow, are those tears forming at the edge of his silver eyes, he raises his wine glass and says, Life is meaningless, and Path sees the scene with Kohler and his estranged wife, Martha, holding each other in a field of flowers and a thousand startled Monarch butterflies and the couple, on the verge of their destruction, tremble and weep; Anne leaves with her boyfriend to go eat pancakes (they will marry on December 31), Aubrey heads back to Pittsburgh, Path rides back to Wil's where Wil and Claire watch a Fifties Western, Path drinks a Bud, he didn't go into town, didn't visit the old neighborhood, instead he hugs Will and Claire goodbye and drives his rental across the south of Erie, east to west, then north, down to the shore and into Presque Isle, the Bay is high and silver gray, it snowed too much last winter, on one weekend alone over eight feet, through the foliage the city spreads out on the opposite shore, he can spot the downtown, the Public Dock, renamed Dobson's Landing by his molester because teenagers kept stealing the L in Public, the spire of the Catholic cathedral, St. Peter's; when he drives to the lake side of the peninsula dark clouds are forming and piling in on the northern horizon, he parks on a beach, he puts on his rain jacket and walks out, a cold rain sprays his face and the lake begins to churn, hitting the shore with waves a foot high, Lake Erie, a Great Lake, is it the smallest of the five, is Ontario smaller, Erie, he knows, is the shallowest, only about two hundred fifty feet deep, it has islands somewhere to the west, islands he's never seen, he should go to them but today is not the day, there will never be a day, he doesn't want to ever come back here, though he remembers now why he came to this beach, off to his right, behind a stand of bushes and trees lies a tiny bay that few people know of, the bay everyone knows is Misery Bay where Perry built his ships and smuggled them out under the British noses in the dead of night, on the backs of logs, at high tide, yes, these lakes are big and have tides and bays, but the sea battle wasn't fought near Erie, but west of here, near Sandusky, closer to Toledo; he should swim, when he was young he couldn't go near water without going into it, it didn't matter the weather, the wet and cold, but not today, in this cold and this rain, on this purple day of sadness, but when he lived here briefly in the mid-Seventies he'd push through the brush and lay naked and alone on that beach, swim nude, though he didn't drive to the Peninsula then, the Peninsula is what locals called it, no one ever said Presque Isle, French, the French were here first, then the British, the French killed fewer Indians though the Erie tribe was rubbed out even before the French got here, by the Iroquois, or the Mohawks, the males tortured and killed and the women and children enslaved, that's what he'd heard anyways, people didn't talk that way about Indians now, who told him that story, was it true, well, was anything true; Path's first airplane ride was on Mohawk Airlines, from Erie to Buffalo to Ithaca where Garvey, who was going to summer school at Cornell, waited for him, Garvey researching his dissertation on the Elizabethan Exchequer, Garvey was a Tudor scholar back then, Path wrote about this in his memoir but he changed the places and names, Erie to Stuben, Ohio, Cornell to Ohio State, Ithaca to Columbus, Garvey to Callahan, he changed every name but his own, why, because then he thought to protect other victims, though people did research, and others remembered, you could figure it out if you wanted to bother, but most of those molested boys, now men, denied it all and signed petitions for the newspaper condemning Path, though in truth Path didn't care about that; the wind kicks up and blasts his face with rain and spray, he hears the sigh of a moan coming from the foliage, though he's heard moans in the woods before, in fact, on the path he is walking in California, when he passes the big oak on his way home, he often hears the groan of a man, a wail, less of pain than despair, a pleading, and he turns but there's no one there, and he calls out, who are you, where are you, but there's no response, there is never another cry, so the first time he dismissed it, but when he heard it again a few weeks later he stopped walking there for a while; he used to walk his dogs there, dogs were illegal, especially off leash, but it was a narrow trail and the rangers never got out of their trucks, if they appeared they parked at the trailhead and there was plenty of time to spot them from above it and leash his dogs, how they ran, what joy, chasing rabbits, birds, squirrels, H.D. even chased deer or cougars, there is a bog up ahead under a walking bridge where Nadine loved to race down and frolic in the wet stink, now she's old, diabetic, and blind, but he looks at her, into her and sees the frolic yet in her heart, but since he's gone back to the path and sometimes hears the moan behind him, always from the same spot, always singular, and not every time, sometimes it doesn't happen for weeks, but like the knock under his kitchen cupboard, he now accepts it as undeniable, if inexplicable, yet undeniable, is it like a vulture swooping down to look you in the eyes, and now here, on the lake, he hears a sigh in the foliage, a woman's sigh and, well, maybe it wasn't a sigh, or if a sigh, then a sigh of the rain and wind, the vulture swerving to him by coincidence, the moan the sound of branches groaning in the breeze, the knock some pan shifting, though here, alone on a cold and windy beach, he feels death stalking him, yet how many times has death had her chance with him, he tries to feel whether death is male or female, in Saramago's *Death with Interruptions* death is female (Shelley has called her female too) maybe death was like Jung's animus and anima, one or the other or both depending, depending like that chicken and red wheelbarrow in the rain, and what he remembers now about this little beach behind the trees, is the day of his brother Wil's wedding to Joan, Path was in the wedding party with Wil's old friends, he wore a tux, a gold tux, the only time he's ever worn a tux or a bowtie, but after the ceremony, when the party jams into Path's Toyota station wagon, he doesn't drive them to the reception but heads to the Peninsula, they smoke hash, the interior of the car fills with smoke, Path parked where he's standing now and the party leaps from the car and follows him through the trees to the tiny beach where they strip nude and yell and swim, the sun is pouring light, the lake and sky shimmer, white caps bash, it is a wild soft day, how many of them were there, he thinks four, he can't remember a single name, a John, a Tom, maybe, though last night with a Bud and Jim Beam, in front of a Fifties Cowboy Western, Wil recalled that two were dead, another harasses him with Trump slogans on Face Book, Well, he said, well, things change, He's a fool, Claire said and Will said, Maybe, How far was Garvey's reach, asked Aubrey, did he molest Tom Ridge (once governor of Pennsylvania, then the Head of Homeland Security, he awarded Garvey's college, Mercyhurst, with a lucrative contract for police training) Ridge is sick now, said Wil, bad heart I think, In more ways than one, said Aubrey, but here in the wind and rain and facing the tumultuous lake Path is thinking of the tiny plane he'll catch tomorrow for Detroit, and then his flight to LA, he longs for Carla, and in his head, his mind, does he believe in the mind, something whispers, it might be death whispering but he can't make out what it's saying; when he had cancer he didn't feel stalked, he felt afraid, he felt how much, how long, he added up his life and thought this is what you've done, there's no more to do, you tried, you failed, you'll be forgotten, Gass said that life was meaningless because meaning was syntactical and life was not, so what meant and what didn't, what meant? the roar of the waves, the whisper in his head, the voice calling from the hidden beach; when he was young he'd have gone in, even in the rain and cold and swam anyway, what would happen now if he did, what would it change, how would he dry off, what would be the point of an old man acting like a young man; he recalls Carla's mother some years back taking him and Carla to her community swimming pool, he tried to remember if Jesus was with them but he can't recall her being there, Path yet loved to swim and he could swim every stroke, freestyle, backstroke, breaststroke, even the butterfly, the pool is warm, it isn't an Olympic size pool, not 25 meters, but the old style, 20 yards, and an old man slides in and begins to thrash the length, not a good swimmer but, in fact, decent enough, and Path watches, his elbows resting on the end of the pool as the man splashes toward him, stopping across from Path he looks up and says, I love to swim, and Path says, Me too, and the man raises his goggles to his forehead and says, I swim every day, That's great, says Path, I'm in great shape, Yes you are, How old do you think I am, and Path, unthinking, says eighty-five, the old man's face dropped like lead, yes, Path, there is no good faith, only bad faith, no in-itself without for-itself, as well as the reverse, he dreamt last night of his mother, as death has stalked him he dreams of his parents more and more, he and his mother are rummaging through shoes on a closet floor and his mother holds a baby, a thick brown cherub tucked under her right arm; are you afraid of dying Path, Seneca says that all we have to do is conquer our fear of death, Buddha said the ego, same thing, that's all we have to do; the wind, blowing in from the northeast, is brisk and wet, death stalks him with neither visage nor words, it has no voice, he feels it palpably, like a madman he feels a big change in the air, he wonders if it's the big change that Saint Jin feels is coming, a cosmic warning, if he walks through the foliage to the beach, will death be waiting there, will he swim, would it matter, he turns his back, he touches the oak tree, how soft the light, last night, yes, it's last night again, he sat with Carla at the glass table recalling how in the winter a silver racoon jumped onto the split system cabinet outside their window, it's where they kept food and water bowls for Mr. Scott, a short haired orange tabby with a white belly and neck, though thin, agile, and noisy like a Siamese, is Siamese and impermissible world now, Mr. Scott lives outside because when their other cat, Frida, was just a kitten, Mr. Scott tried to kill her, five times, a friend in Westchester who fed feral cats took him until an owl swept up Frida and flew away, Mr. Scott, then Path's last cat, was brought home again until a vet called the day after Thanksgiving to say Frida, who had a chip in her neck, had been found in the wild, tail broken and shattered in half, right hind leg fractured, she'd survived a month, then found her way to a cabin porch whose occupant brought her in, puffy gray white Frida came home, Mr. Scott tried to kill her again and now he lives outside, she in, now she's too big to kill, bigger than Mr. Scott who really prefers living outside, Path, who's owned dozens of cats and loved and remembers many of them, thought back to when they had two dogs and seven cats along with kittens, too, and two seventeen year old newts, a frog, a rescued turtle, a python named Eve who performed with Jesus at the Venice Beach Freak Show, and a genius rat named Ratsky, bought as snake food by Jesus but saved by Carla who couldn't watch and ended up as Path's drinking buddy, skittering down from Path's shoulder to a bourbon and soda until Path finally just raised the glass and let him drink and pass out on the back of his chair, this discounting the big, obsidian chicken that wandered into their house one day and moved in, back then Jesus lived with them, too, all of that and somehow life seemed less complicated then, more complicated now, and sometimes, listening to, say, Stan Getz before he went Bossanova and sharing a half-bottle of wine, Path and Carla reminisce, does that mean they're old, am I old, then I'm old, I am large, I constitute millions, as once, in the not too distant past, when out for drinks, margaritas, invented in Texas by the way, not Mexico, gringos the green, green grass of home, with a pair of poet friends, oh Path, you don't have poet friends, Path has always said he loves poetry, it's poets he doesn't like, which is two lies, not one, though that's a lie too, are we tunneling back, in 1995, when Gass published *The Tunnel*, Path published his only commercially successful book though it wasn't successful enough to keep him from being mid-listed, shit-listed as he called it, Path flew through *The Tunnel* without comprehending anything, as Cohen said, the ponies run, the girls are young, the odds are there to beat, you win a while and then it's done, your little winning streak, and when you come, to feel, your invincible defeat, you live your life as if it's real, a thousand kisses deep; the Path—tunnel thing is probably heavy handed and, if it wasn't before I pointed it out, it is now, but this time through *The Tunnel*, aboard the sacred throne, Gass dead, Path stalked by death, Path gets it, gets it, gets it, so we're tunneling now, though that's only one of its metaphors, its allegories, and this is an experiment to see how we tunnel back to where we started last, or last started, last night at the glass table, but let's save the discussion of how Path became the star of the Larry Levis documentary, Larry, who slept with Carla during the first time Path and Carla broke up back in Salt Lake City, those are two stories in themselves, the third story would be Path's discussion of the Fuck Off Clown joke which, in its first context in *The Last Book of Everything*, Path claimed to be the metaphor of all narrative development, since Path never published that I might permit tunneling there, but not now, now we're back in the bar, Lula's, drinking margaritas with the poets, Bertha and Wolfgang, and Wolfgang, learning that neither Carla nor Path has watched TV since 2013, Wolfgang staggers back in his bar stool and asks them, If you don't watch TV, then what do you talk about, and Carla says, We rate our cats; okay, that's one version of the very very long joke that ends with Fuck Off Clown, get it, though we've not circled back to the glass table yet, not back to last night, and though I'm not going to let Path go back to any Larry Levis stuff, neither the documentary film that Path and Carla are in, anybody can go see it, nor Carla's affair with Larry, Path, in his gentle way, hates Larry, not inexplicably, because, he says, there are men, women too, he supposes, who will unconscionably fuck anything, anybody, and Larry was like that, although Larry didn't have to seduce, or his aura was already seductive, slurry eyed, salacious by instinct, and famous, Carla would add that he was also a really good poet, maybe a great one, though Carla had slept with many great poets, though great poets generally don't sleep back, you don't sleep your way to the top in the poetry world, you just sleep your way, where, anywhere, and anyway this story's been broached, if surreptitiously, if by elision, in a novel that Path published about Carla's career before she met him, i.e. Path; yet several mornings after that last night we're heading to, Path, on the throne, read from *The Tunnel*: I . . . publicly maintained a whole series of beliefs I privately put no stock in, among them: Santa Claus and Shirley Temple, the fun of birthday parties, scouting, Ferris wheels, and baseball, the uncertainty of future happiness, all honesty, the therapy of work, what a pleasure it was to go and how nice it would be to have a sister, the peacefulness of Sundays, roller skating, the perils of chewing gum, the prize in Cracker Jack, anything at all three miles from me, each of those rules my father described as summing up common sense or Herbert Hoover, and every one of the so-called laws of God, Man, Nature, and the State; why Path and Gass got along so well, though you have to know where metaphor and fact cross each other's lines here, and is he referring to Three Mile Island, did that happen twenty-five years before Path's current students were born, and Path has two sisters, when was it nice, sometimes, Fuck the bastards, says Aubrey, work till you die; so not watching TV is a bit like being a vegetarian, inevitably it poses as a moral high ground whether you want it to or not, people immediately declare that they only watch Netflix or PBS, though Path likens it to his Ice Cream Theory of choice; Try this fruity ice cream, I don't like fruity ice cream, Yeah, but this is great, just try it, I only like chocolate ice cream, Just try this, Okay, I'll try it, and he tries it and doesn't like it, he likes chocolate, he'd take bad chocolate over great fruity every time, no accounting for taste, does everything have to be justified, need we always do what's best, just do what you do, don't theorize, argue for, mollify, though vegetarianism, now veganism, or raw vegan, or fish-vegetarian, tend to have moral overtones which, in general Path agrees with, when he was kind of a hippie he was kind of a vegetarian, grew his own vegetables, baked his own bread, he's vegetarian sympathetic now, and Path is in fact TV sympathetic, Hollywood movie sympathetic too, but now they've just become so much fruity ice cream, though he understands that anyone could accuse him of taking any number of high grounds, moral, aesthetic, intellectual, even political, yet if shit comes to shove, as he likes to say, he quietly takes all that high ground, thus the Gass quote, I mean, Path means, like really, can you spend a day, an hour, any time at all watching football, booze breasts and cars amidst what little football is played, well, football is the metaphor for the rest of that wasteland, right on up to CNBC and CNN, points repeated over and over with commercial breaks as long as an anaconda, PBS taking a half-hour to disperse a sentence of information, the radio isn't much better, NPR dragging out tedious interviews, yes we're starving here, yes we're drowning here, yes the lava is hot, the bees are dying, the sky is falling, but watch or listen if you must, he'll take early Stan Getz, Bird, Miles, Monk, Bill Evans, and conversation with Carla; they rate their cats, who had the greatest tail, a tie between the inestimable Mr. Puff, the Great First Cat, though he was closer to Path's sixth, let's go no deeper, and the other, Mucha Plata, tails like feather trees, they could lay them down over their noses; ugliest, Kih-hen, irascible, pale beige, three gray smudges on one side, a gray patch over one eye, a thin half tail; Romeo, the most passionate, who grew into a huge, long haired mackerel, who spotted Carla from the lap of a homeless man at the Malibu Coffee Bean and Tea Leaf and never took his eyes off her, he held her in that gaze for twelve years, even if he had to sit across from her or place himself in front of the television screen to do it, facing off with Nadine over Carla's lap, each occupying a thigh, Romeo gazed at Carla, unfazed, undaunted, anything else remarkable, not too much really, though Path once timed him climbing a tree to hunt a bird, he climbed ten feet per second, and well, he hunted squirrels by watching them cross the telephone lines and waited for them hidden behind a fence where the line descended, okay, smart and tough, because pound for pound you'd likely bet the squirrel over a house cat, though Romeo had disproportionate forearms almost triple the size of most cats, but at the end of his life, sick almost to death, his kidneys failing, he fought off a raccoon bigger than him at the upstairs doorway, took a horrible beating, but did not let him enter the house, his house, Carla's house, the raccoon retreated, fine, home court advantage and he had more at stake, but so much for the maxim that a house cat will only pick a fight he's certain to win, ask Lee, who won at Gettysburg, who won, Robert E? he didn't go up there to win, he went there to distract, he was a big distraction, fifty thousand dead men, and a hundred cats, a thousand stories, so anyway, they told their stories and rated their cats, like that, and one day as they sat there listening to Miles Davis' "Bitches Brew" drinking gin and tonic and smoking home grown pot, a silver raccoon appeared at the window, she put her paws on the pane and looked at them, black starry eyes, black stripe across her silver face, had they ever seen something so gorgeous, so wild so close, for a month or so she came every few evenings, eating Mr. Scott's food, washing her face in his water bowl, standing, her black palms against the window pane, and how did they know the raccoon was female, well, she stared at Path, not Carla, and Carla said, She's coming to look at you, which makes as much sense as you want it to make of it, but Path believed, and Carla came to believe it, too, that sexual attraction crossed species lines, male dogs loved Carla and were suspicious of Path, mares liked Path and stallions didn't, male birds and once even a bull elk squared off on him, this silver raccoon came to look at him, not Carla, and her behavior toward him, for lack of a better description, was furtive, so they named her Sylvia, and one day she disappeared only to return some months later with a silver kit in tow, so it turns out she was female after all, and what a cute baby raccoon; the two of them visited then for a while, though now Sylvia was less concerned with Path, became more business-like about eating and doting on her kit, but then, during a horrible heat wave, the worst in history, the temperature in Topanga Canyon soaring to 109, she disappeared again, and that, it seemed, was that, for months, Carla guessing that Sylvia had another litter but the heat wave got them and only the night before last, when Carla took a breath of cigarette, a sip of tonic, exhaled and said, I guess that's it for Sylvia, and Path sullenly agreed until last night, suddenly, yes,

Fuck Off Clown, Sylvia appeared at the window, and then a little silver head next to hers, and then another, and then a third, Sylvia glanced at Carla through the window and went to the food bowl, her affair with Path over, her eyes were not as bright, but one of the kits stood on his hind legs and put his paws on the window pane and gazed at Carla, mesmerized.

HAPPINESS RUNS (AWAY)

I'M UNHAPPY, SAYS CARLA.

Have you ever been happy, says Path.

When I bought my convertible. She pauses. He waits. Everybody has more money than us. They buy new cars all the time. They take trips.

We don't take trips?

They have bigger houses. They remodel their bathrooms and kitchens.

Swimming pools, says, Path, movie stars.

They send their children to Harvard or Yale. They put in new hardwood floors.

When I pray for paradise, says Path, Vishnu tells me I'm living in Paradise.

Living with you is not paradise, says Carla.

Do you want to buy some new clothes?

All the women around me have more expensive clothes.

Jewelry, says Path.

People just steal it.

They steal the agave plants out of our front yard, he says. They steal our mail and our newspaper. I put in a video camera, somebody stole it. I had to put a lock on my gas tank. It's pretty simple. You have it, they don't. They take it.

Then they have it and we don't, says Carla. Why doesn't it work the other way.

They even steal our cats, he says.

Not the shitty ones.

What does that say.

Have shitty stuff no one wants, she says.

And the less the better, says Path.

Corporations and utility companies are like Medieval lords, says Carla. Even at school, the other women dress better than I do.

Speaking of Medieval, says Path. Their older sisters or brothers got the land, the factories, they got sent off to the convent. The academy is a monastery.

Everyone we know is more famous than us and has more money. My brothers are bums. They ignore their mother.

Do you want to ignore her.

Yes. But I can't. All my friends inherited or married money.

Not you! says Path.

Not you either. That's the problem.

Are they happy, asks Path.

Of course not, she says, but that changes nothing. They're still better off. Better off is better off. Don't go dialectical on me.

We've got each other, says Path.

That's the problem, Carla says. Don't compare us to the rest of the world. I'm not talking about the rest of the world. I'm tired of your condescending.

To the rest of the world?

To me.

Path hesitated. He couldn't think of a response that couldn't be regarded as condescending. To respond would be condescending. To not respond was condescending. Carla, he said softly, I don't want to fight.

This isn't a fight, she says.

He gets up and goes to the kitchen wine rack, selects a $15 French Bordeaux, pulls the top and fetches a cork screw. The Australians don't use cork anymore, he says, the Spanish and Italians are moving away from it. He draws the cork and gets two wine glasses, pours into them, brings them to the glass table. Do you want any club soda?

Diet tonic, says Carla.

He fills two cocktail glasses with ice. That was it for the ice. He'd have to make more. He opens a liter of Canada Dry Diet Tonic over the sink, lets the fizz calm down, then pours. In his glass he pours gin. That's it for the Canada Dry and the ice, he says. He'll have to fill the ice trays now, because they don't have an ice maker. Everybody he knows has a refrigerator with an ice maker. All their ice makers are broken. That fulfills his world view concerning moving parts. He brings the drinks to the glass table. Then he pulls three ice trays from the freezer and fills them with tap water, stacks the trays and puts them in the freezer. Routine he thinks, you have to embrace the routine. That might be true, but Carla doesn't embrace the routine. After all these years they are yet so different, but here they are. Are we good? he says, but she doesn't respond.

Back at the table, he raises his wine glass. She touches his with hers.

I'll drink Schweppes if I have to, Carla says.

DESIRE
MIND THE GAP

IN THE END WE THREW THE TIVO OUT THE WINDOW. Let it spend some time in the wind and the rain. It had grown unruly. Bored, somehow, with our viewing patterns, it seemed to have created, like Kant, categories of viewing, and changed our channels at will, to please us? to please itself? (what is the "will?" certainly something my "mind" needs to think about, when and how is volition, whether demonstrated by human, animal, or machine, determined, conditioned, or free?).

I am trying to explore the gaps inherent in the necessary adhesion of fact and explanation, even when facts themselves are necessarily explanations, the gap between J. L. Austin's sense and his sensibilia. In London, when I'm notified (mindlessly?) by a machine, to be aware of transferring myself from platform to train, or train to platform, I am told not to "watch my step" from one to the other, but to "mind the gap." Though obviously recorded, the voice is female, not male, not a digital monotone machine voice, however digitally constructed, it authoritatively suggests, not commands, though it is everywhere, in all the subways, ubiquitously the same, it is the GAP we are minding, the space between, though you can't really fall into the gap, and it isn't a thing, it's that no-thing between where I'm leaving and where I'm going, and yet I must mind it to do either, like the space between the material and the spiritual? the space (is it space?) between the sub-atomic quantum world and the world of gross materiality, a reason why Alfred North Whitehead has been accused of mysticism?

Would that be Buddhism?

Plenty of us have been told many times that on the sub-atomic level there is far less material than there is space. The table that I'm writing on is in fact a webwork of buzzing movement. As Whitehead contended, the stuff that we perceive around us as *things* are better described as *events*. Whatever tiny bits of thingness there are "down there" (a metonym) it buzzes about, possibly in and out of the space occupied by this particular universe (existence?) according to the laws spawned in the first instances of creation, right now known as the notorious cosmic cliché "The Big Bang." As the matter and light of this cosmos runs away from itself, runs away from us at its maximum (and only) speed, 186,000 miles per second, no more, no less, though I imagine that measurement is only grossly approximate, somehow entities, quasars, galaxies, stars, planets, us, don't come apart, there are forces, laws, habits, traditions on the sub-atomic level that hold the phenomenal world together (mind the gap!). Now, cosmically, we have dark energy and dark matter, neither of which can be observed. However one wishes to explain that, we are pushed toward metaphor, toward what Whitehead would call *feeling*, and that's how existence as we seem to know it survives in the tension between such-ness and nothingness, because nothingness is not nothing, or, if you're a Buddhist, what-ness and nothingness spring, moment to moment out of nothing or emptiness, thus "emptiness is empty too," (and what and where is a moment?), or let us reverse the spiritual/material dualism and say that spirit, soul, even God, are emergent characteristics lying at the beginning or end of Time, or both. God(s) does not so much create the cosmos or cosmoses as They are created *by* them—much less anthropomorphic than Freud's view - more pluralistically, say Gods, or even souls, are emergent characteristics like natural laws, as real, at least, as dark matter, as any significant metaphor, or as Bachelard might suggest, an image, any metaphor, is as real as any fact, a metaphor can run you over, burn you down, blow up the world, can blow up this incomprehensible world. Take that, Ayn Rand.

This is not to elevate metaphor to the status of reality, nor to elevate reality to the status of metaphor, nor a way or means of "minding the gap;" but then I must ask myself, what am I trying to do? To somehow find the axiom, a fulcrum, that unites my personal longing to the thing longed for, if only I knew what that thing was.

While trying desperately to avoid religion(s), I think most serious religious thinkers, that is, truly philosophical ones, would say that I have to spin this once again, that the wrong questions have been asked, for am I not, in this longing, really asking for salvation? Does every particle, every molecule, clinging within itself, reach out across the abyss, wishing, willing, to be saved? From what? For what? To what? As Leonard Cohen asked, when did the suffering begin? I hesitate on the edge of this digression. Then again, the moment that I'm writing this is not embedded in immutable time, nor even on the page. Yet if you are reading this, then it was not thrown out. Says Dee to Dum, That's logic.

BAD MIRACLES

PATH WAS A GREAT BELIEVER IN TITLES, not the royal or secular ones held by people, but titles of literary or artistic things, he figured titles sort of set the mood, the direction, even if you wandered away and had to replace them later; in the header of this text, we originally placed the word 'Nexile,' a working title, though we're thinking about making Nexile a subtitle and changing the title to *The Time Before Land*, something that makes even less sense; some time in this literary now, in tomorrow's yesterday, the Jin phoned and said she was on the floor of her bedroom and couldn't get up, didn't know how long she'd been down, maybe since she'd awakened that morning, she fell out of bed, it was now 3 pm, what had she been doing since she fell, how did she get to the phone, she doesn't know, she can't get up, could Carla call Prison Village, Jin-Jin, you're on your phone *in* Prison Village; Path steps in the shower and all the water in the house goes dead; so there are those who believe miracles are a good thing, well, what is a miracle, where did the universe come from, asks Path, if space and time, space-time, were created at the moment of the Big Bang, what was it created into, what was the difference between empty space and nothing, were parts of universes or multi-verses disappearing in black holes and reappearing someplace else like quantum particles, didn't some cosmologists say that the universe was impossible; Carla has packed up and is racing down toward Prison Village, she called their resident nurse, they break into Saint Jin's apartment and find her on the floor, one leg too weak to move, Carla calls her younger brother, a talent agent with MegaMuse, his secretary tells Carla that he's on the phone with Mick Jagger and what could he do anyways, besides, this is likely the Jin's karma, let Jin and the world work it out, Carla calls her big brother in Topeka but he's at a trade show in Chicago, trading what for what, it's hard to know, meanwhile, Carla sits in a traffic jam on the 405, she bluetooths Path who thinks it's a stroke, the Jin fell two weeks ago, too, off the couch, how do you fall off a couch, now, falling out of bed, how do you fall out of bed and lie there for hours, she must have blacked out, her sister died of strokes a year or so ago at age 89, Path turns the house water off, then on, gets it flowing but the shower explodes again and goes dead, their plumber to the stars, Ernesto, is in Oaxaca, Mexico incommunicado, so says his cell phone message, Path calls another plumber, Jim Green, recommended by Topanga Neighbors, Jim Green says, I don't go up there, I don't go to Topanga anymore, try Dave Willsome, he lives up there, but Path has been in Topanga for almost thirty years and Dave Willsome has never responded to a phone call, never summoned the will, loosely speaking; Carla reaches Jin, It's my heart, Saint Jin says, The doctor says it's my heart enzymes, when Carla phones Path he tells her heart enzymes doesn't make any sense but what does he know, Buy me a cellphone, the Jin cries to Carla, You have a cell phone, But I don't use it! inside the miscommunication triangle Path tells Carla to get Jin a JitterBug, who does she call other than you, Then she'll Shopping Channel herself, and then us, into the poorhouse, Carla says, then an email from outer space arrives, a small press in Utica, New York tells Path they'd love to publish his animal book as long as he gets rid of all its ideas, what's left? stories, stories!

Carla has reached the hospital in Lake Forest where Jin-Jin shrieks that dozens of children are screaming in her room, her roommate—she doesn't have a roommate—is a plotting transsexual, plotting what, who knows, it's a secret plot, the doctor is ignoring her and making out with her boyfriend on the balcony and the nurses are trying to murder her with neglect, that she, Saint Jin, has been a martyr to her children all her life and why aren't they there for her, why, if Carla broke a leg, wouldn't she miss work, is she, Saint Jin, Martyr Mother of All Time, less important than Carla's broken leg, and Carla says, Mom, my leg isn't broken and I did skip work and I'm here, You're not here, you're not, you're not here for me, the transsexual is here, the screaming children are here, and then, anyway, the doctor phones the Village and declares that there's nothing wrong with Jin-Jin, old people just get disoriented sometimes, fall down, go to the hospital and act a little crazy, so just leave her alone where she spends the night screaming at Carla, back on the home front Mr. Scott breaks into the house and Frida ignores him while he eats a baby bird in the bathroom, some kind of detente has arisen, Counterpoint Press rejects Path's Trotsky book and the molestation lawyer from Philadelphia leaves a message that Path should call him, something about Pope Francis; with Carla sitting with her in her room Saint Jin calls and leaves a message to say she wants Carla to take her Writings and give them to Rick Warren at the Saddleback Television Mission; Carla weeps, I hate my mother, she says and her older brother finally calls back and says, I wish Mom was dead, Baudrillard states that seducers know how to let signs hang and Bachelard claims that alchemy was penetrated by sexual reverie the way that earthquakes are rather more common on earth, and where else would they be common, those French; a woman phones about buying Nikki and Path, weeping, meets her at the ranch and saddles his horse for her, she jumps on and Nikki takes off like a rocket and bucks her off, worse than selling her, he might be stuck with her while Angela from the HR office at the Society phone calls Path and Carla to remind them that they're financially doomed; I'm changing my name to Ludwig Abramosky Path tells Carla, Go with Stanislaw, replies Carla, I like the name Stan, says Path, Path is dead, no more Path, You've tried that before, says Carla, If I've failed once, says Path, I can fail again.

WHY DON'T YOU WRITE ABOUT AFGHANISTAN, Path, why don't you write about Pakistan, why don't you write about Palestine and Israel, how about China, that would be a big topic, what about the California Indians, the Spanish mission system, the Comanche, the casinos, global warming, Hurricane Katrina, Hurricane Maria, Hurricane Eric Dolphy, California wildfires, sexual assault, child molestation, the Wild West, Ghost Town and Venice Beach, the homeless, the minimum wage, the techies, the way the camera follows us in slo-mo, the way we look to us all, the way we look to a distant constellation that is dying in the corner of the sky, these are the days of miracle and wonder that Paul Simon sang about in 1987, the year Jesus, nee Marlena, now Trans Kafka was born, Simon got the constellation thing wrong, constellations are not places but made up picture outlines of stars seen from earth, stars millions of light years away from each other, so don't cry baby, don't cry, don't cry, don't cry, why don't you write about that, why don't you write about aliens coming to earth, aliens staying put, illegal aliens, alien abduction, immigration, President Rump, Roe v. Wade, the Supreme Court, the Me Too Movement, Black Lives Matter, police brutality, Russian espionage, the Russian Revolution, the fall of the Soviet Union, Karl Marx, animal consciousness, dogs, rats, birds, cats, Black people, red people, yellow people, brown, women, white men, non-binaries, the C.I.A. in South America, the drug wars in Mexico, insurance corruption, corporate extortion, drug makers' monopolies, opioid addiction, the Jesuits, the Hindus, Hindustani Arianism, Tibetans massacring tigers, Vajrayana Tantric harems in the Himalayas, Tibetan monks running orphanages and fucking the little girls, how about the Holocaust, Costco, Frankenstein, past times, Charles Shaw wine, credit card fraud, identity theft, the wicked, the holy, the bereft, assisted suicide, the dead, earthquakes and flooding, rainstorms and fire, fire, fire, how about horoscopes amidst those distant constellations, midgets and ropes, the shrinking Salton Sea, Orville and Wilbur Wright, the melting ice caps, the expanding Ozone, species extinctions, AIDS in Africa, Ebola too, the Jesuits, the Franciscans, the end of nuns as we know them, the Mormons, the Jesuits, the Jesuits, the Jesuits, why don't you write something Path, how about Trotsky in Mexico, the siege of Vicksburg, because you already wrote about all that and no one knows?

THE OLD WOODEN CRISS-CROSS

PATH PLACES HIS PALMS ON THE OLD OAK, its bark at the trunk stripped away, by whom, who would vandalize an old oak tree, Path touches its bare skin, heal, heal me, heal you, he stands and hears an inaudible female voice, he lowers his hands, he hears his name, Path, and looks up; above him a girl sits on a thick branch, a young woman, really, he supposes, though now he thinks of his own students as kids, when he was nineteen did he consider himself a kid, he did not, and at the time the women his age, in that dawning of contemporary feminism, insisted on not being called girls, girl was diminutive, he agreed, though now that battle of words has passed, though his daughter battles with, over, new words, she has gone non-binary, wishes to be addressed as they or them, not she, not girl, though this girl in the tree looks younger than his daughter, could she be 25, 21, though there's a way that this girl's eyes, one brown, one blue, and her smile, look eternal, is that the word, or internal, is that the word, there's a way that he doesn't see her as in the world at all, but in his mind, whatever that is, wherever that is, he's pretty undecided about the mind, remembers, as he meets the visage above him, his mother on her deathbed, eyes like stormless clouds, in a coma now for days and his father saying, She never responds to anything anymore, and Path, remembering deathbeds past and future leans over his mother and whispers in her ear, I love you, Mom, I'm here with you, I love you, because hearing is the last thing to go, and in his book, his book about his childhood, the very end of the third of three, his sister enters with her newborn daughter and places her on his mother's chest and his mother, Eleanor, awakens, that's how that book ends; years later, at the funeral of one of his first students, this one died on a motorcycle at the Alpine Crest on Rt. 2 in the San Bernardino Mountains, only 40 years old and leaving a wife, a daughter and a son, the wife approached Path and said, That was his favorite book of all, he kept it next to our bed, and isn't that who you write a book for, Not for nobody, not like this book for nobody, says the girl above him on the tree limb, think of your molestation memoir that saved your younger brother's life, an audience of one like Thoreau's audience of truth, write your book for one person other than yourself, the girl has brown hair in pigtails over her shoulders, wears cut-offs like they all do now, cut so short that they expose almost everything, and an embroidered blouse like from a Sundance Catalogue or Johnny Was, her brows are thick like Frida Kahlo's and she wears short, clunky boots, a slightly wedged heal, again very much the style, why haven't we ever described Carla in such detail, well, Carla is more complex, too close to his heart, besides, he has in other books, he's done it too much, she dislikes it, let her live her own life, leave it alone, leave her alone, but where did this limb girl come from, how did she get out on that limb with smooth, naked legs unscathed, It's kind of a miracle, Mr. Path, she says, like the teenager in Murakami's *Windup Bird*, a book, and a character that, in the end, Path didn't like, Mr. Path, repeats Path, How do you know me, Did I go to school with your daughter, Did you, he says, and she smiles quixotically, I'm Veronica, she says, you talk to me every day, she pauses, then, You wanted me to look like a nun, I didn't want you to look like anything, says Path, you were a metaphor, if vague, of someone who might help me, Help you to not panic, help you to calm down, help you to disappear, help you to not disappear, why not go to a Zendo, I don't like groups, says Path, What if I brought you up here with me, says Veronica, and held you tight, what if I took you to a mountaintop and offered you might, offered you night, offered you the world, Like Satan and Jesus, says Path, I thought you might say that, says Veronica, but Jesus says aren't we all the sons and daughters of God, Do you know God, asks Path, and Veronica giggles, she says, To Know God is to disappear in God, I'm tempted, but I've chosen to stick around, so to speak, to help out, Like Buddha, says Path, like Tibetan Gods, You're mixing metaphors, and religions, she says, when each religion is a metaphor for the others, don't you think, And every metaphor is as real as another, says Path, Or unreal or true, Veronica responds, shall I come down there, Are you a saint, says Path, Do you want to fuck one, she says, fuck a saint, No, he says, But you already have a thousand times, though you've fucked the devil, too, and Path, now realizing that he has been mesmerized, sees that Veronica doesn't move her lips when she speaks to him, or maybe she does, he sees her lips moving and then can't remember seeing her lips move, maybe this encounter is telepathic, or he's making it up, what does the Great Unreader think, the audience of one, the audience of not one, Were you once alive, he says, Never alive, never not alive, I'm here whenever you think of me and whenever I think of you; Path looks away for a moment, then looks up again but she's gone, what can happen after that happens, he turns and looks up at the hilltop above him, once he rode Jackie O to the plateau on that hilltop every day, he let her loose underneath him, let her run, a rush of pounding wind and sound, though the day before she died she didn't want to go and, puzzled, he yet urged her and she capitulated, then the next morning suffered a horrible, painful death, he found her in her pasture rolling on her back and screaming, he got her off the ground and walked her and walked her, each step she tried to lie down and he had to whip her to make her stay on her feet until the vet arrived and emptied her intestines by flushing her insides with a hose, which did no good, he remembers following her as they trailered her to the hospital, watching her back end sway, and at the hospital they flushed her again to no avail, they x-rayed her, and while he waited an older horsewoman walked up to him and said, I've been watching, how old is she, Twenty-one says Path, and the woman says, Let her die, don't make her suffer, let her die, and when they brought Jackie O out of the x-ray stable she refused to move until she spotted Path and the surgeon tells his assistant, Let her go to him, she steps, falters, Path goes to his horse, and the surgeon says to his assistant, Let him take her, she'll do anything for him, and Path leads her to a stall where she collapses and Path kneels, then sits, she puts her head on his lap, then the surgeon appears at the door and tell him they could try surgery, it would cost tens of thousands of dollars with success and recovery uncertain, Let her go, he says, and Path hugs his horse, I'll see you tomorrow, he whispered to her as he did every day, she mutters, groans, and that was the end; he thinks of Nikki now, if he sells her he won't have to watch her die, he thinks that those are the kinds of decisions he has left; back home in his office he scans his book shelves and notices a small journal, he picks it up and it opens to a page with this: October 25, 2006: Kanchenzunga shows her face at sunset, glass blue in the northwest; to the west the mountains are shadows beneath the red sky, a narrow crescent moon sinking above, and near it, to the right, a planet; it must have been from his balcony in Gangtok, Sikkim; we dream the nightmare of Brahma dreaming, he and Carla were just back from Kathmandu, he doesn't really remember keeping the journal, and Veronica, Saint Veronica, whether you are only in Path's head, in my head, or only in God's, or whether somewhere in between, Carla, now at the glass table says,

What a wonderful thing the mind is and how horrible its thoughts, his older
sister wants him to call her, the lawyer who has offered to represent him if the
Pennsylvania congress decides to lift the statute of limitations on childhood
molestation has sent him a contract, his firm wants 40% though they cover all
fees and services, the fiction board of his tiny publishing endeavor, What Books,
is about to throw him out like Stalin did to Trotsky and frankly he doesn't care,
he wishes they'd just get it over with, he wishes he could just quit but he can't,
Think of all the good you're doing for so many writers, Carla says, besides I need
the press, and now Saint Jin is on the phone, Help me, she pleads, please help
me, she's old, she's insane, and she's alone, it's Carla's mantra of forgiveness,
unforgivable sins forgiven, Path fears Saint Jin will outlive him, turn to your
right, disaster, turn to your left, pain, behind you failure and humiliation, fear
and death ahead, for everything, turn, turn, turn, there is a season, and a time
for every purpose, every purchase, every surface, at 2 a.m. when Garvey drove
him home he went through red lights, there was no one on the streets of Erie, PA
at 2 a.m., he remembers sitting in front of an editor at Simon & Schuster pitching
his memoir, she suggests that he alternate the chapters on two time-lines, the
first the story of his grooming and molestation, the second his coming to
remember and realize it, which he does, and six hundred pages later when she
looks at the book she decides that really that wasn't such a good idea; Bill Cosby
was sentenced today for one of his rapes, he's 81, three to ten years, he'll be out
in no time, months, and Garvey is dead, the bishop of Erie holding the Attorney
General's list of creditable molesters and now, several months after Garvey's
death, he offers his sympathy to all the victims, begs for their forgiveness, It's
time to heal, heal all the unacknowledged wounds, and Path wrote to the Erie
Times, first justice, then forgiveness, and the bishop tells a local reporter, off the
record, that Path could bankrupt the diocese, schools closed, church doors
chained shut, Catholic children forced into the horror of public schools, the
Church, admitting guilt before anyone is found guilty asks for forgiveness as a
means of covering up its cover up, and as Path waits for the attorneys in
Philadelphia to make a counter-offer for representing him, his brothers in NYC
suddenly fall silent to his emails, Path writes to Simon who suffered the symptoms
of molestation for decades, joblessness, nervous breakdowns, Path writes, I
sympathize with your caution, I approach all this with reticence and no joy, yet
it must be done, but Simon is silent now, as the state congress in Pennsylvania
mysteriously mulls the statute of limitations while in the U.S. congress a woman

testifies to a rape attempt by President Rump's Supreme Court nominee, the congress, Path can testify, will not believe her, Path once testified, too, on PBS and the local television outlet of ABC, what did he say, he doesn't even remember, yet now, as his dream life is invaded by the metaphors of rape and threat, he doesn't want to go back to it again, he'd drop it, leave it alone, though Carla points out that if he won some money maybe they could retire, where, somewhere, if he lives, he points out, if he lives, though they tried, a month ago, a lifetime ago, to reinvestigate Mexico where in the 80's and 90's they travelled frequently, the Baja, Mexicali, El Ciudad de Juarez, Puebla, Cholula, Guadalajara, Pueto Vallarta, Manzanillo, Oaxaca, and many times to Mexico City, once for over a month, stopping their Mexican sojourns briefly when the drug gang wars heated up, though again, recently, to El Ciudad de Mexico to do research for his Trotsky novel, mostly in Coyoacán, only to find both Casa Azul and Trotsky's fortress completely museumified, everything moved around and placed behind glass, he stood in Casa Azul pointing out what used to be where, he'd researched two other novels in Mexico City, one about the Irish deserters, the San Patricios, during the American invasion in 1846, particularly the battle at the Churubusco where the San Patricios, the artillerists, fought hard and deadly but ran out of ammunition, surrendered and were hung for treason, that's what you get for being right, it was a book he never finished, and another about Kerouac's stay with William Burroughs on Orizaba Street where he wrote *Dr. Sax* stoned on Burroughs' toilet, Path published some of that in his Kerouac novel, the only book written about Kerouac that isn't carried by City Lights, a testimony to Path's irreverence and outsider status even unto the Beats, so much so, Path, that you have to be proud of it, don't you, that's why he's going to Vicksburg, his dedication to the inapproachable, but now he and Carla fly to San Miguel de Allende to investigate their retirement, a three hour flight to Guanajuato, two hour crowded van shuttle to San Miguel, Path had an ex-student, Ron Alexander, a fiction writer ten years older than him who'd retired there, who took them to El Santuario de Atotonilco, a 17th century church on the outskirts, its inside walls covered with intricate murals, its alcoves filled with larger than life statues of Christ's passion, during the revolution of 1810 the revolutionaries hid in the church under its floorboards, in San Miguel, Path and Carla sauntered on the cobblestone streets, Carla shopped for jewelry, silver, in a kind of infinite and desperate quest to spiritually, if not materiality, replace the Matilde Poulat that was stolen from her by a homeless couple they'd befriended, they sat in café's and drank mezcal, perused real estate office windows, dreamed a possible dream until Carla got sick, stricken, likely, by the parasite she'd acquired in India, when they returned her doctor told her she could not move to Mexico or almost anywhere for that matter, Path took that right between his nexiled eyes, a fire engine roars by the house, his blind dog howls, another agent rejects his book, so what, you say, but thank the Gods you aren't there or here to say it, he picks up *Infinite Jest* again and again he puts down *Infinite Jest*, as he prepares to teach "The Concept of Character in Fiction" from Gass's *Fiction and the Figures of Life*, he feels like he can't teach it, has nothing to say about it, he sets aside *Omensetter's Luck*, the novel he read in 1982 before he met Gass, maybe he's through with Gass, tired of the harangue of nominalism and metaphor, and now, having read almost every word of him, sees that even Gass could stoop or fall to the banal and ordinary, whatever his dedication to alliteration and rhythm (just like Kerouac, though Gass would never admit it when Path brought it up) sometimes he didn't sound so good, sometimes his descriptions fell flat, the details didn't dance and, as if proving what Gass himself had to say about detailed imagery, they were vague and unexciting, never became poetry; the phone rings and it's Trans Kafka, two weeks ago she called from a car on her way to the Melbourne Fringe Festival, she was driving with a friend, where was her husband, Space, well, he flew down, she was carting equipment for her show, Space, flying without her, and when Carla put down the phone Path said, That's not good; these things Path knows, he's no longer a Behaviorist but he still follows behavior, watch what they do, don't pay attention to what they say, it's just another thing they're doing, and this time when Carla picks up the phone Trans confesses that things aren't so good with Space, a tough week in Melbourne, Space's acrobatics collected bad reviews and an award, she performed a show a day for a week, each one got better, she said, each one drew larger audiences, but Space wasn't in any of those audiences, too busy with his own show, yet he expected her to be there for him and now, he flew back to Sydney alone, Sydney, where she's famous and making money, collecting Federal and Provincial arts grants, piling up performance dates and zooming across Instagram and You Tube, Space is living on Centrelink, the Ozzie dole, and in the doldrums, contemplates going back to Melbourne to live, Will you go with him, asks Path, No, she says, I'm famous here, I work here, I have work, Come home, wishes Carla, but she doesn't say it, there's too much determination, confidence in her daughter's voice, though she can't use daughter anymore, use child, her child lives in Sydney, Australia and married or alone they're not coming home, Simon finally emails Path, he doesn't want lawyers to get rich off his pain and suffering, well Simon, it's that or nothing, meanwhile, Gary, his contact lawyer at LBK tells him the firm will reduce its take to 33% if they settle out of court, 40% if it goes to conviction, plus fees and services but no hourly wage and Path signs, emails his brothers that he took the deal; Gary tells Path that the Pennsylvania House has voted to drop the statute of limitations while the Senate mulls opening a two year window and the Catholic Church, backed by some big money, will sue the state for an unconstitutional action if the statute is dropped, more delaying action, but they offer arbitration, and while they battle over that, more delays, the Church, says Carla, over a glass of red wine at the glass table, is waiting for you to die; she's been through it before, after her defamation lawsuit against the Society within a year everyone at the university was gone, the President, the Dean, three associate deans, the English chair, only the African-American perpetrator who reasonlessly screamed at her in a meeting that she was a mentally ill racist, remained, Carla won the lawsuit after five years, 90% of her money went to the lawyer, so it was a classic Society maneuver to rub out institutional memory; the same thing happened in 1990 when Hank Gathers, an All-American basketball forward died of heart failure on the basketball court during a game, Path knew he was a coke addict, Gathers drove a convertible BMW, his family was given an apartment, and when Hank died they threatened to sue the school for the housing, the school settled quickly and silently, soon quietly accepted resignations from the President, the Athletic Director, the head coach, Paul Westfall, and his assistants, and moved on to quiet decades of losing seasons, the Society had been at this game for over 500 years, the on-campus rape of Jesus and the beating she and her boyfriend took in a campus parking garage at the hands of four marines on their way to Iraq could just be ignored, so why didn't Path quit, why did the world watch while the Nazi's murdered 8 million Jews, is that too implicit, why risk the loss of life and limb to suffer the loss of life and limb, in the world, a world in which Path and Carla have just returned from a trip to New Orleans and then, yes, the ill-fated Vicksburg, Path's novel will be a metaphor of 47 days of siege (why not 49 days like the Bardo, that's what Antoine Volodine would do), the book and the city will die of starvation if not surrendered; despite his college days rapes Kavanaugh is on the Supreme Court and the noose will tighten around women's rights; while they were gone it rained, wet rained goodness fell, but what must follow the first storm will be the first Santa Ana and the ugly dry warm winds will circle back from the desert and you can only hope or even pray that the land will not dry out too fast, the winds will calm, it will rain again before the next winds, this circle of danger in southern California that Path has suffered through for 30 years now, the battering of disasters, storm, flood, wind, fire, mudslide that he's lived amidst for so long, as the warm wind whips around his little writing cottage he wonders why he hasn't left and then thinks of silver Sylvia and her three silver pups who visited again last night to snitch Scotty's food, one, the largest and most curious, Carla names Sergei, then Butch, the other two are more narrow-faced and timid, she thinks they're female, if she can be so non-non-binary, so they drove back home through these verdant hills and glorious cliffs to their animals, only three now when once there were so many, seven cats plus kittens, two dogs, a turtle, a frog, two newts, a snake, a rat, and a daughter, now child, their dog, Nadine, now blind yet joyous, a year has passed, it is 2019, they sip diet tonic tonight because there was nothing to do in the South but drink booze and eat fried food, and Path asks Carla, Will we get another dog, more cats, how long can we live in this house with its sixty twisting steps; the electric companies are talking about turning off electricity in the wind zones to prevent fires starting from grounded wires, and yet there are stories to tell here, Carla's lawsuit, why not, and the trip to Vicksburg, start in the middle, start at the end, so the African-American man who spawned Carla's suit, let's name him, D. M., but the shadow, the ugly web of the academy, shall we go there, Path, it doesn't interest either of us, while on the throne this morning, Gass's narrator, Kohler, tells of the Kristallnacht when he helped loot, trash and burn Jewish shops and synagogues in Berlin; Let's stay here as long as we can, replies Carla, Can I count my time to the end in dog lives, says Path, he must have a crown replaced on a molar this week, then a physical, his liver checked for alcohol deterioration, his blood searched for cancer, he could really use a drink under this volcano, a book Gass dearly loved, so let's go back to Vicksburg, now dying at its center; they fly into New Orleans, rent a car, Enterprise is out of intermediate sized cars and Carla points at a white convertible Mustang, Can we have that, Yes, so they drive to the edge of the business district on the border of the French Quarter, a hotel called The Pelham, a tiny 3rd floor room without windows, it costs $38/night to park, the Pelham brags thirty three rooms, though some have windows, there are no amenities but for a soda machine on the bottom floor, only three workers, a parking valet, a desk clerk, a cleaning woman, but the clerk points them to a restaurant around the corner called

Mothers, Carla eats soft shell crab, Path crawfish etouffee, sides of fried spinach and garlic, red beans with rice, they drink Abita, a local pecan ale, sit out the night in their blind room drinking Knob Creek Rye, yes there is a television in the room, a small, flat black screen, but neither of them is tempted to touch the remote, even with the Dodgers in the playoffs, the bars will all have televisions, there will be too much television regardless, cars, beer, breasts, legs, scare'em-sell'em insurance commercials, and even if sports is the only unscripted TV, it's millionaires vs. millionaires playing for billionaires, rabid fans rooting for guys who have never lived in their town, and in the end someone will win, someone will lose, and it will all fade away, Path asks Carla if she remembers who won the last Superbowl, she cannot, Philadelphia beat New England, he says, the year before New England beat Atlanta with a huge second half comeback, can he name any of the players, only two Patriots, Tom Brady and his tight end, Gronkowski, and Path follows sports in the sports page, but the black and white print leaves no pictures in his head, thank the gods, he doesn't want them, Path plasters it all onto his Wall of Not Mattering, a phrase he recently discovered at the Glass Table, he's working at plastering his personal universe there, sometimes it works, sometimes it don't, in the morning he wakes Carla, holds her, kisses her hair, he had nightmares, villainous children following him and threatening him, but Path and Carla get up, there's pod coffee in the lobby, they grab croissants at the Starbucks around the corner and cross Canal Street in the Quarter and walk down Decatur to the Café du Monde on the River, they wait a half-hour in a line a block long, then drink lattes and chicory with their sweet powdery beignets, afterwards they walk up the steps to the balcony over the Mississippi, Path remembers eighteen years ago, standing in the River with Marlena in a bayou above Vicksburg, the truck drivers honking at his child, then, Carla was fed up with everything and tried to leave him then, why didn't she, God knows, God doesn't know, she tried, she is yet a beautiful woman, but then, at age 46 men became speechless in front of her, students tried to copy her dress, and men fell silent before her razor banter, I would have left you, she told him upon his return, but there wasn't anyone as interesting, confirming one thing, Path believes, that no one jumps ship into the naked sea, there has to be another ship, and even the real ocean is no longer so full of other fish in the sea, so she's with him now, through cancer, through humiliations in job and career, does she yet think sometimes of leaving him, yes, she's thinking about it right now, but here, together, they stare over the mile wide green brown Mississippi, she only needs to touch his arm, in India, on the Ganges, he jumped in with the petitioners, the current surprised him and almost swept him away, but he swam back in, dunked three times like the Hindus around him, children jumped into his arms though he doesn't really like children, all his sins were forgiven, besides, then he was fifty-four and would still jump into almost anything, now he is sixty-eight, another thing he's left behind, will leave behind, like his horse, like this book, every day we write more, every day he leaves more behind him; they take Decatur Avenue all the way to Jackson Park, sit with the vagrants, then walk up Royal to Frenchman Street, drop into bars twanging and blowing with Sunday afternoon jazz, Frenchman the music street now, better than tourist saturated Bourbon, less spread out and confusing than Tremé, they stop for a beer, walk on to Bourbon Street, it's the eve of Columbus Day, still Columbus Day in Louisiana, in California it's now Native Peoples' Day, a long weekend here, in California only the post office closes, they wander back to Colony, down to the Pelham, share a rye on the rocks, eat out down the road at Luke, oysters, raw, fried, broiled, Carla will saturate on oysters before they're done with the South; the next day, as they leave New Orleans, a rainstorm hits so hard the inner city freeway is brought to a stop, a wall of rain, it lets up, they drive a little, get hit again, drive again, a dance of automobiles and rain, they are perched on a crowded bridge filling with rain and wind, but it finally ends, they move, Carla says, I've seldom been so frightened, and Path remembers driving out of New Orleans in the spring of 1973, chased by a hurricane and driving through the night in driving rain in Mississippi and Alabama, he had just learned he wouldn't get a fellowship to study for a philosophy Ph.D. at Tulane; now they wander the outskirts of New Orleans until they find the U.S. Route 61 to follow the river to Vicksburg, Carla's cellphone doesn't want them to take the 61 and continuously tries to divert them back to New Orleans to take the I-55 North and then the I-20 West to Vicksburg, they make five U-turns before they figure what Siri is trying to make them do, but eventually they find the 61 and travel across the barren bayous of western Mississippi to their cottage outside an antebellum mansion, The Cedar Grove, built by Steven Klein in 1840, marble, wood, and glass imported from France, Who built this, says Path, Who built this, and Carla says, Slaves, slavery surrounds and fills Vicksburg like a shadow, like ghosts, unspoken, the middle of Vicksburg, including the historical district is poor and black, a few extant churches, the home of General Pemberton who lead the Confederates defending the city, Pemberton himself from Philadelphia, retired and died humiliated in Norristown, Pennsylvania; Path and Carla go to the battlefield to tour the Union lines, they stop in the tourist center, watch a movie and a display of Sherman's failure to the north at Chickasaw Bayou, the failed attempts to build canals to divert the Mississippi, Path has read about all of this already, Grant's trail down the west side of the river in Louisiana to cross into Mississippi at Hard Times, he battles eastward across Mississippi to Jackson where he defeats Johnston and levels the city, then heads west, defeating Pemberton at Champions Hill and Black River, the Vicksburg siege lines are now a national park, the accounts are one-sidedly pro-Union, then the siege, 47 days, Path has read several firsthand accounts, so they drive with the top down past the cannons, the monuments, the memorials to the Union regiments that mark the Union trenches, but the Confederate lines are closed for repairs, so they head into town and find Pemberton's home during the siege, across the street the Catholic convent that served as a hospital, they go to the original courthouse that's full of Confederate memorabilia and a gift store chock full of Confederate flag souvenirs, on the second floor, a hallway behind the original courtroom is lined with paintings and homages to Jefferson Davis, yes, the South did not lose at Vicksburg, they were pounded by artillery from the river on the west and the trenches on the north, south, and east, starved out, the population living in caves behind the Southern lines, reduced to eating mules, rats, kittens, leather, crumbly cakes made out of peas, the soldiers too; Carla and Path eat at a restaurant just off the main drag, Washington Street, they eat on a porch overlooking the river and watch the trucks and barges and trains moving cargo, and that night, in a spacious cabin with a whirlpool tub, in a line of cabins where once the slave quarters stretched out instead, they drink rye whisky and stream the Society's student radio station in Los Angeles, KXLU, it's the modern world, the post-modern world, the world has never been more modern; it's raining in the morning and they cross the street to a cooked breakfast in the mansion, Southern biscuits and eggs, deep cured bacon, then head back to the battlefield to cruise the Southern lines, Path gets out of the car three times, once to walk to the Stockade Redan where Grant was repulsed on May 19 and 22 and again at the Great Redoubt of the Third Louisiana Redan where on the 22nd the Confederates took heavy losses but repulsed Grant again, the park's Red Southern lines and Blue Northern ones meet where the combatants fought hand to hand, after those failures Grant settled into his siege, it being said that he realized then that a well-entrenched position could never be taken by assault;

back to the city through a maze of construction work on Washington Street they crisscross the downtown and find the bar atop the tallest building in Vicksburg, ten stories, and gaze at the sunset over the river, the food isn't very good, afterward they try to find a bar, but it's October, the off-season, and half of the establishments are closed, though the next day they find an open bookstore and a young clerk from Maine shows Path some books about Vicksburg, one, *Becoming Southern*, by Christopher Morris, appears to be a published dissertation about the material culture of Warren County and Vicksburg from 1770 to 1860, that's just the thing Path was looking for, but the kid also tells him that the number one expert on Vicksburg, Gordon Cotton, works at the Courthouse, back they go, they get in just before closing and find out that Cotton only comes in on Thursday mornings, now it's late Wednesday, they eat that night east of town at a place called the Beechwood, a populace hangout, oysters, oysters, Carla eats so much she passes out, and in the morning, instead of taking off for N.O. first thing, Path and Carla go to the Courthouse where Gordon Cotton is waiting and spends two hours with them spinning Vicksburg folklore in a voice as sonorous as Shelby Foote's, he ends every story, a litany of love, chicanery, and greed with the refrain, Nothing changes, Cotton is an unabashed Confederate, They'd've never beat us, he says, they didn't beat us, they starved us out, and here, inside and outside Vicksburg, masters and slaves were partners and friends, slaves received shelter, food, medical care, affection, Affection, Carla is thinking, Path knows it, she was a founding member of the Sally Hemings Society in Charlottesville, now wasn't that affection Mr. Jefferson, anyway, Cotton was darn colorful if darn racist, he signs books for Path and he and Carla head back to New Orleans, the freeways get them there in half the time, they hit the bars on Frenchman, jazz at the Spotted Cat, Reggae fusion at the Negril, Path gets so drunk that he passes out, the next day they wander in Tremé and the Quarter, Carla buys nicotine for her Vape (she's stopped smoking cigarettes), but the streets are packed with Georgia Bulldog fans because Georgia is playing LSU in Baton Rouge on Saturday, a sea of red, like Chinese tourists in Oxford, England on a summer's day, then Carla and Path Uber out St. Charles Avenue to a famous rooftop bar that's full of more drunken Georgians, a view of the River, girls in red dresses, legs, legs, ten years ago it was cleavage, too much hooting, downstairs the old bar and restaurant are supposed to be gorgeous, but they're not, not anymore, they fly home, fly back to Nexile; Path's Trotsky book is rejected by another agent, one more to go, he goes back to work on a last draft of his book on animal cognition, begins reading *Becoming Southern*, but half-way through he finishes a chapter, "Households Within Households: Masters and Slaves," the institution was brutal, cruel, and barbaric, founded on humiliation and rape, he turns to Carla who is sitting with Nadine on the couch, shuts the book. She looks up from her laptop, spies the book on his lap. Slavery, she says. He says, I can't write about Vicksburg.

Path has walked away from a lot of things. A lot of things have walked away from him. He's been reading and re-reading about the Civil War, slowly circling in on Vicksburg, about two years of research, a pile of books over two feet high, several thousand dollars spent on four nights in Vicksburg, and now he's done, he can't walk around slavery, can't walk into it, can't walk through it, it's a job for a person of color. How done are you, Path? Mary Gass has sent him the posthumous *William H. Gass Reader* with a sweet note, in *The Tunnel* Kohler is fighting bitterly with Martha, his wife, at the Society the College of Liberal Arts has doubled his class sizes from 15 to 30, Path will face ninety students next semester, age 68, he'll have to recalibrate, and when he tries to postpone his sabbatical, what would be his last one, so he can take it simultaneously with Carla, the Dean emails him and tells him to come in for a talk about his legacy and the timeline for his future, his legacy? his future?

THE SHEPHERD RELIGIONS

THE MONOTHEISMS THAT SPRUNG out of mid-east Asia some 3,000 to 1,500 years ago, Judaism, Christianity, and Islam would appear to arise in order to, out of the desire to, place and placate the myriad of crises and problems of human existence, though, as well, offer somewhere to send our gratitude for the moments of joy in between, and unlike polytheism, to do it simply, in one fell swoop, with one source, one mystery. It allows "the believer" to answer it all with God and then get on with things. Recently, as recent as the end of 2019, it has come into parlance in the States to explain a good result, most often one that has followed a bad one, with the phrase, "I believe everything happens for a reason." Following Voltaire, the first question is whether or not the explanation covers the original bad results, or unfortunate results that arise from good ones, or bad results that continue to occur. Next we might ask if the reason is one big one, either the result of God's perpetually creating the world omnisciently, moment to moment, ala Descartes, or if it plays out to the articulation of a great plan, theistically like Calvin or Mohammad, less so as in Leibniz and Spinoza. You might accuse me of attacking a Straw Man here, but sometimes a cliché is a window into complexity. Commonly, the speaker of the phrase, "I believe everything happens for a reason," is not a philosopher, more likely a sports star, and has made a vague expression of faith, explicitly, and hope, implicitly, that there is a guiding hand, some supernatural entity who looks after them as an individual, disregarding others less fortunate, who continue on in their suffering, i.e. the speaker hasn't thought through what they really meant or the consequences of it, they caught a touchdown pass, what of the millions dying now of Covid-19 (go long!), nor have they examined the questions just raised, though much of that can be mitigated by the religious impulse, prayer, church on Sunday, a candle (now a light bulb in most churches) lit for a dollar, don't cheat and light without paying! well, one wouldn't. Admittedly, those impulses are equally present in polytheism, e.g., a sacrifice to a god or goddess whose domain covers one's request or adoration. The religious impulse goes deep—touring Pompeii, I found it impressive how devout, on a daily basis, its residents were, though that didn't stop Vesuvius—and long pre-dates monotheism, and polytheism demonstrably exists inside monotheist belief systems, saints, angels, genies, the Holy Trinity, and Mormon telestial realms, if the Lord helps those who help themselves, then let us give Them some reason to help out. Saints and angels bear the brunt, if not the scars, of Christianity. The problem of evil is not an aside, if Plato solved it on the level of human volition by calling it the absence of knowledge, Augustine called it the absence of Good (one more "o" than God), though absence doesn't sit well with omniscience. How much of the Void was filled with creation? Did creation create the nothing or create into it?

William James, in *The Varieties of Religious Experience*, reiterates examples, one after another, of individuals who find themselves in God's presence, who become ecstatics, if not mystics, capable of turning the other cheek to human evil, if not existential misery, catastrophe, disaster, illness, loss, death, as well. A pluralist, James finds subjective reality as good and real as any other reality, i.e., objective reality, if that exists. He almost seems to fall into Christianity as if, for now, it's the best of all bad solutions, one that at least allows for expiation, and free will, because determinism is, complexly so, existentially unacceptable, given that he cannot believe in a providence that is both all-powerful and all-good; again, better, on the spiritual level, if there were more than one individual responsible for all this beauty and chaos (let us remember, St. Augustine was once a Manichean). In my edition of the *Varieties*, in the "Introduction," Reinhold Niebuhr back handedly forgives James for being a 19th century human being; having not experienced two world wars and the Holocaust, the pallor and threat of nuclear massacres, among others, his "naivete" might be forgiven. Or as Ken Wilber suggests, God is joy, God is forgiveness, God *is* the nuclear bomb. But Wilber is neo Advita Hindu, if not Hegelian. God is everything and everything is God. God is unity, diversity is illusion. As Cohen says, "You live your life as if it's real." The Islamist terrorist who holds the head of his beheaded victim by the hair, is as equally God or Satan or Jesus. And what do they have in common besides our passive, voiceless God? Our God, working from within our souls as well as without, speaks all languages.

WHO'S THERE? (GHOSTS)

THEY HAVE A KNOCK IN THEIR KITCHEN. Would you call it frequent, almost every night, one discrete knock in the corner of the kitchen, like knuckles on wood, always in the evening but never at a specific time, always after dark, but any time between dusk and midnight, one knock, but not every night and never if there's a guest, though every guest who's told about it and never hears it has a naturalistic explanation, it's the ice expanding in your freezer, it's not coming from the freezer, a branch against the house, there is no branch near the house, something sliding, falling in the cupboard, Path has inspected the cupboard dozens of times, wood expanding as the temperature changes, lowers, in the night, it's an old house, originally a cabin, 97 years old, that's a possible explanation, but why is it so personal, why do only Path and Carla hear it, and they both hear it; now it is after the great fire, the Woolsey Fire that burned 100,000 acres and 500 homes, there are often fires here, two last year, one at the top of the canyon, they were asked to evacuate but they waited, there was no wind and the fire was extinguished, one at the bottom of the canyon while Path and Carla were having lunch at the Santa Monica Seafood Market, the Canyon was closed on both ends but they circled the city up Sunset to the 405 North, across the 101 West to Valley View in Calabasas and back across to Old Canyon where they sneaked in the back way, it took 5 ½ hours, but the wind blew the fire away from the road and up the mountain toward the Palisades and firefighters stopped it there, still, the bottom of the canyon was closed for five days, then it rained and the mountain fell on the road and closed it for five days more, then it happened again, and again, and once more until it stopped raining and the red flags that went up for fire warnings ended, yes, why do they live here, because this is where they live, it's Los Angeles and they can't live anywhere half the size of their home for less than twice the mortgage, do I have to say Nexile, but the Woolsey Fire was a big one, bigger than the one in 1993, the last time a fire burned from the Valley to the ocean, Carla was at the Society and Path got out of the canyon with Marlena, then Jesus, and her favorite cat, a grocery bag of her art, leaving four other cats outdoors, newts and fish inside to live or boil, they stayed with a colleague for two days, with Path's brother Simon for two more, the fire burned southeast and circled, jumped to the State Park, surrounded Fernwood, their neighborhood, then the winds died down and it was stopped; a week before the Woolsey Fire a fire broke out near the ranch, a woman who claimed she was part Indian and renamed herself Great Snake Feather, said she had a right to open bonfires and lit one, but there was no wind and it only burned two acres, but the Woolsey burned thirty miles in a three mile swathe in half a day, then hit the ocean and spread up and down the coast, Path and Carla received the mandatory evacuation and got out with the two cats, Frida and Scottie, and blind Nadine, landed in Westchester with Flaca Rosen, her husband, Razo Domingo, was vacationing in Chile and Argentina and she worked fourteen hour days in her office at the Society, you can't follow the fires on the television, though they don't watch that thing anyways, nor the radio, or even the internet, everything is gossip and the reporters don't know where they are, the police and fire officials are tight lipped because that controls the residents, the evacuees, through ignorance and fear, for their own good, though up north an even bigger fire is burning that burns down a whole town, Paradise, thousands of homes burn, hundreds die, the fire is quickly renamed the Camp Fire, Paradise Fire is too real, too ironic, those people knew it was coming and stayed and died, so down south here anybody even remotely threatened had to get out; Path and Carla sat in their fear and ignorance for eight days, got back on a Friday and on Saturday A.W. DeAnnuntis and Mary Mammarella flew in from Philadelphia, in celebration Path smoked two cigarettes and momentarily passed out on the floor (two years later, a week ago from just now 2021, an arsonist sets another fire on the hills above them, they sit under it for four days until fixed wing scoopers can fly through the fog), but in the past past, on Tuesday, Trans Kafka flew in from Sydney without her husband, trouble ahead, and a packed house, and on Thursday, Thanksgiving, the five of them pile into Carla's Magic Car and join Carla's brother, Hazlitt, and his wife, Lamby, and they fetch St. Jin of Arc and drive to a Belgian restaurant in San Juan Capistrano where Path eats badly cooked duck and gets stuck with an $800 bill, how does that happen, you might ask, you don't have to let that happen, says a descendant of Ann Landers, somebody like Helpful Amy, Ask Amy, Path later reads in the LA Times, so good guess, but Ann Landers lived in the same universe as Ayn Rand, one they made up, where relatives are put in their place, the great are great and conquer the weak for the good of all, because, as Monty Python has said, What Jesus fails to understand about poverty is that it's the poor themselves who are the problem; the next day Path cooks a twenty pound Turkey and Bertha Barnes and Wolfgang Hermes, Hazlitt and Aunt Lamby, join them for a Thanksgiving, things don't go so badly but for the fact that it was Path who invited Bertha and Wolfgang to Thanksgiving last Friday over margaritas and poblano rellenos at Lula's, forgetting that Hazlitt and Bertha dated in high school in Detroit, Michigan decades ago, but the Aunt Lamby, like Johnny Torch, is that his name, Sue Storm's brother in the Fantastic Four, Path briefly owned that very first comic book, cost him a dime or twelve cents, and as Aunt Lamby verges on fire Path remembers meeting his nascent friend, Al Messina, at Lyon's soda fount corner store on 23rd and Parade, the two of them skipping Sunday mass, they're talking about Updike, atheism, Kerouac and Batman, that's where and when Path bought that first Fantastic Four with money he was supposed to put in the collection basket, anyway, Flame On! But the Aunt Lamby holds, it's too crowded for a fray, home grown pot, port and gin and rye whisky, DeAnnuntis knows the makeup of every jazz band in the history of jazz, every composition, every composer, Mammarella has a wit like a razor, and Trans Kafka explains the Insane Clown Posse and the burgeoning alliance between the Jugalos and Furries, the binary universe imploding, it was fun, fun, fun until Daddy took the T-Bird away; in the first mail delivery after the fire Mary Gass has sent Path a copy of Bill's *William Gass Reader* and Path leaves the room to weep, that night he dreams of saddling La Femme Nikkita, he feels her breath in her chest, the unchartable gracious leather of the saddle, and he fills with deep longing because in this time, this now, he has sold her and longs for her, though in the narrative present of this story, if I can call it such, he is yet on his way, an Iranian carpet mogul has spotted her in Path's ad and his eight year old daughter has fallen in love, though an eight year old will never be able to mount her, ride her, stay on, but now the conversation turns to A.W. DeAnnuntis' new novel, *Terror Island*, a monstrous 800 page behemoth set in the 17th Century where the son of an alchemist goes into the world in search of his vagrant scientist father, meanwhile constantly waylaid and delayed by a giant monster who destroys every fantastical place the boy visits, empires of Mafiosi pirate emperors, convents of vampire nuns, the monster sure looks like Godzilla, Path's artists' collective has rejected the book without anyone reading it so Path and Carla have started a new press to publish the book, didn't Coover and Elkin do the same thing for Gass, yes, what about the Bloomsbury group or Fiction Collective 2, everyone talks and talks but the ghost never knocks, Okay, says Path, don't believe it, what does it matter whether you believe it or not, But the ghost, whether it exists or not, says DeAnnuntis, has followed you here from Vicksburg, They were here before we left for Vicksburg, says Path, using the non-binary pronoun, They followed you here from Vicksburg before you left for Vicksburg, they're a ghost! let the ghost narrate the novel about Vicksburg; Carla likes the idea but for Path it just complicates an impossibility; Come live in Philadelphia, says Mary Mammarella, that solves everything, but they live in a cliff of cement with windows surrounded by a hundred even taller cliffs of cement with windows, it doesn't matter how close they are to the biggest State Store in Pennsylvania and Trader Joe's, and who would the ghost be, a sympathetic Southerner, there can be no sympathy for the South, not in these days, a slave, Path can't write from the POV of a Black slave, even if he could, he can't, identity politics has swept the land, is "Baby It's Cold Outside" sexual harassment, from the Left everything has something wrong with it, from the Right that's all wrong, beatitude is bad attitude and the other way around, Hyperbole, shouts Carla Blacklabel Beer, Everything, agrees DeAnnuntis, is hyperbolic, There is no reality, says Mammarella, only hyperbole, and Trans Kafka, nee Jesus, weeps, but soon everyone will be gone, Path and Carla will be out of money, spent on friends and child, before Dali leaves she'll reveal that the non-binary world is hell, though Path shall not go further, even in a book about nothing written for nobody that will never see the light of day, he will not reveal his daughter's personal troubles, be she nine thousand miles away, when they send her off this time he doesn't cry, he comes home and he drinks soda and a rye, Carla clinks her gin and tonic to his glass, tomorrow he will see the Dean. Knock.

Path finds a note that he wrote to himself. It says Samsara is Nirvana, we live in heaven and hell at the same time, we inhabit paradise in every second and every second we walk away.

FROM DEATH TO MORNING

RICK STARED WEST

TO THE RIVER WHERE the Yankee ironclad gunboats filed in, his friend, Schopenhauer, put a hand on his shoulder and said, Like the Iliad, as the first Confederate salvo unleashed from the cliffs. The gunboats returned fire. They spoke to each other, but under the din, neither could hear what the other was saying. There'll be more, Rick Monty said. More and more. They can build them. The South can't. Vicksburg is the key to unlocking the South, said Schopenhauer. He was quoting Lincoln. But this city can't be taken. It was Christmas week of 1862. Ulysses S. Grant sat with an army somewhere to the east. William Tecumseh Sherman was driving an army toward Vicksburg above Chickasaw Bayou. Rick owned a casino below the bluffs of Vicksburg on the east side of the Mississippi River, between the river and the city, Rick's Dixie Doodle Dandy, self-proclaimed neutral territory since before the secession. He didn't care who came in there as long as they weren't carrying a weapon. He was born in New York City, educated at Johns Hopkins in Baltimore, took classes in philosophy from William James and Charles Sanders Peirce. Schopenhauer was born free in New Orleans from generations of free Blacks. He played the piano, Chopin, met Goethe and Fichte in Vienna. I am the ghost who followed Path to his home before he and Carla Blacklabel ever left for New Orleans and Vicksburg. I saw him on the Confederate battle line as he drove in the rain through the Vicksburg War Memorial Park in 2002 with his daughter, Jesus; he got out of his car and crossed No-Man's Land to the North's entrenchments and, out of sight, took a messy shit next to the marker of the Indiana 11th Regiment, it wasn't an intentional act, let's just say he'd been moved, it were symbolic, at least to me, he wiped himself with a wet leaf as Jesus sat impatiently, anxious to get on to Memphis and Graceland, but

Path needed one more stop, this at the northern Redan where the 17th and 25th Louisiana fought off Grant's first and second assaults. We fought hand to hand. I died there. I am A. Nonymous Nacht. To some, Anon, to others just Nacht. Nacht-Nacht. Who's there? Me.

PRAY FOR ME

PATH ENTERS THE PARKING GARAGE and finds a spot for his truck in Faculty Parking, he pays $700 a semester for a spot, first come first serve, Carla pays $700 too, because even though they commute in her hybrid twice a week there are times when it's inconvenient to drive in together, like now, an early meeting with the Dean; the parking garage is about four stories deep and he doesn't like to use the subterranean floors because it gives him earthquake chills, the garage sits under a giant four storied hall built by Howard Hughes across from the airfield where he built the Spruce Goose; when Path first came here the airfield was extant, now it is covered by miles of million dollar condos, though the Spruce Goose hangar remains in there somewhere, inhabited by Amazon Google Silicon Spielberg Disney Pixar; when Raytheon, who bought the building from Hughes to develop Ronald Reagan's Star Wars, put the behemoth up for sale, Pepperdine University tried to buy it, which would have put them right on top of the Society and turned it into a shadow suburb of those notorious fundamentalist protestants, so the Society bought the building and threw all their administrative offices and, ironically, the school of Liberal Arts in there, they couldn't possibly have meant it ironically, could they, it's festooned with escalators that seldom function, elevators to nowhere, tiny crucifixes, giant crucifixes, live trees, Path always takes the stairs, which ascend and descend maze-like, though they're almost always negotiable, eventually; he watches old faculty like him wandering, bewildered; today he doesn't use his cane, a Leonard Cohen prop he doesn't need, an affectation to connote frailty, but since the Dean has likely called this meeting to imply he should retire, he's decided to appear healthy and spry; when he reaches the fourth floor he encounters the Office of the President, on its outside wall a line of photographs of old, dead, white men, dubbed Famous Teachers and amidst them Path spots Kirk Dicker, the man who was the English Chair (on sabbatical) when Path was hired who tried his best to fire both Path and Carla but failed, another long, convoluted embroilment not worth going into, not even here in a book about nothing for nobody, though it introduced a departmental vendetta that lasted decades, often unbeknownst to Path while it was under his very nose, c'est l'academe, in Path's first week at the Society Dicker brought him into his huge chair's office and opened a photo album filled with pictures of all the undergraduate girls he claimed to have fucked on the roof, La-La Land, said Kirk Dicker, now he's a member of the Society's Great Teacher Hall of Fame, you can't unravel that without a lot of explication but it's a synecdoche for the Society and the Society a synecdoche for the whole damn world, Path spent six years getting fucked under somebody's roof and now, almost fifty years later, the Church and state of Pennsylvania are resisting the facts that it happened to thousands of boys, heal, they say, forgive, the first news of Garvey's sexual abuse record came out a month after he died, convenient, the bishop probably knows that Path had cancer and is holding out for him to die; Path, on his home throne, is reading *The Tunnel* about Kohler's rendition of a departmental meeting, shit floats, though in Kohler's academe, the shits are larger, quicker witted, more complex, and bother to publish, unlike Path's colleagues; the Dean's personal secretary is a pretty, thin blonde woman from Liverpool, fashionable, a cute accent, Path notes that Liverpool is having a good season in the EPL, only two points behind undefeated Man City, Yes, she says, I don't really follow but really you can't not, anyway, the Dean is late for, Path ruminates, a not so very important date, or a show of her power, Path sits, the secretary brings him ice water, he reads from *The History of the Siege of Lisbon*, right now he's progressing at only a few pages a week, what does it matter, and it's the most convoluted and digressive of the six Saramago novels he's read, the errant proofreader will inevitably sleep with his boss, sometimes the inevitable produces tension, sometimes it don't, right now, Path isn't tense, he has no plans to retire soon, Nexile is tough enough without being broke, but the Dean eventually arrives in a pant-suited rush, sorry, sorry, you know, LA traffic, that's why Path left an hour and a half early and barely got here on time, but the Dean is from New Mexico, then Connecticut, she will always be surprised by LA traffic, the mantra of anyone who is always late in LA; this meeting was inspired by Path's application to postpone his sabbatical, likely his last, for one year so he can take his simultaneously with Carla, something, in thirty-three years, they've never done, Never, really, oh my, says the Dean, Well then, just let me know so I can schedule it, and so the meeting is over, yes, no, the Dean must bend his ear for another hour, the books she's reading, mass cultural NPR level novels, the gifts she's been given by retired and retiring faculty, her complicated work with dozens of intra-university bureaucracies designated by indecipherable initials, NFTSA, TAEI, what, what, what, and then, almost finally, the death of English and History in the liberal arts, something his department, English, will have to deal with, They're history, ha-ha, Will it be recorded in English, says Path, As administrators we must understand the difference between what students want and what students need, the MFA market is saturated, English majors might want to take courses in fiction writing, but those needs can be met by Communication Arts, film making, screenwriting, Dramatic Arts, journalism, besides the English Department here is creatively diverse, almost anyone can teach anything or, Path reflects, that none of them specialize in anything or are good at anything or publish anything, it gives them lots of time to teach, teach what, anything, So, the Dean goes on, anyone can do what you do, when you retire you won't be replaced, but Path has published sixteen books, with two more in the wings and nobody else in the department, besides Carla, has punished, he meant published, any, trying to keep it positive Path mentions the bookshelf outside the departmental secretary's office where there are a few dozen books published by his and Carla's ex-students, but all of that is too implicit for the Dean who recommends that he think of the future, think of his legacy, one which she hasn't seemed to notice, besides, he's fed up enough now to tell her, I don't believe in legacy, I'm just not a legacy kind of guy, But what can you do, she responds, for your department, your college, your University, before you leave, well, the department hasn't offered fiction writing in eighteen months and next semester he will teach three introduction to literature classes to a total of 90 students who could give a shit and he won't be able to teach any writing at all or die trying; after an hour the Dean shakes his hand good-bye and he goes to his office where there's an email from his chair asking him to work on a committee for developing an MFA in creative writing and chair a committee for hiring a fiction writer; if this were any kind of dramatic narrative, this would be the place to stop and let the reader reckon, but it ain't, so what we got here Nexiled in the Society is a failure to communicate; Saint Veronica, Path says out loud on the way to his Intro to Genre, Fiction class, pray for me, then he and Carla meet over margaritas and he spills it all out, What do I do, he says, and she says, Don't do anything; he's going to break his four drink quota tonight though nonetheless when they get home there's a pleading message on the phone, Honey, it's your mother, the prophet Josiah has told me to give you my Writings.

FROM DEATH TO MORNING

PEMBERTON IS COMING

TONIGHT, SAYS SHOPE. Rick went way back with Jack Pemberton, when Pem was a cadet at West Point before the Mexican War. They drank together at an Irish pub in Manhattan. Rick was against that war, Pem was going there to fight it. See the guys in this bar, Rick said to Pemberton, they're Catholic, just like the Mexicans, that is, against slavery. If you send them down there they'll cross the river. Pemberton, from Philadelphia, said, Everyone always has a right to choose, but if they're American citizens that would be treason. They'd choose treason, said Rick. Pem said, That's right, they'd choose to die. Die Mexican, said Rick. You have to die something, said Pem. It's war. Rick sipped his beer. In New York you could get a beer. In Philadelphia too. It was harder to get beer outside of the cities, harder to make it, harder to store it, keep it cold. He found that out when he moved to the South. Anyway, Pemberton was smart, if conflicted. Obviously, now, he'd decided it wasn't treason for states to secede, only citizens.

At Rick's Dixie Doodle you could drink rye whisky. Rye aged in eighteen months. Bourbon took years. Something for the cellars of the rich plantation owners, not for farmers, dock workers, now, soldiers. Though plantation owners occasionally came to Rick's too, to gamble. He owned a classless joint. He enjoyed that pun. Just put down your guns and swords. You could sneak in a knife or derringer, sure, I did it all the time, but that generally led to a short, one on one conflict. It couldn't be helped, particularly in poker. Rick preferred dice and wheels. You couldn't blame anybody but yourself when you lost to the dice or the wheel. Anyway, the money most men were playing with now was worthless, Confederate. If you came in with Union money you had to leave it at the door, just like your weapons, and convert it. Generally, they didn't convert it back to Federal dollars when they left because they'd lost it. It was a damn casino. If you came there to win money, well, you were an idiot.

Jefferson Davis had just given Jack Pemberton the task of defending Vicksburg. In a few days he'd likely be heading up to Chickasaw Bayou to meet Sherman in the hilly swamps above the Yazoo River. Pem knew Sherman, and Grant, too, back in West Point. Now he came to the casino by himself, out of uniform. Rick didn't like uniforms, they polarized things. He didn't outlaw them. People just knew. The place was smoky and crowded. There was a section near the bar where you could drink and even eat if you chose, away from the gambling tables. There, men could bring women, an anomaly, but this was a casino, a club, an entertainment establishment, not a bar, not a whisky hangout like the places in town. Though if a woman was unattached, you could assume she was available, but that was none of Rick's business and, if it was business, then he owned it or he ended it.

Jack Pemberton was a tall man with a long goatee, fair skinned, Rick doubted that he had enough beard to cover his cheeks, though later he would let his mustache grow out and comb it into his beard. He remembered Grant at West Point. Back then Grant was nobody. In fact, until recently, he was still nobody, kicked out of the army for drunkenness after Mexico, he failed at business, ended up working as a laborer delivering firewood, Pem bought firewood from him once, then U, they called him U, fell back into the military at the beginning of this war, ended up in charge out west when his superior was killed in Tennessee, then won that Pyrrhic victory up in Shiloh, but it was a victory, the North hadn't had many. Pem could beat Grant. But he'd need some troops from Texas and Louisiana, some cavalry from Tennessee, he'd need Johnston to come west from Jackson, then he could cut Grant's supply lines and surround him. He could save Vicksburg, close down the Mississippi to Yankee transport, end it for the North right here.

Rick poured him a rye and water. What about the gunboats? he said.

Pemberton sipped. We'll sink them, raise them, repair them. Then we'll have boats.

Shope sat down at his piano and began playing a Mazurka in B flat major that rose above the low din of the room, gathering smoke around its tones. Rick's bartender, Molly Joy, opened a bottle of champagne and poured for Jack and Rick, walked to the piano and poured a glass for Schopenhauer. Molly had red hair pinned behind her ears and falling on the back of her neck. She was from Dublin. There were lots of Irish in Vicksburg now, mostly skilled laborers, few, if any, were land owners, or slaveholders, most slaveholders lived on plantations outside of town, they imported their own champagne and wine from France. When the Yankees took New Orleans it looked like that might end, but New Orleans danced to money, it didn't matter where it came from, at least that's the way it was so far, though now, with Grant moving in Mississippi, things could change, but booze could still be landed in Mobile and brought in by train or wagons via Jackson, or you could bring it down the river from the north, or if you had to, you could make it yourself; Rick knew a slave with a trading post just east of Champion Hill who made his own liquor and sold it. The financial arrangements with the owner were a mystery.

Jack Pemberton didn't have slaves. Rick didn't either. People said that Robert E. Lee didn't. That Sherman did. Sherman had a sister living here in Vicksburg. Most of the boys under arms down here, the foot soldiers, not the officers, never owned a slave either, or even a horse, they came from small farms, they plowed with mules, the fortifications that Pemberton had started to build east of the city, just in case, were dug and constructed by Confederate privates and paid slaves working shoulder to shoulder for a similar pittance; word was that any Blacks freed and recruited by the Union were given half-wages and segregated. That was the word, anyway, it was hard to know what to believe.

Lee's going to invade Pennsylvania, Pem told Rick.

Again?

To distract the Feds from Vicksburg. Maybe Grant will have to turn back.

Do you believe that?

No.

Molly returned and placed the champagne bottle on the table. We're a long way from Philadelphia, she said to Jack.

Lee trusts me, Molly, said Pemberton.

Does anybody else?

Would you have deserted to fight for Mexico? Rick said to her.

Thank God, women don't fight.

Secession is a right, Pem said. A state's right.

Until somebody bigger and stronger disagrees, said Rick.

Johnston has sent me a command to leave Vicksburg and meet Grant in the field, said Pem. He poured himself a second glass of champagne.

Rick poured him more rye, too. You'll have to chase Sherman off the bayou or he'll drop in behind you, said Rick.

Jack Pemberton stiffened. You seem to know a lot, he said.

This is the center of the world, Rick said. He got up and put his glass down. The door to the casino burst open. There was some trouble in there. Rick turned to Molly. He said, Trouble in paradise?

DOES DEATH HAVE WHATNESS?

IF ONTOLOGY, IN THE BEGINNING AND END, leads us to a bundle of four antinomies, i.e. Kant, irresolvable contradictions, we are aptly left with duty, not heart. What does it matter if it's the truth, if that the truth is unfigurable, if not unacceptable, contradiction at the core of how we live. Gaps are now epistemological irresolvables, their whatness or suchness are not approachable through either logic or experience.

For Kant, the crux lay here. Whether time and space are limited, having a beginning and an end, or are infinite; whether or not atoms, which he describes as simple parts, make up the experienced world (or for Leibniz, the only logical one); another gap, that I discussed earlier, as to whether the cosmos is ubiquitously caused or contains spontaneity; and finally, whether or not God is a necessary cause of the world. These dilemmas cannot be solved by experience or logic. And that's that. In Europe, after Hegel, no one really tried to step into that space; if the central questions of being were irresolvable, then knowing became even more so; thus begins the circuitous, if not inevitable, path to Deconstruction and analytic philosophy, but as old as the clash between Protagoras and Socrates/Plato. If this is where we've ended up again then the only reason to keep talking is the desire to keep talking.

So let's keep talking. What is the point of knowledge? What do I want to know? Recently, when I was diagnosed with cancer, I found that knowledge didn't mean much. I couldn't see or feel my disease, though I was told by my doctors that they could, in various ways, find indications of it in my blood and, later, after my biopsy, they found cells of it. I was told that if they left it alone it would spread, most likely to my bones.

Poe said (and Baudrillard agrees) that the most primal emotion was fear, so he became fascinated by its portrayal, the evocation of terror. I was never a fan of Poe, I read him at the dawn of my interest in narrative, this after a half-decade after pursuing advanced degrees in philosophy, leaving that not because I was disillusioned with the pursuit of truth, very early I became aware that philosophy couldn't alight on truth—I should qualify that and say objective truth—I read it as metaphor and came to that conclusion on my own some time before I read Wittgenstein's *The Investigations* (yes, I read the *Tractatus* first)—then, in my late twenties, I began reading literature again though it felt, even re-read, brand new, and being an American I began with American literature, and beginning at the beginning I soon encountered Poe. That was over forty years ago and a lot has changed in me, and the world, since, but for now, let's go back to then, and not psychoanalyze that self from my present perspective; if need be there will be plenty of time for that. At the time, narratively naïve as I was, I read literature with an analytic eye of the philosopher, I thought about it *as* I read, and I found terror resting, or more so, embedded, in suspense and found suspense, when it wasn't transparent, at least manipulative (like Hollywood suspense, and do I include Hitchcock? yes). I didn't like Poe. Though now, through the eyes of Baudrillard and Baudelaire, I understand his progenitor relationship to the genre. Yet, even now, Mary Shelley's *Frankenstein* aside, I dislike horror as a genre, unless it's subjugated by literary disregard like in Antoine Volodine, who I yet feel is too arbitrary and his worlds too unexplained. In its basic, naïve forms, in genre it's just too easy to take one step back, or one step outside the frame, like a bodhisattva in the Bardo (M. Volodine), and the horror is gone. Besides, I just don't like feeling horror-filled or horrible, take no pleasure in being scared. I have the same complaint with literary realism, the real is boring and frightening enough, I don't need it to be recreated on the screen of page. I don't need to depict, I write for revenge.

The argument that reading literature somehow prepares us for life was pretty much blown up by those Goethe loving Germans in world War I. Horror doesn't get us ready for the horrible. Nothing does. In my cancer years I spent less time fighting terror, as surgery failed, as radiation failed, each, at first, with its glimmering of rescue, and more time fighting hope. I lost my sense, my ability, to conceive a future. Living in the present is deadly. That's the horror. My younger brother who works with dementia patients, says that is dementia's horror.

When I studied Buddhism I often encountered the Mahayana screen metaphor that to invest in reality, pick a reality, any reality, was as foolish as thinking that a movie you're watching is real, that the present is as evasive as the future or the past, and that satori, Nirvana, was as momentary and illusive as anything else. But unlike a movie theater, you can't step out of reality. Can you? In 2013, with my cancer (yes, I called it mine) rising in my blood, my life partner and I stopped going to the movies, stopped downloading or streaming movies, stopped watching screens altogether. As well, one day my cancer started disappearing, and one day it was gone. My doctor said there was no medical explanation. The movie theater had stepped out of *me*. That was a number of years ago. Recently, at one of my cancer check-ups, an intern, after looking at my chart, my cancer history, turned to me and, looking me in the eyes said, "You are a very lucky man." Yes, now I was available to get hit by a bus, the cliché every cancer victim hears from the healthy—"I could get hit by a bus tomorrow." I know of only one person who was run over and killed by a bus and he was eighty-five. Dancing with ontology, asking the question *why me?* when one contracts it, (I never asked) is no less perplexing than asking 'why not?' when it mysteriously goes away, though oddly, as I sit here writing this in June of 2020, my test scores came back yesterday and for the first time in years my score has jumped. Is it back? As Covid-19 rages around us all—at sixty eight I'm in a vulnerable age group to die if I contract it, 80% of people over sixty-five die from it—what death am I trying to avoid? As my shrink has said, you can't get ready for death by thinking about it. The 'right now' of this sentence is June 2021. The Pandemic in the U.S. is going into remission too,

TROUBLE IN PARADISE

PATH LOOKED UP JOSIAH ON WIKIPEDIA, he didn't usually do that kind of thing, but times were changing, Josiah was an obscure king of Judea, around 800 B.C.E., there were rumors of his death but no records of it, he might have been assassinated in a coup or died during an ill-advised invasion of Egypt, or both, Does she know who Josiah is, Path asks Carla, I doubt it, Does she know she's already given you those Writings twice and taken them back twice, She doesn't remember, Let your brother take them this time, He'll destroy them, he wants her to die, she's old, she's crazy, she's alone, I'll just take them back again and put them in Spider World, And that will be that, said Path, Yes, said Carla, Wrong, said Path, he had one more day of school before the 2019 holiday break, then the horrible barreling toward Xmas; he thought, once, he was through with it, back in Utah, isolated in Utah, on the cusp of Carla, he had to go back to Davis to work on his community service sentence for getting busted drunk on his motorcycle in possession of pot and acid and coke, not enough to sell to anybody, but it put him in jail, then on a work gang, through drug rehab, and finally working as an assistant in the public library, they'd even let him go off to Salt Lake City to start his Ph.D. on the agreement that he return over his breaks to work off his sentence, in fact, after he got his Ph.D. he was still on probation, but that first Xmas break his ex exploded at him for not helping trim her Xmas tree, threw ornaments at him, threw him out of her house, his most recent Davis girlfriend was an Hasidic Jew, no Xmas issues but she threw him out, too, he slept in the bus terminal, went to work in the library where his old roommate, Buzz, showed up to tell him the police came by the house with a warrant for his arrest, Buzz, said Path, I'm *in* jail, right here, Well, said Buzz, you should be easy to catch, so Path got on his motorcycle and drove over the snowy Donner Pass and across Nevada, back to Utah and spent some peaceful evenings with a bottle of Jim Beam and a bag of potato chips, now he was a wanted man in California, Carla came back from D.C., took one look at him, pulled him to the floor and fucked him, he was starting to like her, she had a mind like a shooting star and didn't give a fuck about Xmas until they had a baby, then, then he found some joy in it, seeing his child wake up, eyes agog with wonder, but now she was gone, down under for almost a decade, what was left was Jin-Jin of Arc getting the lyrics wrong to The Little Drummer Boy, pur-rum-pum-pum-pum, it passed fast, poets sent Carla post cards, ex-students sent photos of their multiplying families, familication, his ex, her name was Kara P, kind of out of nowhere sent him an email about her one-woman retrospective at the San Luis Obispo Museum of Art, he thought of her and for a moment forgot why they broke up, how they broke up, all the fights, fights, fights, he couldn't remember what any of them were about, though he recalled how in her nascent feminism she insisted that she could have affairs and he should not because he would fall in love and ruin everything, well, maybe he had that all wrong, could he have had it all wrong, had they broken up after a half dozen break ups and get backs and a divorce almost forty years ago, should he go, and Carla said, Path, you made her an artist, she met you and became a photographer, an artist, Do you think she thinks that, said Path, Regardless, said Carla, it's a big deal, just go, so he did, he jumped in his truck and drove up the coast, it began to rain like hell, he got lost in SLO; didn't know how to use Cruz or Waze or Google maps, he's a techno reactionary, so Kara P's husband, Donald, a retired historian, guides him to their house by phone, Donald looks thin and tired, he's now diabetic, like Nadine, his father just died in Florida, age ninety-eight, he begged for his hospice to kill him so they permitted him to starve himself, then Kara P's father, Rowan, died, the mothers were long dead, Rowan lived to be ninety-three, died pretty happy says Kara P, her younger sister, Luna, just died, too, in her fifties, Down Syndrome and Alzheimer's, a more painful death than it had to be because the other sister, Lola, who lived down in Florida near Rowan and Luna, had become a fundamentalist Christian and no longer believed in pain medication, Mary Mammarella's younger sister had just died the same way and medication helped a little but not enough, Lola and her husband, Roy, had inherited their moving and storage company from Rowan who inherited it originally from his father, that's called self-made in America, and that's one thing Kara P missed out on when she first hooked up with Path forty years ago, quit cheerleading and picked up a camera that one of her early lovers sent to her from Vietnam, she became a freak, at the time her older brother had just died in boot camp down in the Carolinas somewhere, never even made it to Vietnam, Path was a protester and given all that, Rowan hated him, let's forego the stories of his abuse, so when Rowan died and Kara P projected his smiling face all over Face Book, Path ignored it; when Path and Kara P broke up and she got back on Rowan's money wagon, she bought a Nikon for starters and gave her old camera, a Petri, to Path, that's pretty much what he got out of that divorce, he took some photos of his dying mother, developed them and printed them in a darkroom, they were sad and horrible and he regretted it, the camera broke and Path was through with photography, never took another photograph ever, I still have that camera, says Path, he'd found it during a clean up of Spider World and put it on a bookshelf with his Kerouac books, You have it, Kara P says, he says, It's broken, she says, I'll take it if you don't want it, he says, I wouldn't have it if I didn't want it, that's kind of their relationship in a nutshell, though still, in the rain, she drives them to the museum, sans Donald who says he's spent hours with the exhibit already, Donald is a discreet being, and in fact, the show's quite good, forty years of her life in black and white, in diptychs and triptychs organized thematically, not chronologically, one series, in color, of photographs taken from the second story window of Vesuvio's in North Beach of people standing in what is now Jack Kerouac Alley, her first time there, she says, was with Path, in '76? but she's good, she's a good photographer, he somehow finds that gratifying, though there's one photo of him, a profile, from long ago, he fails to recognize himself, he likes that metaphor, in coincidence they run into a poet, Archie Rollo, and his wife, Katie; Path knew Rollo in Davis about thirty-eight years ago, later Donald takes everybody out to dinner and later still he retires early and Kara P and Path stay up drinking rye whisky, he looks at her, her hair is still thick and wavy, she's lively, aesthetically informed, a leftist, kind of, an NPR leftist, are her eyes blue, and for a moment, for a brief moment, he sees the girl he fell in love with in 1970, he remembers sitting on a bench over the Ohio River, reading Plato and listening to a Pirates game on the radio, waiting for Kara P to get out of her job selling women's clothes at a nearby mall, now she pulls out old pictures, photos of their gang parties in Erie, in Davis, nude photos of Path, memory as seduction, he remembers, she needs the attention of the man across from her, any man, not just him, in the morning she makes breakfast for him now, shows him her spacious house, her work space, huge darkroom, her personal gallery, all the building and rebuilding, she must, he thinks, be pretty well off, they touch lips at the door and he drives home, it hurts, why does it hurt, Path, he's glad he came and is sorry he went, his past collapsing like a top hat, he returns to Carla, he holds her, he holds her, he holds her, this life will disappear too.

Time is leaping now, turning his life into blank gaps, I'm ready to write his death, Path is ready, too, he's finished *The History of the Siege of Lisbon* (Carla picks it up and reads it in a bounce), finished another history of the siege of Vicksburg, he reads *The History of Roman Warfare*, Bachelard's *The Psychoanalysis of Fire*, puts down Baudrillard's *Seduction*, rereads *The Turn of the Screw* and *The War of the Worlds* for his classes, Kohler is tunneling into a despotic rhapsody of malice against his colleagues, his father, his mother, his wife, Path, who's reread both Whitehead's *Science and the Modern World* and *Process and Reality* picks up a secondary source, May's *The Philosophy of Whitehead*, begins Bachelard's *Poetics of Space*, dives, slowly, into Thomas Mann's *The Magic Mountain*, he can't read *Being and Nothingness* right now, his brain is too thick filled with thickness, and slower still, a new cusp of Nexile's maw opens before him: Nadine dies, finally, the gap in her joy blankets the house, everywhere now becomes a place where she is not, where she had been, next to their bed, at the top of the stairs where she waited for him to hug her before she descended to be fed, to receive her shot of insulin, he can't come home without expecting her, her dogsoul haunts; Jin of Arc calls, her apartment has been infiltrated by gremlins, singing children, the coroner is at her door, is she dead, a choir outside her window is singing "Found a Peanut," how absurd, she says, that they would sing that, he and Carla make the drive to Prison Village, when they arrive the jig is up, the Jin is down, the coroner put her in a coffin and drove her on a train to heaven, she saw her father, he looked good, her mother was short and fat and mean, Jin loves men and hates women, now Jin's back from heaven, from death, the room fills with blonde baby girls but when she goes to them they disappear, frightened, Carla calls a nurse, the nurse calls an ambulance, they sit with her in the emergency room for six hours while she babbles on and on until a psychiatrist shows up and she straightens out, he finds nothing wrong, she can't hurt anybody, she's not hurting herself, he sends her home, now what, let's do it again and again, madder than *Groundhog Day*, and the Diocese of Erie has created a fund to recompense its abused men, but time is short and the money is limited so get ready, be bewared, Mercyhurst College where Garvey worked as dean, as President, announces that they are not a part of the diocese, baloney, says Path's Philadelphia lawyer, Gary, besides, as Dean of Mercyhurst Garvey transported Path to Cornell in Ithaca, New York, and to the World's Fair in 1965 and fucked Path every day for two weeks, the state of New York has dropped the statute of limitations for eighteen months, a window for us, says Gary, but now the tsunami of memory, of six years of rape, hold me close and tell me how you feel, tell me love is real, mmm, mmm, mmm, day-do run run run, day-do run run, day-do run run run, day-do run run.

FROM DEATH TILL MORNING
A COTTON RUNNER NAMED WALLY

A SHORT, STOCKY MAN who wore a black long-coat and a gray, bowed scarf at his neck, had cheated somebody again, but he was a regular, he drank and paid for high end whisky from Scotland and lost plenty at the tables. The gambler he'd cheated, at poker, Rick doesn't recognize him, stands at the table and holds a derringer on Wally who turns to Rick, palms up, and pleads, It's cards, Rick, if you're not cheating you're not playing, while Shope, who is a good deal bigger than Rick, moves in quickly and without hesitation disarms the gambler. The piano aside, Shope boxed and fenced in Europe.

He can't touch me, says the gambler. He doesn't have a southern accent, but a rural drawl, Rick's guessing Missouri, maybe Ohio or south Illinois.

Rick says, He already touched you. And you brought a gun. No guns. How much did you lose?

The man stammers. His hands make fists at his side. Check his sleeves, he says.

Wally crosses his arms over his chest. Check *his* sleeves, he says. He hid a gun, Rick. Who knows what else he's hiding.

Rick always carries a fountain pen and paper. He writes out a scrip for $100 and hands it to Shope who offers it to the gambler who glances at it contemptuously.

Federal? says the gambler.

You played Confederate, you lost Confederate, you get paid in Confederate. Take it and get out.

They're surrounded now by a circle of men.

Everybody get a drink on me and calm down, Rick says.

Molly is already there with a shot of whisky and offers it to the gambler who takes it. He nods toward Shope and says to her, you hand me the scrip.

She ignores him.

I'll have a scotch, please, Wally says to her.

Get it at the bar, Wally, Rick says. He turns to the gambler and says, You've got about thirty seconds to cash out that scrip and get out of here.

My gun, says the gambler.

I just bought it, says Rick, it says so on the scrip.

Shope steps between the gambler and Rick and holds out the scrip. The man grabs it like a snake strike.

If you fail to leave immediately, Shope says to him, I'm going to touch you again.

You can touch me any time you'd like, Master Shope, Wally says to him, and Shope brushes the back of his fist across Wally's cheek.

The gambler sidesteps Shope and heads out of the casino parlor and Rick follows him to the cashier window, lets him collect his money and leave.

I'm never coming back here, the gambler says to Rick.

You can bet on that, pun intended, Rick answers. Shope is back at the piano and begins a variation form Mozart's "Don Giovanni" in B flat major. Men settle back down to the tables in the casino, most of them have seen Rick and Shope settle things before. Pemberton was still at his table where he sat stoically with a glass and a half bottle of whisky. When Rick sat down again, he noticed Wally hovering near the piano with an ear cocked toward him and Pemberton. For Wally, it could be important to know where Pemberton might deploy his troops, whether running his cotton to New Orleans or Memphis would encounter the least chance of interference. Cotton was money, as valuable as gold, more valuable than Confederate currency.

Pemberton stood and eyed Wally. He's burning both ends, he said to Rick.

Yes, but both ends are buying into it, Rick said.

Not forever, Pem said. He stood, nodded to Rick and left.

Now Wally came up to him, sipping his drink. He's a dangerous man, Rick, said Wally. He has too much integrity.

Dangerous to the likes of you?

Well, if you force me to say so, yes. I think I'll duck underneath Sherman and head to Jackson.

Well you better get in and out of there before Grant does, said Rick

DUST IN THE AFTERNOON

ASK THE DUST, SAYS CARLA, A Handful of Dust, says Path, The NEA is for prose writers this year, Carla says, you apply on-line now, Did you apply last year in poetry, asks Path, Almost, but I couldn't figure out how to submit my work, they say they've simplified it this year, I'll send you the link, Dust to dust, says Path, It's anonymous again, she says, Path says, The anonymity is a sham and has always been a sham, the insiders know who the judges are and the judges are familiar with their work, the insiders notify them that their work is coming, And you're not Vietnamese, says Carla, Vietnam is hot right now, even Trump went there to meet with Kim, That's what I need, says Path, a nuclear missile, Just do it, Path, what have you got to lose, Well, time, pride, so he takes four maddening days trying to figure out the Kafkaesque website, the trials, the castles, are not worth repeating, it's Groundhog Day all over again, but he blunders through somehow and submits, it's raining and the house is leaking, Path turns to me, Stop writing me, he says, I can't go on, But I'm just following you around, Path, you're out of my control, You're God, he says, But God is not in control, I tell him, God is an afterthought of the sentient universe, regardless, Path had to teach that day, it was the day that he had to teach seven hours straight, part of the dean's incentive package toward convincing him to retire, next week he'd meet with his chair to find out he wasn't going to get a full raise, the 1% he'll get won't cover the rise in his parking fees, then the Society Alumnae Fund will ask him to contribute money, then the Trustees will ask, then the President, he can just have it withdrawn automatically from his paycheck, but on the escalator down to his first floor classroom, coming up the escalator across from him, he spots St. Veronica, she's carrying a skateboard, wears a blue sweatshirt with white lettering that says Society of Jesus, skinny jeans, dark hair on her shoulders, she's wearing those soft, flat slipper-shoes they're all wearing now, all the girls anyway, if he can be so gendering, she winks at him, students never recognize you so she must be a saint, not a student, somehow when he reaches the bottom of the escalator she's there, waiting, A miracle, says Path, You want miracles, she says, Yes, he says, miracles, she drops her board, flips it with her toe, jumps on it and rides away, then she appears at the top of the escalator, jumping on its downward moving railing and rides the board to the bottom, skids to a stop in front of him, Can you get me an NEA, he says, she squints, smirks, tilts her head, No, but I'll help you deal with not getting an NEA, Like last time, he says, You weren't talking to me then and I wasn't even born, she replies, he tells her, It's a measly $25,000, See, she says, you're doing better already, I'm a better doing red Teddy, says Path, I'd have been more impressed if you'd gone down the up escalator or, better, up the down escalator, and my mother-in-law, for lack of a more expedient description, has conversations with her hallucinations, Some people believe in the devil, says St. Veronica, some don't, what's the difference, Not much, says Path, I'll be late for class, but how about God, he says, How about God, she says, I've seen you out in the woods pretending God exists for five minutes, It's all I have in me, says Path, you know too much about me to exist, then a grungy boy, he's on a skateboard too, rolls up, kinky hair, scant beard, floppy pants, he puts out his hand, St. Jude, he says, you ask me to help you control your drinking, Path shakes his hand but the kid doesn't have a very firm handshake, You're doing a lousy job, says Path, Jude takes a silver flask from his back pocket and offers it to him, Path says, Not here, not now, not in the afternoon, See, says Jude, you're getting better already, I never drink here, I never, okay, I seldom drink in the afternoon, Gather momentum, says the grungy St. Jude, Veronica has disappeared, just like one of Jin of Arc's gremlins, though at the time Path didn't see them appear or disappear, he just had to take St. Jin's word for it, When I saw my dead friends in heaven, she said, grinning wryly and madly, an index finger pointing up, reaching for the ceiling, I knew I was destined to end up in a place much higher than them, but of course I said nothing to them about it, Jude takes a long draw on his flask, licks his lips, Path wonders how many of his students will have actually read "The Dead," Did V ask you to sleep with her, Jude says, I don't sleep with youth, says Path, and they don't sleep with me, She's a thousand years old, she just looks young, I don't sleep with the aged, says Path, but I'd like to levitate like St. Teresa of Avila, You're baiting me, says St. Jude, You know she didn't really levitate, Path says, It was hyperbole for meditate then, or at least a rhyme, Don't mention her to Veronica, V hates Teresa of Avila, Jude says, Path is thinking that he needs to take his brain through the car wash, he wonders if he should take his wares, his prayers, to a different pantheon, ancient Greek, Hindu, Doesn't St. Veronica know who I pray to, he says, and Jude says, You think we're on a party line up there, Up, Path says, A metaphor, says Jude, If you said party line to my students they wouldn't know what you were talking about, Well, says, Jude, that should tell you something, but Path knows any time someone says something should tell him something else he won't know what he's being told, St. Jude holds up the flask again, You sure you don't want a swig, he says, I bet it's your favorite rye, but Path turns away, how would he know what Path's favorite rye was unless Path made him up inside his head, Limited omniscience, says Jude to his back, maybe you should be talking to a different crowd, Augustine, Aquinas, St. Jerome; Path teaches his seven hours and through it he hears the snow falling in the graveyard, falling on the crosses and the headstones, on the spears of the gates, on the barren thorns, falling faintly and faintly falling, falling upon the living and the dead.

Gaston Bachelard meditates on his first home, the home he was born in, and all first homes, the first home of us all, oneiric in our memories, the special essential: the heaven of the attic, the cellar of hell; in one of Path's books his mother, his fictional mother, more essential, more real, less real, descends into a labyrinth of broken appliances where she lives behind a wall of fire with a statue of the Infant of Prague, the steps to get there were rickety and wooden, the floor was cement, before they had an automatic washer and an electric dryer, he remembers helping her wash clothes in an open tub with a spinner, then placing them in another tub, pushing the clothes through two rollers to squeeze out the water, in the summer you carried them outside through a back door, up some steps to a slanted trap door, a hatch, he used to love to hide there on the stairs between the trap door and the cellar door, in the dark, but he carried the wet clothes through there to hang them outside to dry, stick clothes pins, he envied the neighbors who had the ones with a spring that you squeezed, whose mouths opened and closed like an alligator, those were more expensive, in the winter they hung the clothes in the basement, the clothes lines strung on the rafters, the sheets and towels almost touching the floor, like a maze, he didn't like that work, how did she do it, his poor mother, as Carla says, your poor mother, dead from a brain tumor at fifty-six, birthed and raised six kids and never saw a grandchild, this is how the world ends, this is how the world ends, there were no lamps down there, no ceiling lights, just an occasional uncovered incandescent bulb screwed into a fixture that you lit by pulling a chain, the floor was cold, bare cement, there was a corner of the basement near the foot of the stairs where his father kept old cans of paint and tools, a Charley horse, screw drivers, wrenches, pliers, hammers, hand saws for wood and for pipes, tape measures, hand drills, too, nothing electric, part of Path's cultural inheritance, suspicion and anathema for automatic anything, for moving parts, the first thing to break on any device will be its moving part, things that move break, things that sway swoon, power pales, the body, like a machine, survives on regularity, beware its power source, beware its moving parts, your father, his mother told him, would live in an unmovable world (like Parmenides'), nothing would move, not even him, that's why nothing gets done around here, which was only true metaphorically and so more true than ever, what do you want to do, Red, what would you like to do, I just want to sit here, I just want to sit, here, I just want to sit, while his mother, if given the chance, would conquer the world, but not in this body, she'd say, dropping her hands, not in the body of a woman, Path's wishing now he'd known her longer and better, but it didn't happen; near the steps there were two musty rooms that led beneath the front porch, no windows, light poured in through the lattice work underneath the porch floor above, through that crisscrossed sheen he saw a different world, a jungle of haphazard lawn, ants, bugs, dragons, ghouls, the base of their giant maple, aah, when the street was lined with giant elms before the Dutch Blight hit, the neighborhood was basked in shade, now it burned in the summer light and soured in the winter gray, the room to the right held shelves of canned fruits and vegetables that they'd brought home fresh, nothing was brought in that wasn't canned, tomatoes, beans, peaches, Bartlett pears from the tree in their backyard, plums too, crocks of sweet gherkins, strawberry and grape jam, a pile of potatoes, fresh, if you could call them that, they kept all winter, hence the room's name, the Potato Cellar, though Path recalls another name, too, the fruit cellar, in the other room, what, picks and shovels, an ax, a sledge, screens or storm windows depending on the season, though they were always behind the season because Red hated changing them and if there was a person who hated it more than Red it was

Path who stood at the bottom of the ladder, holding things, holding things that Red might need and seldom needed, there was a wheel barrow, a hand pushed lawn mower, not a power mower, Red would have none of that, but Red didn't push it, Path did, and Path hated that, too; the step ladder was in there, the extension ladder wouldn't fit in the room and lay behind the paint cans and tools, the wooden steps that descended into that netherworld were open, just thick boards hammered into a frame, that's where the broken stuff went, the broken machines, you didn't throw stuff out, you never knew when you'd need it again, you never knew when the new stuff would break, the newer the breakier, nothing lasted as long as the old stuff had, you never knew when you'd need a part, a hose, a belt, a ringer, a washer, a gasket, a screw, a nut, a nail, a scrap of steel or wood, an old bike, an old toy, stuff made out of metal, not plastic, that's why his mother, Eleanor in life, Helen in his book, hid in there, you couldn't get rid of anything that was down there and, in fact, it lasted longer than she did, now Path's remembering the piles of football helmets and shoulder pads, footballs, baseballs, bats and gloves, doll clothes, Chatty Cathys and Suzie Walkers, the cellar was unheated, a labyrinth of labor old and cold, games, no, discarded games were in the attic, the attic with its hotter, higher, deeper memories, though equally as dark, unpainted, a peaked roof, you had to stoop to move, a tiny window peered into the limbs of the maple tree, chests of things, a wooden marionette, hands and face painted white, Red made it in high school, he could make it dance, he'd been an artist, Eleanor's wedding dress, a photo of their wedding day, Path has a photo of his mother on his office wall now, my god, my god, she loved him so much she crossed her faith to fuck, he signed off on religion till the day she died, Red's dress marine shirt, two corporal stripes on its sleeve, a sergeant's badge lying near, he left before he put it on, rode an aircraft carrier home, home, there was a naval uniform, too, all white, and a captain's cap and sword, his Uncle Ray's, two medals, the Legion of Merit and the Croix de Guerre he got in Normandy, though they were worthless in the insane asylum, shell shock then, PTSD now, his law diploma he never used, he flunked the bar twice when he got back; there were racks of clothes that his sisters played in, draping themselves in oversized dresses and coats, like scarecrows, like ghosts, who cares, who cares, Path, there's no one to care, no one now, if ever, these are lives beneath graves, Path thinks, I am a grave, I am here and gone; Path just got put on a panel for the 2019 Associated Writers Programs in Portland, the panel is called Writers Over Sixty Talk About Death, no kidding, he had to write a presentation, here it is:

Well it was supposed to go here, but I'm working with Path's new computer that he had to get because a tiny piece of plastic, a moving part, broke on his old laser printer and it couldn't be replaced so he had to replace the whole printer, then his old computer couldn't communicate with his new printer so he needed a new computer and though all we do here is word process we couldn't buy a simple computer because it would become incapable of communicating with any new technology almost immediately, so now we're typing on a computer that could send a robot to Saturn but simple word processing, what used to be known as typing, is almost impossible to unearth underneath all the complex abilities of this machine; it took us weeks to be able to do what is happening right now, typing, then saving and retrieving, but now, after a half-hour of brain battering we still can't figure out how to copy one document and paste it into another, which was once a simple task; this super powered mother fucker doesn't even have a simple edit command, won't even execute simple line spacing within a paragraph without descending through myriad hidden windows, so in that half-hour we managed to select a whole text, i.e. the AWP Death Panel, we can't copy it without it disappearing before we try to add it to this one, under all this capacity lies incapacity, simple tasks hidden under complex rubrics, just select all, copy, paste, what happened to that, this is the story of our lives, we can neither copy nor paste, meanwhile, back at the ranch, Carla has unplugged the phone because Jin of Arc calls fifteen times a day because she forgets that she just called, Carla drove her to a shrink where tests revealed that Jin remembers almost nothing, she can't subtract seven from anything because she forgets what she's subtracting seven from, all she can remember is ancient folklore of her own beatitude, her days of motherhood and martyrdom, seems to have completely forgotten locking Carla in the closet or the garage, you think you find it tedious to read, trying living in it, it's a really good thing that none of this matters; yesterday was the first day of spring, 2019, World War One has been over for a long time now, time for a new one, Path's book about Leon Trotsky rots on some computer file in New York, Carla is compiling a manuscript of her new and selected works, *The Arc Between Two Deaths*, that title will change a dozen times, suddenly there's a burst of rain, Path remembers 1993 and '94; but first, the AWP Death Panel, here, finally, it is:

I don't know if I think about death more now than I ever did, though maybe now, at sixty-seven, sixty-eight, sixty-nine, I think about it differently and, often enough, think differently enough about it depending on what time of the day it is and who, particularly, I'm thinking about. Generally, and bluntly, there are deaths I've mourned, deaths I ignored, and deaths I, well, celebrated.

Recently our dog died and I feel her around me almost everywhere, in my house, on the property around it; what I feel is where she used to be, where she should be, though now she is irrevocably gone. I would like to believe that she has moved on somewhere, but there aren't many moments when I can make myself believe that, even though I often practice many things that I don't believe, just to feel what it would feel like to believe in them, say, a providential deity, or some pantheon of helpers between that great soul and we human souls, say Hindu gods, Catholic saints, Islamic angels, Hebrew messengers, Vajrayana sub-deities, maybe a paradise, like in *Genji*, where great lovers share eternity; usually it doesn't change much of anything, and maybe I started to do this just before I turned sixty, some nine or so years ago when I was fifty-nine and diagnosed with cancer. It was then that I discovered that I was coward about death. Anyway, as you see, I'm not dead yet. Though now I know, undeniably, that I'm a coward about it, and often stalk my own life like a shadow, feeling myself in places that I don't occupy anymore, the tennis court, the top of a wave, the space above the rim. I'm more tentative about my plans five years from now, for ten years from now I have no plans.

Just before my mother, a devout Catholic, developed a glio brain tumor she told me she was ready to die. She was fifty-five. She wasn't ready. Sad and disabled by her surgery, she suffered and died in about ten months. She was bitter. A mother of six, she never lived to see a grandchild. I had a camera then, a 35 mm. SLR. I took a photograph of her on her 56th birthday, developed it and printed it, tore it up and threw it out. I never took another photo. For her part, as my mother fell into her death she abandoned many of her religious practices. What was the point? My mother's son, when I began my cancer treatments, I drank more booze. What was it going to do, kill me? I discovered Buddhism when I was twenty-one. I was pretty fervent then. I'm less fervent now. As the extinction of my *dukkha*, the end of my clinging to my precious selfhood becomes more inevitable, I've become less holy, more contrary. What am I doing with my time? What am I doing with this whisky? Is someone (me?) enjoying it? Or not?

What am I afraid of? The unknown, I suppose. How much I'll miss myself when I'm gone. I'm less scared during the day when I'm busy, less scared when I'm drunk, more scared when I'm facing my cancer detecting blood tests that are coming up next week, most scared in the oneiric territory of the preconscious, in the morning, just before waking, when reality and inevitability wash over me like bright light, when I fear my lover's death more frighteningly than my own, because then I might be left waiting, decrepit and alone. In those shivering moments I invite death. Bring it on, I say. But I don't know if I mean it.

I'm sixty-seven, likely seventy if and when this ever sees print, if I live. Old enough to be wise. Where is my wisdom? Where is it, Carl Jung? Socrates didn't fear the nothingness. Neither did Buddha, who took comfort in the escape from the illusion of desire and pain. Whatever comfort Jesus took in the intimation that he might be the son of God, it didn't help him much that night in Gethsemane. When you throw suffering in with death things get really depressing. I try to think about late August on the Great Lakes when the leaves turned down and started to dry. The wind rattled them with the first whisper of winter and despite the warm and gentle days still ahead, I felt winter, white, cold, and dreadful in my bones. As horrible as some winters were, that fear was more visceral than in the actual winter, the winter, inevitably, that we got through. Maybe, maybe, it's like that.

As more people around me get sick and die, ones who meant a lot to me who I didn't even know, David Bowie, Leonard Cohen, others whom I knew, like Bill Gass, Chuck Kinder, and Francois Camoin, now, in 2021, the physicist, Bob Hellwarth, of covid-19, I gaze at those around me who are still alive, the still alive club. Do we congratulate ourselves? Whew, glad that didn't happen to me. Though I notice people my age trying to get healthier. What's the trick? Less meat? For the gift of long life and infirmity? If I hobble around at sixty-seven, what do I tell myself about the next ten years, do I quote my dying father, almost crippled to immobility? "I'll be playing golf in a week!" Things are going to get better? Do I clean up my past the way I'd clean the cat litter? Do I accept my life of hidden accomplishments? Do I line up my truths like duckpins? My failures? *Mea culpa*, not? Bleed optimism? Ooze despair? What do I got, a bad attitude? Okay, I should be happy I'll be dead before the really bad environmental shit comes down. Let the kids worry about it. I'm starting to think that I'm not the person who should be writing this essay.

I'm reading *The Magic Mountain*. J. -K. Huysmans' *A Rebours (Against Nature)*. Researching the siege of Vicksburg. Writing a novel about a man lost in the sea of over-existence. Reading Bachelard, Whitehead, and Sartre. Suzuki. Always Shunryu Suzuki, the Zen Master whose last words were, "I don't want to die." On the commode, at the rate of a page a day, I'm re-reading Gass's *The Tunnel*. On my first reading, when I was in my forties, I didn't get it. A tunnel to nowhere, out of house and home and life, out of the past and out of the future. Now I'm in there with him, digging.

With a fresh mind of a new day he figured it out, something he did by putting it on the Clipboard, he doesn't quite know how he did it, copied to the Clipboard, pasted from the Clipboard to Nexile, from Clipboard to Nexile, and you can't go back, there's freedom to all this, after forty years of crafting his fiction with thoughtful phrasing and architectonic, even *The Last Book of Everything* had a kind of rhythmic repetition of thematics, woeful resonance, that's not what we wanted to say, but it doesn't matter what you want to say, say first, then matter, if it matters at all, the difference between not mattering now and not mattering back then is that then he thought it might matter, when Gass told him, once over wine in the afternoon, and again late at night, the two of them on the living room floor on either side of a coffee table, that life was meaningless, he meant that meaning occurred in language, no language, no meaning, life was ontological, not syntactical, meaning was imposed on it, life did not mean, life did not mean itself to language, language meant itself on life, though on the other hand, late at night, the cognac flowing, it meant that ontology was meaningless too, as Carla would say, spring, spring, the bird is on the wing, why that's absurd, the wing is on the bird, the burden of a Jack Kerouac sentence, the pound of sound over sense, but let's return now to 1993 when it felt like it would always be 1993, time could never advance beyond 1993, Trans Kafka went by the moniker Luke Skywalker, though on Halloween she dressed up as a mermaid, a group of Topangans and their children trick or treated on the back streets off Old Canyon, there was a lesbian couple, Didi and Ingrid and their adopted daughter, name forgotten, a hot wind howled from the northeast and an electrical wire fell in Calabasas, a wildfire swept into Topanga, up Old Canyon and to the hills above the town, it stayed in the hills and ran toward Malibu, burned an acre every three seconds, burnt to the ocean, then turned back into the hills, heading up the box canyons, Rambla Pacifica, Las Flores, Tuna, burned at the top of Fernwood, Path's neighborhood, and jumped the road to burn in the State Park across the way, Path got his daughter out early, at the start, drove to the Society and found Carla coming out of class, he pointed toward the mountains where a plume of smoke rose a mile high, angry flames beneath it lining the tops of the mountains, What did you get out with, said Carla, Marlena held up a grocery bag full of her drawings and paintings, Nothing, said Carla, Nothing said Path, One cat, the rest are still there, even the newts, Carla dragged them to the Sears and bought clothes, they urban camped, stayed with brethren, friend, and foe, watched the burning hills, how long had they lived there, then, about two years, across the town television sets burned with images of fire, no one knew what burned, no one fighting the fire knew where they were, sirens screamed, helicopters whined, before the fire started Path was writing a short story about it, in the story he owned a big gray horse, Carla was in Denver on the cusp of an affair, peddling her cowgirl persona in an era of her beauty that dropped men where they stood, and she was there in Denver dropping men, Path took his daughter and the horse up a fire road to a cave in Red Rock Canyon and waited out the fire, then rode the limping gelding, Luke/Marlena on his lap, into an evacuation center in Woodland Hills, after the fire he sent the story to C. Michael Curtis at *The Atlantic*, What about the affair, said C. Michael Curtis, short stories have affairs, but Path forgot to write about the affair, Did you have an affair, Carla, did you, but Carla said Path's big mistake was not her affair whether she had one or not, it was playing pick-up basketball with C. Michael Curtis at a high school gym in Park City, Utah, it was at the Park City Writers Conference and Path was Curtis' host, Curtis fashioned himself a good street player but Path crushed him fifteen-zip, That, said Carla, was the beginning of the end of your career, your fade away, your step back jumper, your left-handed jump hook, what good do they do you now, not long after the fire Bill and Mary Gass were in LA because Gass had a Getty Fellowship, they walked through the charred hills of Red Rock Canyon, disintegrated eucalyptus, felled pines, blackened oaks, deer carcasses, Gass took photos, Mary took pictures of him taking photos, then that night the Northridge Quake struck and the next night after the earthquake William Gaddis read at the Pacific Design Center, Gaddis insulted Gass, ridiculed his own daughter who sat in the front row, called her a failed artist, how old was Bill Gass then, sixty-eight, like Path is now, and now Gass is dead; the Death Panel in Portland was packed, SRO, people lining the back of the room, the walls, the aisles, half the audience wasn't even old, Carla talked about T.S. Eliot's *Four Quartets*, his last work, you just saw what Path read, and afterward the panel was swarmed, people approached them on the conference floor, in their hotel lobby, waved or shook their hands and thanked them, for what, Path didn't know, he wasn't used to communicating with people, Gratifying, Carla asked, did he feel better because of it, worse? A year later, 400,000 Americans, young and old, would be dead in a pandemic. His older brother, Wil, age 75, comes down with a rare nerve disease and rots to death.

PEMBERTON MET SHERMAN'S ARMY

NORTHEAST OF VICKSBURG ON CHICKASAW BAYOU. He entrenched us, his outmanned, outgunned army, on a ridge. Sherman sent his men at us, slogging through the swamp, a wave of blue, cut down under blistering fire.

Think that'll do it for them? I said to my companion, Josh. I didn't regard him as a friend, friends die, brother in arms, I suppose, though if you had a family, like I did, then you weren't really that fond of them either, they fought for money, land, sex, my brothers and sisters were probably already scheming for my patch of desultory subsistence right at the moment. I say probably because at the time I could only surmise, now, of course, I know that I'd surmised correctly, once I became a ghost I wouldn't even bother to haunt them. People came to say that we fought better, harder than the Yankees because we were fighting for our homes, but we were already fighting amongst each other for our homes, being human and therefore greedy; we were fighting the Yankees because they came down here with their guns, if they hadn't have come down here we wouldn't have been fighting them.

No, said Josh. He filled his pipe. Sherman just likes to fight. We whip him here he'll just come back somewhere else.

He's not fighting, I said. He's not dying.

Well, neither is Pemberton, said Josh. Such is war. At least all this gun smoke is keeping the mosquitos down.

For now.

For now.

I don't know what Sherman thought. Maybe he wasn't expecting us to be waiting for him out there in that swamp. Maybe, regardless, he thought he'd have too much firepower. Thought we'd see the numbers and get up and run.

Wouldn't be the first time for that on either side. In any case, we didn't. We didn't have much artillery, but we were entrenched. He couldn't go around us on either side, the bayou was too deep. And at least for that battle, we had better guns, British Enfields, as good a muzzle loader as there was at the moment.

I guess Sherman had thought about things a little bit because next time around he started with a bombardment, most of which made a lot of racket but passed over our heads. The Union boys weren't bad artillerists, they'd figure things out and begin hitting us sometimes soon enough. Seemed like they had about ten guns, not big ones, they had to drag them through the brush for miles to get to us, they were good at that kind of thing, smashing shit up. Our cannon fired back. You couldn't tell who was hitting who or what, but Josh stuck his head up over the abattment and bingo, a ball knocked his pipe out of his hand.

Whoa. Cool, he said. Guess they got snipers. He shook his hand at the air like a match had burned his fingers.

Next came the skirmishers. Things were going much more by the book this time. We sent out ours, too. I never liked that work myself, out there in the open playing cat and mouse in rifle range. Sometimes that's as far as things got, armies lined up and gauged each other's strengths and weaknesses for days, fronts shifting, flanks changing, though here there was pretty much nothing to be done but fight or not. When their troops came at us this time, it wasn't in a thick line, but in separate, spaced groups of about a dozen men, two rows, the first six shot, knelt in the swamp, then the next six stepped forward. Separated like that it was harder to just mow them down, though if any of them broke through our lines it would be harder for them to consolidate the breakthrough. In fact, one bunch of them actually made it up the hill. Then it came to bayonets. But there weren't enough of them. They died there.

When you're fighting like that, you don't think about the fact that you're fighting men, boys, fathers, sons, husbands, uncles, nephews, brothers. I can tell you, from memory, that when you die you just die, you don't have time to think about those things, the hell must come when you're fatally wounded, dying alone in no man's land. God given hell. No need of Satan's hell after that. That's how it was after we repelled that second assault. The cries of the wounded and dying. A symphony of devils. I mean that sympathetically. You could hear men crying for someone to just come out there and shoot them, but you'd have to risk your life to do that. When you put on your coat and picked up your gun, marched around prancing to Dixie or Yankee Doodle, whoever thought they'd end up like that.

Josh was on my left. Just a kid. A couple feet to my right was an older guy with a red beard. He wasn't much of a talker. One of those just shut up and kill or die types. Probably believed in God or something worse.

The sun was setting. We sat with our backs to straw and logs. Our fort. You couldn't hear much now but the wall of moans.

You got family, I said to Josh. A girl?

He didn't say anything.

Workers? I said.

Them who can afford workers are wearing boots and sitting on horses behind us, Josh said. He meant behind the lines.

I suppose there's a lot to explain right there, but since I'm writing things down now, in the quiet void with my ghostly hand, I have time; while Josh and I sat in that pit of death waiting to see the stars, maybe for the last time, I have time to explain how we were considering what we were considering. If you could afford it, you weren't out here behind a wall, the only other thing between you and an army trying to kill you being your bayonet and a few rounds of bullets, and you might, as well, be barefoot. If you could afford it, you owned a horse and a pair of boots and maybe even a fancy hat. You had a sword and a repeating pistol. Not that the cavalry didn't fight, they fought hard and plenty, but they fought out in the open, wind in their faces, not the putrid stink of corpses reminding you every second of what you just did. Admittedly, there was no place for them here in the swamp. If we were lucky they were circling around Sherman's right to hit him from behind, though in fact we weren't that lucky, Bedford Forest, or one of his types, would get distracted and head up to Arkansas or Missouri to tear down telegraph wire, burn farms, pull up railroad lines, safer, if useful, combat, I suppose, the work of knights not peasants. We all have our place in the world, mine was where I was.

Anyway, if you had a horse then you likely owned land or were the son of a man who did and likely, then, you had workers. Those workers were more than likely Black Africans and unpaid but for food and lodging. In the North they called it slavery. We didn't use that word. It had a bad sound. I heard one woman say that it was a kindness. They got to join a family and learn about

Jesus. All that, I suppose, before they got sold to somebody less benevolent. Anyway, it was an assignment they couldn't refuse, not that I could get up and walk away from what I was doing without getting shot in the back, and my enlistment period was over and I hadn't seen a paycheck in memory, not that the Confederate dollar was worth anything. Word was that Lee wanted to enlist Black Africans and free them after the war, then they could buy some land and fight over it with their relatives, maybe get some workers of their own.

Josh pointed up into the sky. I think he spotted the Dog Star. I got a dog, he said.

A good dog?

She's a good dog. She'll fight anything.

Well you should be glad she's not here. We'll be eating dogs and worse before this is all over.

Turns out he had a girl once, too, but he lost her to one of those cavalier types on the horses. There was a tale there. I had some too, girls, dogs, but the sun came up and so too the fusillade of cannons.

MAY DAY

PATH LIKED THE OLD SOVIET MAY DAY, that dreadful Red Parade of stomping soldiery and giant nuclear missiles, Khrushchev, who slammed his shoe on the podium at the U.N. shouting We will bury you! under nuclear fallout, Path supposed, he never wondered then how those images from behind the Iron Curtain ended up in his living room on the tiny black and white Zenith, who would let that kind of evil out, shown to the American public, he guessed, maybe, to scare us, though later, soon enough later, it was ourselves scaring ourselves to be afraid of the Red Menace, look at them, look at them tromping evil and destruction, we better be careful, they're setting a bad example, we better build more and more nukes, holy shit, they even had a satellite in space, what if they put one of their nukes up there, why the hell did we save their asses from Hitler, even though it turns out that we didn't, they saved themselves from Hitler, good old Zhukov, inventor of mechanized warfare, one of the few generals Stalin forgot to kill, Path had always, well, not always, but since he crawled into political consciousness, preferred Trotsky to Stalin, kind of a long story, but he'd just finished writing a novel about Trotsky's years in Mexico, his affair with Kahlo, his amazing lover, Natalia Sedova, little did Path know that he'd be identity politic punched out on Frida, he, himself, not being Latinx, though she was half-German, like him, and no one knew or remembered Trotsky and the ones who did hated him, lousy Communist mother fucker, stick that armored train up your ass, but those big fat brown missiles with the red hammer and sickle on their cones, coming to a city near you, ka-boom, but it didn't take long for Path to turn around on that, one draft pick away from Vietnam, Path yet had a poster above the glass table that he found in a back alley dumpster in Prague, a golden hammer and sickle over the eastern hemisphere, rays of sunlight blurting out, banners with the name of every member country of the Soviet Union surrounding the globe, in Cyrillic, of course, you bet, he loved those Russian hockey jerseys, plain as day, with CCCP on the chest, he still didn't know what that meant, he assumed USSR in aberrant Coptic, it was on the space capsules too, but that poster it turns out was from the first post-war International convention of Soviet Republics in 1948, in Prague, tromp, tromp, tromp, who were they kidding, Path had been to Prague several times and once took the subway to the end of the line because when he looked out his window from his apartment he saw tall buildings shimmering hazily in the distance and when he asked a local what they were he was told, Don't ask, Can I go there, he asked, and was told, Don't go, so he went, and there he found that Prague was surrounded by bunches of fifteen story apartment complexes, bending to each other, convex and concave, like crescent moons, villages of apartment complexes, and at the center of each of them the ruins of hospitals, playgrounds, libraries, schools, empty and abandoned, the complexes themselves now packed with poverty, clothes drying on the balcony railings, but once, once upon a time, filled with workers, where do they go now to read, to play, to learn, to heal, he stops outside a playground, yellow metal monkey bars and swing sets, he surveys the gifts of totalitarian rule, were they better off now in their poverty and freedom, who was it who appeared to Bernadette, was that in Fatima or Lourdes, put down that screw driver, that hammer, and pick up a rosary, say the rosary every day to keep the world from going Communist, the Virgin Mary, like Mighty Mouse, appearing just in time, meanwhile, Carla comes down with pneumonia, Path finds out they're $11,500 short on their taxes, the septic backs up and spews its guts in front of his kitchen door, his refrigerator dies and the microwave blows up, the dean fires the only other fiction writer and slaps Path with three introductory level writing courses stacked one right after another, five straight hours of teaching, teaching, teaching, sixty ignorant badly formatted and punctuated essays a week, their brains have turned into Google, they don't know the difference between present tense or past, how did they get into college, the plumber uses a magic electronic wand to discover a second secret septic pit under Path's office, must tear out the floor and start digging to find it and Path, throwing books out the door shelf by shelf, epiphanizes the metaphor, he's been reading and writing on top of a sea of piss and shit; his life is waste, he's Willie Wasteful Life, he begins to gather up the books in trash bags and put them in the trash, he gathers four boxes and sixteen huge trash bags of books and he's only half done, all of Woolf, all of Waugh and Maugham, Ford and Forster, all of Twain and Faulkner, Burgess, Graham Greene, Dickens, Sterne, Defoe, George Eliot, George Sands, he keeps Hemingway's short stories, Joyce, Gass, Bolaño, Kinder and Camoin, both of whom just died, Gass, Camoin, Kinder, the knockout punch for his mentors, none left now, he keeps one book by Alice Adams because she signed it for him just before she died, was sweet enough to say she remembered him from a workshop in Davis, he thinks it was at a party thrown by Carolyn See, who recently died as well, she lived in Topanga with John Espee and when he died she told Path, Don't let them die at home, it's a nice idea but a bad idea, Path throws out Carolyn See, he'd thrown out Lisa See a long time ago, and Greg Sarris after he ridiculed Path for writing about an Indian, out with Updike, Bellow, even Barth who once recommended Path to his students, Gaddis, Barthelme, both Donald and Frederick, Coover, too, Berger, O'Conner, Atwood, Acker, Duras, Cather, Porter, Henry James, Cooper, Hawthorne, Melville, Poe, he keeps one volume of Chekhov for now, Marquez gone, though he's got Flaubert next to his chair, just finished *Three Tales*, reads *A Sentimental Education, Bovard and Puchacet, Madame Bovary*, will he keep them, who knows, he threw out Cortázar's *Blow Up* and *Hopscotch* but he's got *Cronopios and Famas* lying around somewhere, a realtor spots him lugging bags of books to his trash down his front steps, What are you doing, Throwing out books, Any cookbooks, No cookbooks, only literature, I once read something by Dickens, I've thrown him out already, says Path, The library? Doesn't want them, says Path, Leave them in your driveway and I'll notify the community, so Path left a six foot tall pile of garbage bagged books in front of his house for three days, nobody touched them and he threw them away, he's throwing out sci-fi, he's throwing out religion, a bunch of Beats, a glass of wine, a cigarette, an old banjo; if in doubt, throw it out.

WALKING AWAY

IF THE BUDDHA RADICALLY WALKED AWAY from metaphysics and ontology on the very practical grounds that all such questions were unanswerable, many of the Buddhist schools that sprung from that realization seem to have found it just too true to accept. Yet if attachment is the first cause of human suffering, it very well may be the first cause of everything. As Bertrand Russell said, in the simplest refutation, there's just too much denial. Various Buddhist schools, and Buddhist logic, anticipated that. On the human level, a close examination of consciousness reveals a moment to moment co-arising of percept—object, of percept—concept—awareness; there is no mind, no soul or self observably involved in the process. William James reiterates this in "Does Consciousness Exist?" Well, if consciousness is a *thing*, then the answer is "No." We do experience (whatever "we" are) the flow of these confluences from one moment to the next, a phenomenon his brother, Henry James, described as "the stream of consciousness," a term often used in both literary and philosophical circles to mean the opposite of what the James brothers meant, i.e. the stream of consciousness, for them, did not imply an entity that possessed said consciousness nor, as I've said, grant consciousness substantial existence, for William ontologically and psychologically, for Henry, personage. Not so long after Buddha, some 500 years later, around the time of Jesus, Nāgārjuna, the founder of the Nothingness School, extended that analysis to all substance, observing and dialectically arguing that all existence, all phenomena, results from spontaneous, moment to moment co-arising and there ain't no turtles underneath it. Later Buddhist thinkers, dissatisfied with that, pondered the reasons for this co-arising, and supposed it was desire, the acquisitive desire of any individuated stream of consciousness to impose *thingness* on the process, a form of idealism, that mind, or minds, create reality, and clinging to that creates suffering (karma, a concept Buddha, a Hindu reformer in the way that Jesus was a Hebrew reformer, accepted but couldn't be justified by his agnostic nihilism), consciousness, desire, create reality, but, of course, not a reality that is really real. Now we're back in Plato's territory, or Berkeley's, or Royce's, whether or not there's a turtle under there, say, Plato's mathematical laws (the Forms), or God, or Nothing, phenomena, the world, still falls together in remarkable agreement; mew, you, my cat for that matter, we seem to be delusional in the same ways—we all see that table over there, sit at it or on it—we all make the world up in remarkably similar ways. To deny the realness of the world is hard to do, and to postulate the really real, whether it's something or nothing, grows increasingly unsatisfying. To quote David Byrne, "How did I get here?"

THE BLIND EYE OF GOD

THEY STAYED IN AN APARTMENT IN PRIANO on the Amalfi Coast, a small town sitting between Positano to the north and Amalfi to the south, large windows overlooked a yard that hung over the Mediterranean Sea, on a clear day they could spy Capri, other black rock islands sat in the bluest water Path had ever seen; they went with some friends, now old friends, the political poet, Flaca Rosen and her partner Razo Domingo, both had been on Death Row in Argentina after the military coup of the Seventies, thirty thousand others, Montonero compañeros, did not survive, they were shot, beheaded, thrown from helicopters, crushed under tanks, how had these two escaped, dumb luck and Amnesty International, said Flaca, married to another man then, had her daughter kidnapped by the military, her husband was dropped from a plane, she became the only survivor of a prison camp, then spent three years in prison, Razo was placed in front of a firing squad four times, he said he got used to it, they were both deported to Seattle, met there, Path, who'd been at Kent State, did you see him in the photo leaning over the dying girl, he couldn't compare it, tin soldiers and Nixon, four dead, not thirty thousand, the current Pope, Pope Francis, was in Argentina then, had he whispered a single protest, no; the sea is so blue, the sea is so blue, where is God, over the horizon, if, like Vishnu, they were to open their eyes, if they were to blink, would it all disappear, then who would know, where to go.

I stopped following Path around for a few months; he's reading different stuff now, now the wind is howling, now there is blood where there used to be water, water where there used to be blood, now the arms of time are extended madly now that time has gone; I'm not planning to live as long as you, Path, I'm waiting for the sinister saint sisters, typing on blisters, rounding up resistors, transistors, are there any transistors anymore? have they gone the way of tubes? why, in a world of absolute and near infinite singular specificity, does so much end up looking the same; Carla goes in for a routine colonoscopy, she comes home in pain, Is it supposed to hurt, Path asks, Gas, says Carla, but it continues into the night, into the morning, Urgent Care, says Path, but Carla is stoic, she takes some gas meds and gets no relief, on Saturday night Path says, the Emergency Room, I'll just sit there in pain, waiting, says Carla, but on Sunday morning she's still in pain, Path thinks she's bloating, she tells him if she's still in pain in the morning she'll go to the doctor, and in the morning he insists she call the doctor, he drives her up the coast to their UCLA clinic, the doctor takes one look at her and says, Go to the ER immediately, I'll call ahead, Path drives her there where they admit her on the spot, they start tests, x-rays, scans, two interns say they're puzzled, there seems to be blood in her stomach but they don't see bleeding, Are you in pain, says Path, I'll be all right, Carla says, she gives him a list of things to get from home, her phone, her brush, a book, Path drives home, but he's upset, something's wrong, he's been at death's door with Carla before, her cesarean when the anesthetics didn't take, she screamed, begged them to let her die, when Marlena emerged, bloody, Carla couldn't look at her, then Carla shivered for hours as the misapplied anesthesia wore down, they never told their child about that, Trans Kafka still doesn't know; later Carla had an ectopic pregnancy that ruptured, she went to the ER by ambulance, again, maddening pain as her blood pressure dipped to 40/20, when they wheeled her into emergency surgery Path said to her, I love you, and she flipped him the bird, You did this to me, you bastard, she said, Path waited, imagining life without her, when the doctor came to the waiting room he said to Path, In twenty more minutes she would have been dead; recently she fell ten feet from the top of their outdoor steps, landed on her shoulders and head, of course, at the hospital, they were convinced he'd beaten her, he was interrogated six times, Carla, too, but she tells the same story, she'd backed up, pointing at a horned owl atop one of their cypress trees (the one that flew off with Frida?) and now, heading up the PCH for Santa Monica, he's thinking of it again, if she died, how could he live? but one day one of them will die, this haunts him, that certainty, haunted by certainty, the breath of an owl, the life of a tree, he reads Volodine's *Bardo or Not Bardo*, picks up the *Bardo Thodol*, where the worn pages and pencil markings indicate that he's read it several times, but like his life it lives in vague packets of memory; when he arrives at the ER he's told a surgeon came in and took Carla into emergency surgery; he removed the blood, she'd bled internally, her spleen had been nicked, but miraculously heeled itself, if not, she'd be dead now, or wearing a colostomy bag at best, her colonoscopy doctor apologizes the next day, it was an accident, no one's fault (but three weeks later he's fired), out the hospital window the sky is the color of the ocean, in the distance lies meaning and fire and panic; this is your God, Path, this is the shape your God is in, the shape of God, is despair, dreaming Death's dream dreaming death, we won't find out what happened while we were away; stop trying to not make sense, it can't be done, not even here, even Gertrude Stein flailed, sit here now with me, let's pour rye whisky over ice and set our clocks back one hour, Carla and Path will be sitting at the glass table again, Leonard Cohen sings, "Democracy is coming . . . to the USA," Carla says, Ontology is coming . . . to the USA, write that down, Path, and Path grabs a small yellow tablet and writes it down, Everything needs to be done, he says, and she says, Nothing needs to be done, So let it be done, he says, day-do run run run day-do run run, but he can't remember any more words to the song, There's a guy named Bill in it, Carla says, yes, Bill, Path has put down *Cartesian Sonatas*, he thought, after *Eyes*, Gass' last published work, he'd re-read *Sonatas* but he can't, he's Gassed out, couldn't fight through Flaubert's sadomasochistic *Solommbo* either, he's started a book of philosophy, philosophy? (you can find it here, among the rest of this) philosophy of what, like an old time metaphysician he wants to think about what's underneath stuff, how the stuff underneath stuff becomes the stuff we see and hear and touch and taste, not smell because Path can't smell, I've been hanging around him so long that I can't smell either, can't smell ether, does ether have a smell? some time ago, like the knock ghost in his kitchen, there was, purportedly, reportedly, a smell ghost in an upstairs bathroom who apparently exploded into his living room, people held their noses, well, Carla did, Jesus did, they hired a plumber to clean the pipes, a carpenter to search the cabinets, for dead animals; oddly, the bathroom was connected back to back to the bathroom in their bedroom that had no foul smell at all; they sought the aid of an acquaintance, an Armenian named Raffi, who had experience with ghosts, met a lot of them in Armenia where there are yet a lot of sad ghosts, he walked into their house and said, This place is rife with ghosts, thick with ghosts, you have to yell at them, fill the place with anti-ghost yells, but they're harmless, said Path, what about upstairs, and they went up, yup, stink ghost, said Raffi, the remnants of some pack rat, you know, those types who never throw anything away, now everything's gone but they themselves, an irony of the afterlife, you have to be careful of how ironic your afterlife might be, but here's the thing, Raffi, says Path, I don 't believe in ghosts, got no place in my ontology for ghosts, You have an ontology? I have ontologies, said Path, I'm a radical pluralist agnostic, a poly-agnostic, I believe everything and doubt all of it, back downstairs Raffi points toward a Moroccan half-moon shaped coffee table, on it sits a huge wooden Ganesh, lavishly painted and a smaller Shiva dancing on a devil, a rat sits at the feet of Ganesh, all the Gods have traveling companions (Vishnu's is the serpent-bird Garuda who sits on top of Path's desk computer, Vishnu-less), ironic that the elephant-headed Ganesh travels on a rat, that's Hinduism for you, Path and Carla bought these statues at a state run artifact store in Varanasi in 2006, Path wrote a whole book about that four month trip to India, between Ganesh and Shiva stands a small brown wooden horse, a little bigger than the rat beneath Ganesh, a saddle is painted on it, there was once a rider but he disappeared one day, Path conjectures that he was kidnaped by a cat and stashed somewhere, wherever that particular cat, Path figures the big mackerel Norwegian Forest Cat, Romeo, now dead, took it, but Path never found his stash, another mackerel, Italo, raided and stashed a good deal of Carla's jewelry before she started hiding it, and now that we're dealing with the subcontinent, one of the things Italo stashed for good was a ruby ring that Path bought for Carla one evening at the Annapurna Hotel in Kathmandu, the hotel was bombed by the Maoists later that night, when Path wrote about it he imagined Carla and him standing in the lobby, the ashes falling upon them like snow, then they lie down and make love in the ashes; the rat has been roughed up by a number of cats, his tail is loose, teeth marks festoon his body, one of his molesters included Italo, whom Path loved, he died on the road one morning at dawn during rush hour, well, he didn't die on the road, his back legs were paralyzed, Path and Carla rushed him to a 24 hour hospital in Santa Monica, but his back was broken, he clung to Path as he was put down, Path wept, now a new cat, Frida, is playing with the wooden rat, the rat is played with, not stashed, because it's not a thing but an effigy of a rat, cats don't hide rats anyways, they play with them until they're dead, Frida leaves the rat out in the open near the glass table just like she'd do with a real rat, an example, to Path's mind, that she thinks in icons, i.e. sense signs, visual, olfactory, gustatory, tactile, auditory, he just published a book about it, it goes to show that he's not pathetic, neither is he heroic nor tragic, this is Nexile, not exile, Nexistential, not Existential, not paradise, not epic, neither Uruk nor Troy, I only follow him around because I have to, just like the narrator who is following you and writing you down right now, I'm making Path up, Path is making me up, in the impossible first person present my mind follows me everywhere, we never go anywhere without each other, but that aside, on the rose wall above Ganesh hang ten Mexican retablos and a thin iron hand, palm out, or is it palm in, it's flat so hard to tell which, but Raffi is pointing to some books on Ganesh's left, books about the Inca and Aztecs, Where's the Maya, says Rafi, Upstairs next to my reading chair, Well you got a lot of ghosts, Well I don't see them, You mean you can't or won't see them, So what's a ghost, Anything you can't or won't see, Or smell, says Path, Exactly, smell ghosts are particularly insidious, Unless you can't smell, Ghosts are the most real unreal thing, and then Path said, More real than real, says Sappho, More gold than gold, Sappho wrote about ghosts? Raffi said, Would it matter; there was a time when Path pretended to believe in ghosts, though pretending to believe was a game he played with himself all the time, Let's take ten minutes and believe in the Greek Gods, Let's take ten minutes and pretend you're famous, let's take ten and talk to the trees, let's believe you can change the weather, before his cancer when he felt less mortal, he'd take a cigarette outside and sit under the avocado tree and let the figures form in the smoke, he saw his Aunt Orva there the night she died, one night he saw a gang of unrecognizable ghosts who were unhappy with some change he was making in the house, Don't worry, he told them, now he remembers neither ghosts nor change, what about those saints, Path, well, thinks Path, what constitutes existence, my thoughts exist, if for only a moment, if only for me, when he was in India and he and his students spotted a cow beneath the lights of the big cricket stadium, their guide, Ravi Shankar, said, You cannot be seeing a cow, Then what's that, It cannot be a cow because there are no cows in Kolkata, There's a cow right there, There are no cows in Kolkata, you must be thinking you are somewhere else; when Jin of Arc said she saw babies and gremlins, heard children singing, what was their ontological status, might we, as some Buddhists say, hallucinate the world with our desires, what of Plato's criteria, it must be more than perceived, it must be conceived and permanent, the perceived world is real enough, it's just not really real, what is the ontological difference between the laws of nature and the phenomena that they govern, how about those saints you've been talking to, Path, and suddenly Path isn't home with Raffi and the ghosts anymore, he's on the Santa Maria trail and a voice cries out, a moan in the trees, he turns and there stands Veronica, a flowing skirt, a flowery blouse right out of Johnny Was, she's braless and he can see her hardened nipples, I never imagine you like this, he says, then, she says, When you pray to me, would you rather I look like a nun, do you want to fuck an old nun, would you rather I have blue eyes, and her deep brown eyes turned dazzling blue, I don't need it, says Path, and for the first time in Nexile, the first time in all these pages, he feels certain of something, Have you ever been unfaithful, says Veronica, in your imagination, in your dreams, you can't control your dreams, It's all a dream, Are all dreams the same, no, they aren't, call this a dream, what if I come to you every night in your dreams and stretch out upon you, give you the biggest hard-on you've ever known, what could you do about it; Path turns away from her, he's near his favorite tree, the wounded oak, one of its three trunks has broken off and fallen to the ground, its bark has dried and crumbled, he touches the trunk still standing where her bark has been peeled away, by who, who would do that, a wave of life pours into his hands, he can feel a hundred years pouring into his hands, he feels his mind intruded, not by the tree but by something behind him, he turns again, he sees fire in Veronica's eyes, now brown, and knows, 9,000 miles away a huge fire is raging in southern Australia, twelve million acres have burned, 500 million animals have died, he remembers now, while we were away from this page in the fall, three fires surrounded Topanga; ordered to evacuate, he and Carla packed up some art, some clothes, threw the cats into carriers, it's time to leave; that night, in a cheap Woodland Hills motel that permits pets, dogs bark in the rooms around them, Carla says, It smells like dogs in here, dog piss, Yes, Australia could burn down, even if they save the cities, they could be left without animals, both domestic and wild, their farms burned, their water depleted, his old friend, Bob, an aging eco-activist, called him on the phone, This is the beginning of the end, Bob said, this is how it's going to be, Is it real, Path says to Veronica, What's real, Veronica says. How about the Plague.

PEMBERTON IS BACK

AT RICK'S, STILL IN HIS MUDDY BOOTS AND SPURS, a rye in one hand and a cigar in the other, he sat at his table. The club was crowded and the mood, given Sherman's failure to breech the bayou, was spirited.

Rick approached Pemberton. You stopped Sherman, he said.

This time, said Pem. They can't come over that swamp.

Word was that Grant was headed north, back to Memphis, but Pem knew that was impossible. If he went back to Memphis he'd be back to square one leaving a hundred thousand dead. Lincoln would have to remove him. So Grant wouldn't go back to Memphis. Other spies had told Pem that Grant was going to try to dig a canal through the swamps

Johnston should attack now, from behind, on his right flank. I could move up the river and take his left, trap him in the swamps. But it has to happen fast. Speed is everything.

But you're sitting here, General, said Rick.

And Johnston sits in Jackson, said Pemberton.

Why don't you drop in behind Grant now? Rick said.

Then *I* would be trapped in the swamps. He has triple my manpower. Half my men don't have shoes.

Shope broke into a Schubert sonata.

Did he know Shubert? said Pem.

Maybe his grandparents did.

Over the tinkling of the piano Shope said, I'm a Romantic.

Pem finished his rye. He mumbled, We all must be.

Just pass by, said Shope. Pass without conviction.

A good philosophy, Shope, Rick said.

Shope's voice did not sing with, but counterpunched with the sonata. Don't wait to be hunted, I say, hide now.

Now there was commotion at the front door and Wally burst in. He ran to Rick, grabbing his lapels. He screamed, Rick! Rick! You must help me!

Two men in waistcoats, boots, and riding hats stood at the door. Undercover agents. Rick found it ridiculous that undercover police dressed so uniformly, so recognizably.

Do you know them? Rick asked Pem.

Pem said, No.

No guns, said Rick, and Molly went to the men and received their pistols.

The two men stepped in and saluted Pemberton who faced them now without getting up. The bar bustled. Shope played. Wally slipped behind Rick, using him as a shield. Pemberton saluted the men. At ease, he said.

It's too late, Mr. Wally, said Shope. Hide before the hunt.

The taller of the two agents spoke. His accent sounded New Orleans. We caught this man running cotton, he said.

North, said the other.

Rick, everybody runs cotton, piped Wally, or there would be no money, no economy.

Not everybody gets caught, Pemberton said to Wally. How did you catch him? he said to the agents.

He sold it to us.

I was entrapped! said Wally. They're as guilty as me!

Where's the money? said Pem.

If I tell you that then you can just kill me, said Wally.

We can kill you in any circumstance, Pemberton said to Wally. He looked at the agents again. Confederate? he said.

Federal, said the taller one.

Rick could read the consternation on Pem's face. Federal money was floating around under his jurisdiction. These agents with Federal cash were purportedly under his watch, but this wasn't the time or place to address that. He stood and asked for the men's papers. Glanced at them. Do you have the cotton? he asked them.

There's a ton in Natchez, under guard now.

Rick could feel Wally sizing things up. He'd stopped clutching at Rick's bicep.

Give up the money, Wally, Rick said.

My life! said Wally

Rick looked at Pemberton.

We won't kill you, Pemberton said.

That could be worse! screamed Wally. He broke from Rick and scrambled through the crowded barroom to the door. The shorter of the agents, in Wally's wake, caught him and brought him down, Wally screaming, Rick! Rick!

Now the other agent had Wally, too. Rick and Pem followed. Rick knew Wally's haunts well enough. He went to the gun check wall and gave the agents their pistols. I'll find the money, he said to Pem.

A trial! yelled Wally.

Pemberton's chest heaved. You're a military prisoner of war, he said to Wally. So act accordingly, he said to the agents.

Shope started playing "Dixie" but Pemberton put his hand up. The place was pretty quiet now. That was it. The agents dragged Wally out. He ended up in Andersonville where he ran a black market for a while, but he died there. Most did.

Pemberton turned away and Molly was there with a glass of straight rye. They say Grant's a drunkard, she said.

Then we should all be, said Pemberton. He turned down the rye and stepped outside and signaled his attendant for his horse. He and Rick stared at each other in silence. A soldier rode up to the casino with a dispatch. Pem read it. Grant had crossed into Louisiana and was heading south.

He can't get here from there, said Rick.

But he's coming here, said Pem.

He going to fly? said Molly. Swim?

Maybe, Pemberton said.

After Pem left, Rick perused the casino, then went to his table at the back of the bar. It had a chess board inlaid on the wood and Molly brought him a glass of sherry and a box that held his chess pieces. They were red and black. The Red and the Black. Shope tinkled out some Scarlatti as the noise in the bar picked up again. Molly sat across from Rick and moved the black pieces perfunctorily as she watched him set up a castle move for his king. It was just practice. She knew that. Then a man and a woman, new customers, came through the door. But one of them, the woman, he recognized.

THE OSCARS

PATH DIDN'T WATCH THE OSCARS THAT NIGHT, in fact he can't remember
the last time he watched the Oscars, he hadn't seen any of the movies that
were nominated for Oscars, he didn't follow the Emmy Awards either, hadn't
watched TV since 2013, Carla got Grammy tickets every year from her brother
but they stopped going, they never listened to the kind of music that got awards
at the Grammys, besides, they only got one radio station in their house, an
FM jazz station out of Long Beach, but recently, as if the cosmos had adapted
to their inclinations, that stopped coming in, too, sometimes, when Carla
left him to see her mother or attend meetings, Path put the TV on mute and
watched stuff like women's soccer while he read or wrote, you never missed
anything on TV sports, if anything at all happened it was replayed over and
over, besides, the commercials were intolerable and repeated again and again,
sometimes back to back to back, that's why women's soccer was a reprieve,
the game was never stopped for a commercial, they broke from hockey for
commercials, even during play, basketball played commercials in the corner of
the screen during foul shots; TV culture dripped with mediocrity, cliché, and
repetition; there was a student run FM radio station on campus at the Society,
they only played non-label alternative stuff and some of it was okay, but their
signal was weak and idiosyncratic and so were the DJ's, often sophomoric,
often real sophomores, but Path listened sometimes in his truck; he practices
flash meditation, he'd just read some Suzuki where Shunryu said the mind
was a garbage can and you had to empty it as often as you could, though
unlike a real garbage can the trash just kept right on coming even before you
put any in; everywhere he went the people around him recommended movies
and TV shows, no one ever really believed that he and Carla didn't watch

anything, even, as everyone everywhere said, especially on TV, he was told, that it was the golden age of television, that there were hundreds of shows and movies and documentaries, the argument for documentaries was that they were documentaries, i.e. informative, and thus somehow real, though Path had seldom seen a documentary, back when he watched documentaries, that you couldn't encapsulate in a paragraph, more fundamentally, Path disliked entertainment because entertainment didn't entertain him, he and Carla sat across from each other at their glass table and wondered what could be better? Carla sipped a gin and tonic or some wine, besides gin and tonic (Path made a good martini), Path drank bourbon or rye whisky on the rocks with a little soda, Path made pizza from scratch, even the dough, good pizza, there wasn't a food he or Carla made at home that anybody anywhere could make better, and for his part, there was no one anywhere anytime who was more interesting than Carla Blacklabel; last week Path scoured Los Angeles and finally found a twenty pound frozen turkey, being February it was hard to find, and he cooked that bird to perfection to celebrate Gertrude Stein's birthday or Lesbian Thanksgiving, he still baked the stuffing inside the bird, they had five guests, got drunk, the poet Wolfgang Hermes suggested he watch a PBS documentary on Nova about the solar system, Don't you want to know about the solar system, said Wolfgang, it's amazing, what do you know about the solar system, and Path said, Everything, Path even once owned a telescope, saw the moons of Jupiter, the rings of Saturn, the ice caps on Mars, the phases of Venus, learned to find star systems by star hopping from visible stars to find invisible ones, Have you seen the giant storm on Pluto? said Wolfgang, You can't see the giant storm on Pluto, you can't even see Pluto, Path said, have you seen the Elvis head on Mars?

DESIRE/SNOWFLAKES

ONE RECENT EVENING, AFTER DINNER, seated at our iron and glass bar table, Gala and I sipped wine and she said, "Lately I've been overwhelmed by specificity." It took a while to unpack that poetry, but she meant that everything she perceived and encountered seemed absolutely and definitively unique in and of itself, this chair, that table, this rug, that cup, that chair. Again, the best metaphor might be Platonic. We tend to think in forms and categories. 'Horse' might be a species or category for a kind of animal, but this horse in front of me is peculiarly unique.

"Snowflakes," I said.

"Okay," she said, "snowflakes. "Do you believe it? That not one of them is like any other?"

"I guess I accept that, but in fact it's hard to believe, by that I mean it's not possible to imagine. Possible to conjecture but not picture."

"Have you ever seen one? A real snowflake?"

"I've seen photos. I've looked at some briefly on my palm through a magnifying glass. They were different."

"So you've seen it."

"An example," I said.

"All the snow in the world, in the past, now, and in the future, not one the same."

'But is it significant, are the differences significant?"

"Atoms," she said, "electrons, too?"

"I guess Whitehead might say that," I said, "but they're as much a motion as a thing."

Back in the days, that was an ideological falling out between Whitehead and Bertrand Russell. Russell was an Atomist, a Logical Atomist, adapting the then current discoveries of subatomic particles to the ancient atomist theories of Leucippus and Democritus (later, the Stoics and Epicurus, too, I think). For the Logical Atomists, all material reality was composed of protons, neutrons, and electrons (the sub-atomic world has much proliferated since, though the principals are the same). Qualities in our level of the phenomenal world arose from the myriad combinations of quantity. If that world is deducible from math, and logic, calculus, then syntax should be derivable, explainable, using calculus. Russell, on the back of Wittgenstein's *Tractatus Logico Philosophicus*, attempted to break down language, i.e. syntax, into quantified logic, or calculus, from which statements could be objectified, truth statements, that could be tested in the world for truth or falsehood. Alfred North Whitehead, at the time, the early 20th century, joined him to write the *Principia Mathematica*, a sister to the *Tractatus*, to do just that. Ground breaking as it was, in the end, they failed. Wittgenstein responded to that failure by reversing field and writing the *Philosophical Investigations*, where the pursuit of truth, in terms of language, was abandoned, and meaning seen to arise as a combination of syntax and context that he called "language games." Contemporary analytic philosophy was born and philosophers were left to discuss meaning in language, i.e. the language of science, the language of ethics, the language of art, and the search for factual truth left to science, at least in Britain and America. Arise Positivism—even in Austria Wittgenstein became a Positivist, though other directions arose as well, Husserl's phenomenology where analysis of truth was "bracketed" by circumstance; language and cultural issues grew from Saussure's semiology, from which followed Structuralism, Levi-Strauss and the semiotics of anthropology, and then the taking apart of that level of analysis in Post-Structuralism (Roland Bartes) and eventually Deconstruction, which does not mean "to destruct" but, loosely, to try to reconstruct the meaning of an unrecoverable event, yes, nominalism and nihilism.

But back to Russell and Whitehead. Russell, though a diehard humanist (atheist, pacifist, socialist, and a believer of free love) never backed off from his hard-fact, scientific view of fundamental reality, but Whitehead did.

It's often difficult to know what Whitehead is saying, often, particularly in *Process and Reality*, he seems to be inventing and re-inventing a language and vocabulary as he goes; sometimes it seems that he means different things when he uses the same terms, but he clearly backs away from the concept of substance in the Aristotelean or Cartesian sense. My desk is not a thing but a series of events, one following the other, its makeup being composed of momentary "actual entities" that follow the traditions of their predecessors, guided by, but not necessitated by, habits that have mutually evolved; these occasions or events should be viewed organically, not mechanistically; in a sense they *feel* each other, Whitehead called it "prehension," rather than cause, specificity is an occasion, not a thing; what we perceive as enduring objects are really a conglomeration of events in time. God is the logical necessity of organization that arises with the evolution that is this universe—though likely there were ones that preceded it and others that will follow, if not other universes co-existing with ours—the multiverse—God didn't or doesn't create, God is immanent in all events, the universe creates God or, like everything, God co-arises, though that isn't the God we long for. The Laws of Nature, he calls them "eternal entities," similar to Plato's forms, they have co-arisen, as well, and are particular to this universe. This is the core of Whitehead's Organicism, though the social-psychologist, George Herbert Mead, advocated an organic view of the natural world, as well. Whitehead admitted his affinities to Buddhism and Hinduism. Bertrand Russell called him a mystic.

CORONA DEL VIRUS

WHEN IT CAME, WHEN IT CAME ROARING ACROSS CHINA, Path and Carla were in the desert, hiding, they knew they were hiding, they just hadn't known what they were hiding from, In a Dark Time, said Carla, hiding in the dark from the dark, the maw of the virus began to eat America raw, and not knowing what to do, Americans did what they did best, they consumed everything in sight, unblinking, trying to get it all for themselves and fuck everybody else: bottled water, frozen food, canned vegetables, by the time Carla and Path got back the Society had shut down, faculty told to finish their courses online, the power pointers went into a frenzy, finally they would have their pedagogical field day, they would teach everyone the point of their power, how to fill an hour, if they lived so long, what better way to light up the end of the world but on Brightspace, Carla even thought about it, for a moment, but not Path, he emailed his classes Theodore Roethke's "In a Dark Time," in a time of peril, try a rhyme, but it's a pretty good poem, here it is:

In a Dark Time
by Theodore Roethke

In a dark time, the eye begins to see,
I meet my shadow in the deepening shade;
I hear my echo in the echoing wood—
A lord of nature weeping to a tree.
I live between the heron and the wren,
Beasts of the hill and serpents of the den.
What's madness but nobility of soul
At odds with circumstance? The day's on fire!

I know the purity of despair,
 My shadow pinned against a sweating wall.
That place among the rocks—is it a cave,
Or winding path? The edge is what I have.

A steady storm of correspondences!
A night flowing with birds, a ragged moon,
And in broad day a midnight come again!
A man goes far to find out what he is—
Death of the self in a long, tearless night,
All natural shapes blazing unnatural light.

Dark, dark my light, and darker my desire.
My soul, like some heat-maddened summer fly,
Keeps buzzing at the sill. Which I is *I*?
 A fallen man, I climb out of my fear.
The mind enters itself, and God the mind,
And one is One, free in the tearing wind.

Atman is Brahman. Or as Carla would say, The person inside the person I am. The nation is shut down. There's a run on toilet paper. Toilet paper? Trans Kafka Instagrams the world. Don't they have left hands? As people start to die by dozens a day, then a hundred, then a thousand, President Rump proclaims the Corona Virus is no different than the common cold; when the death rate doubles and doubles again, Newsom in California and Cuoma in New York put their states in quarantine, but for food, drugs, and gasoline, no one should leave their homes (so who needs gas?), in LA everyone immediately runs out of their houses, they get on their motorcycles and into their race cars and zoom through the streets, running from themselves like a cat in labor, the gun stores defy the law and stay open and people drive to them to buy their guns! they're going to shoot the virus down, or anybody who tries to steal their toilet paper, a man is shot in a grocery aisle over a single roll, what a way to go, I'll tear myself from self and then I'll know, Angelenos are running in the streets like in *Go Dog Go!* trees are picking up their skirts, Angelenos flock to the beaches, the governor closes them, he closes the gun shops, they flock to the state parks, the governor closes them, the county parks, he closes them, the hiking trails get closed, the bike path on the ocean, the newspapers scream out, wear masks! don't wear masks! wear masks! don't wear masks! 100,000 will die, 200,000 will die, 2 million will die, the disease first attacks the lungs then goes for the rest, the older you are the more vulnerable, in some situations it might be airborne, wear masks! there are no masks, and the U.S. is unprepared, no masks for health care workers, no ventilators for the breathless, wear masks! where are the masks? there are no masks! meanwhile, back at the ranch, Path and Carla make sure the pot store is still open, they venture out, buy some spaghetti, rice, they find one chicken, no toilet paper but for now they don't need it, Path stocks the liquor cabinet, determined to stay one bottle deep, but the wine and liquor stores are closed, he'll have to go to the Ralph's where there's customer rationing, only ten at a time let inside, a line outside, everybody trying to stay six feet apart to abide by Social Distancing, in the morning they wake up and glance at the paper for their dose of misinformation, Path goes down to his office shack and works on the editing of his Trotsky book, Carla is reading the Russian Absurdists and writing blatant small poems about Gronk paintings, posting them on Instagram, in the Society they're each conducting fifty independent studies, Carla defiantly trying to use Brightspace, which Path abandons, too bright, the abbreviation is too obvious, BS, colleges and universities across the land are doggedly trying to pretend this can be done, the NBA shuts down, MLB shuts down, the NCAA shuts down, tennis, soccer, shuts down, the Dummer, I meant Summer, but maybe the Dumber, Olympics are postponed for a year, Rump proclaims this is stupid panic, it will all be over in two weeks, after two weeks he says Easter, after that he says two weeks more, well, maybe two months after that, the economy is falling like a dark meteor, the stock market looks like a carnival after closing time, Path and Carla take the truck and cruise the area of trails roped off with yellow plastic ribbon until they find an open fire road, they walk; in many ways, for Path, quarantine is much like their normal life, and yes, is it time for Jin of Arc to jump off the Ferris Wheel? yes it is, she wants Carla to take her out of Prison Village and let her live with them, she wails, she screams, she never cajoles, she threatens, she bitches, she blames Carla for ruining her life, she claims that Josiah predicted this, the end of the world, in her Writings, she now pronounces it Wry-Tings, she calls, she calls, she calls, every phone call a better argument for denying her what she wants, finally Carla unplugs the phone again and weeps; afternoons it's back to school, reading student short stories about murders and car chases, poems about puppies, while the world melts around them, then they have a glass of port and read, descend to the glass table, a gin and tonic, Carla is cutting back but Path cannot, he drinks soda water between his cocktails, Rump turns another corner and predicts 100,000 American deaths, the virus explodes in New York, Detroit, Chicago, New Orleans, Boston, and up the road Aunt Lamby begins making designer masks, though she and Hazlitt have gone into absolute quarantine, the masks have to bagged and tossed from six feet away, Path won't wear matching masks and trades his back, bag and toss, bag and toss, in no time he's lost his mask, after three days Carla plugs in the phone and St. Jin leaves a message, she wants her Wry-Tings back, they're hers! the Chinese and the South Koreans say they've turned the corner as the virus attacks everywhere else in the world, devastating Italy and Spain, China begins sending masks and ventilators to everybody but the U.S. because of Rump's trade war, at war with California, as well, he drops emission control standards for cars and lowers requirements for MPG, oil has dropped to $20 a barrel, somebody's got to use it! but who in the world will buy these smoke spitting cars? China claims to be getting back on its feet, opening factories, the U.S. economy dives, a million unemployed, 350,000 applications for Food Stamps, in LA the pandemic hits the homeless, hits the nursing homes (St. Jin screams on the phone, take her in and return the Wry-Tings!) if the American economy is gutted for more weeks, months, China will eclipse us, it will be, says Path, the end of the American Era, he might be right, Rump will usher in the fall of America, quote the Bible to Mr. Rump, the First shall be Last, the nation is rudderless, we need a leader! outside the glass table window, Silvia the silver raccoon, after three years and three silver litters, has stopped returning, stopped pressing her black nose and paws against the glass, Carla looks up the lifespan of raccoons, it's only two years, she had it good, but now her son has arrived, a little more gold than silver, Carla names him Silvio, a little more univocal and mercenary, he only taps the window if there's nothing in the bowl, then follows Path with his eyes as Path goes to the back of the kitchen for kibble, Path turns, Silvio jumps to the avocado tree and waits only feet away and begins his descent to the bowl as soon as Path turns his back, in New York, Path's younger brother's wife comes down with the plague, her temperature hits 103 the first day, and Path turns to his inner friends, St. Jude and the Taras, Green and White, and prays for Simon's's wife, Lucia, he prays, then Simon gets sick too, and suddenly Path feels the grip of his own old age, over sixty-five, considered vulnerable; it is April 2 now, 2020, in the year of the New Corona Virus, Covid-19, last week

Path thinks of the lonely chicken he found last week in one of the grocery forays, empty-shelved grocery stores, his friend, Jazmin, calls and says, America, welcome to the Third World! Path roasts the chicken, they eat breasts one night, legs and thighs the next, soup out of the wings, back, and carcass, with not enough soup and too much rye whiskey he awakens at 6 a.m., reads Suzuki and has a flash satori that lingers until he returns to bed and dreams he is writing, like the dreams in which he speaks French fluently he has a million interesting things to write but when he wakes up again it's all gone; Path and Carla get out of bed at 10 a.m., enforcing a new policy of sleeping in, Frida jumps up on the dresser chair and purrdles to be brushed, Carla brushes her and then goes to the bathroom and urinates, then Path urinates, they don't flush the toilet so often since the draught, he brushes Frida, too; downstairs Path takes allergy medicine, though nonetheless his eyes will itch all day, he puts food in the cat bowls, maybe some kibble in the outside bowl for Scotty or Silvio, he takes out the recycling and gathers up the newspaper, comes in and washes his wrists and hands, Carla has mopped up some of last night's dishes and starts the coffee, Path pours juice, he adds club soda to his, then distributes some vitamins, as they do so they share their sleep and dreams, then after carrying the breakfast board upstairs, they split a bagel, cream cheese, lox, they glance at the paper that clocks the spread of the virus, the rise in cases, the diminishing supplies of gowns, ventilators, and masks, the hospitals filling with the dying, the morgues filling with the dead, Carla gets on the internet, hears faint ringing from some phone and her ears perk, her mother, her mother? her mother, her mother? Path hunts it down and finds the kitchen outlet plugged in, he unplugs it, he doesn't know if Carla is finally taking some pleasure now, after sixty years of her mother's domination, is she finally stepping away, finally stopped forgiving, in some ways one's heart must ache for St. Jin, but she lives in some insidious pleasure dome of cruelty and discord, stewing in the hot fog of the next accusation, now she proclaims she's begging God to let her die, Path, in the bad part of himself, wishes he could beg for it, too, he doesn't tell Carla that he found the source of the ringing and shut it down, but he hasn't shut it down, somewhere something is ringing, the ghost? they even hear it in their dreams, Path descends to his writing shack, and writes, it doesn't matter what he writes, it doesn't matter if it's any good, did it ever matter? what can matter now? if it were up to Path he'd stop writing, but it's not up to Path, it's up to me, Carla, in the living room, works on her poems about Gronk's paintings, then, after an hour or so, if they don't need the pharmacy or grocery store, they dress for their walk, Carla foolishly plugs in the answering machine, then they go outside, down the steps, through the gate, down more steps, and throw out most of their mail (the Fire Insurance wants them to cut back most of their trees, strip their yard of vegetation, then pay $5,000 for the privilege, well, not now, all inessential labor has been banned), Path drives his truck north, up the Canyon, to Santa Maria Road that passes intermittently through private and county land, they pass the ranch where he once kept his horses—yes, we're in the future now, in the present he's still on the way to selling Nikki—in this future Jackie O is dead and Nikki gone, It makes you sad, says Carla, Path says, Yes, they drive past a private home where there are horses and a burro in the pasture, the burro is cute and mischievous, he chases the horses, sometimes he sneaks out of the pasture and walks down the road, Carla snaps pictures of him on her cell phone and names the burro Platero after the burro in Juan Ramon Jimenez's *Platero y Yo*, she sends it out to her Instagram network, there will be many many likes, the poetry world ignites, pictures not poems! then they cross back into county parkland, at the top of the hill the fire road, that only last Sunday was filled with dirt bikers and hikers, is closed, though a few bikers and hikers yet disregard the red signs and yellow plastic ribbon and charge in, Carla and Path park and go left, down a city dirt road, technically an extension of Mulholland, that leads into Woodland Hills via Canoga Blvd., due to the quarantine there are fewer cars out now, less traffic, the brown smog air has lifted and they can see the Valley below them bright and clear, they walk down the road aways to a hill where a wooden bench sits, if no one is there they walk to the bench, gaze out, I'm sad too, says Carla, About your mom, Yes, What else can you do, says Path, we can't take her in, she can't climb stairs, she shits and pisses her pants, she would take our bed, play the TV all day in the living room while talking nonsense non-stop, she's crazy, she's mean, she understands nothing, and then there's her Wry-Tings, it's impossible, And she's my mother, Carla says, She has sons, says Path, Who hate her and ignore her, says Carla, I'm all she's got, She should realize that, says Path, these are hard times, Path says, people all over the world are dying, economies are crashing, she's safe, she's fed, she wants to get here, here with her Wry-Tings, and then she has you just where she did fifty years ago, trapped with her and her horrible Wry-Tings, dominating you again in your own house, and I won't let her; Carla takes a picture of the bench, someone has carved a heart with P & C inside it and Path says, we were here, in love, before we ever got here; And where is here? thinks, Carla, nowhere, a bench on a hill, Is she in love? she is no longer in love, but it's not time to say it, if only she could escape, escape everything, go to heaven or hell or Santa Monica, she stares at Path, Is something wrong, he asks, she whispers, No, not something, everything, they walk back to the truck and drive home where there are messages from the Jin, her voice a wicked cranky whine, You have ruined my old age, you have stolen my life's work, well two can play that game, I'm calling the police, I'd like to hear that phone call, Path says, he unplugs the phone but Carla plugs it in and picks it up and calls her mother, Mother, she says, and the Jin hangs up; so Carla and Path begin their online school day, reading and commenting on student work, Carla working on poems and essays, Path on short stories and a grad class with fifteen M.A students each writing a novella, that's a lot of reading, then the phone rings, but Path has unplugged all the phones and put the four receivers in a pile, none of them ringing, it's not his cell phone, it's not Carla's, but somewhere, a mysterious phone is ringing . . . schoolwork done they read for a while, then eventually go downstairs to the glass table, Carla has a glass of sherry, she's off hard booze, Path pours a gin and tonic, they make dinner, they've been lucky to find food at the Trader Joe's and they've been innovative, stretching out portions, eating leftovers, they split a half-bottle of wine, eat some pot, Path drinks a glass of soda water between drinks, but he can't stop, he must drink now, he can't stop his own bashing around in his own head, empty it, it comes back, empty it, it comes back, like a cat, but he tries again and sometimes, for a moment, he's watching, not bashing, the two of them listen to music, Bill Evans, they laugh, talk about what they're reading, what they're writing, they're co-hermitating, says Path, he holds her, he holds her, these are their days, but she's suffocating and hasn't told him.

EQUUS

PATH'S PHONE RINGS. It's the re-plugged land line, he seldom uses his cell, the number on the screen is unfamiliar, so it's not Jin of Arc, he suspects a robo call but it's not, he hears a man's voice, the accent is Persian, he's calling about the horse, so Path picks up, Yes, says Path, The horse, the man says, is she available still, and Path hesitates, maybe he should say, no, he's adding up his losses, I've seen her photo, my daughter has fallen in love with her, How old is your daughter, says Path, Eight, he says, Path says, Too young, she couldn't ride without supervision, When can we see her, this weekend? Supervision, says Path, I'll bring it, the man says, Sunday afternoon, and Path gives him directions.

Path remembers sitting on Jackie O, they're at the bottom of the ranch trail, a section that breaks from the woods in a patch of sunlight, the day is warm, his horse is calm, it took fifteen years to get here, the years of riding Jackie almost every day and here, in the woods, she was at her worst, shying at a gust of wind, spooking at a flurry of woodpeckers, voices in the distance, shouting, she hated that the most and could spin and break for home at full gallop, white foam bursting from her neck, there were days, back when he kept her at a huge ranch in Fillmore, then there were pipe corrals along the trail and he'd run into one and let her rip, round and round, one way then the other, for an hour? who knew? both of them drenched in sweat, and every so often he'd pull back and say, walk Jackie, walk, and then she'd burst out again and they ran, and ran, until finally, finally, she walked, though sometimes when she got out of the corral she'd break out again and he'd turn her and take her back in, until, exhausted, she'd finally walk home, days of that, days and days, he read all the books by all the experts, he spent hours on the ground, in the bull pen, pushing her flanks, bending her neck, even now she could spook, but he had a routine that she recognized, he ran her backwards, side passed right, side passed left, and she knew he was there and would push her, and she'd capitulate, she'd walk, she was magnificently agile and smart, climbed up and down stairs, danced, kicking out her forelegs, changed leads on the fly on any beat, even every other step, she ran and danced, and because he was there every day, her fury changed to passion, she came to love him, love him solely and passionately, she waited for him in her pasture and when he showed up, came to him, sometimes at a run, sliding to a stop in front of him, nostrils flaring like on the cold April morning he first saw her, her fury, nostrils red, her sweat, steam rising from her back, If I could ride that, If I could ride that, and then, to stand in a pasture with 1,200 pounds running at you, to stand there knowing she'd stop inches from his face, her fury now his heart, he stepped forward and put his arms around her neck, the horse who once would not let anyone touch her chest, who had hurt her so badly? he held her and her throat rumbled, it took him ten years to get her to let him do it, put his arms around her neck and hug her, all that, for this moment in the sunshine, man and horse, he, sitting on that explosion that she held inside her, for him, he, breathing slowly, praying to no one, thank you, thank you for this moment, thank you for this horse, how lucky he was, but then he was young, young compared to now, and when she died, he came apart, not till this moment did he put together her death and his growing old, his hips hurt to walk, hurt to stand, hurt to sit, hurt to ride, then his back, he couldn't climb steps, couldn't stoop, couldn't lift, surgery made things better, but not all better, they never tell you that, then his cancer, found when his child left for Australia, found when Carla bought him Nikki, but when he sat on Nikki now it hurt, and when she challenged him, he couldn't meet it, couldn't risk falling off, and she loved to run, a gallop choppier than Jackie's, it hurt, though she came to him, too, every day, he never had to chase her down, she saw him and walked to him, nuzzled, her eyes were soft, but if he couldn't ride her now, she, thirteen, what would it be like in another few years when she would be too old to sell, he with a pet horse he couldn't ride, and he, on retirement, could barely afford, Valley of Death, Dark Night of the Soul, his horse, his horse, would be gone.

But he goes to see her again. Maybe this child can't ride her. Maybe he'll be stuck with her. He parks his truck and his horse walks to him.

IN SOME WAYS

THE BUDDHISTS WERE AHEAD OF WHITEHEAD, he acknowledged that. At the dawn of the Christian Era, in India, Nāgārjuna wrote a complex dialectical thesis that argued against the possibility of all substance, advocating the co-arising of reality moment to moment in complete inter-dependence, a view that Whitehead held on the sub-atomic level, not the phenomenal one, though some Buddhists might have held that approach as well, particularly in the analysis of perception and conception, the rhetoric being that analysis of the moments of consciousness does not reveal a self or soul. Much of that rolled out of Gala's and my discussion that night, that everything is absolutely specific, as well as new, from moment to moment. But how long is a moment and what occurs in between them? For Whitehead, Time. For the Buddhists, the dissolution of causes through time created the mystery of continuity (Why doesn't my refrigerator turn into an elephant? Well, it could). Beginning with the Mahayana and culminating with Zen, it's mind, with a small 'm' that holds it all together with *desire*, if we can let that illusion fall away then Big Mind or Nothingness will emerge, a kind of radical, almost Berkeleyan idealism in some cases. Buddhism, as well as Hinduism, have many views or schools that argue about how this occurs—even Zen has various schools, ideologically the hard-headedness of Soto Zen has the most appeal to me, though I don't like group practice—and Berkeley, like Descartes, on the verge of solipsism, falls back on God to hold it all together; the Buddhists don't fall back, they quietly accept nihilism, though Buddha himself seemed agnostic even about that.

Let me recap. In the West, as Logical Atomism failed, Whitehead roared in with his Organicism; Russell accused him of mysticism and, if you're following, you can see why; post new-new-Wittgenstein, who was once

Russell's pupil, Russell was more comfortable with science and analysis, that is, that the job of philosophy was the study of language, not ethical theory but the language of ethics, not physics but the language of physics, etc. He struggled with his ambivalence, perpetually agnostic about many things, though he practiced humanitarianism and pacifism actively, if hopelessly. Though sentience is doomed, we vow to save all of it, says Shunryu Suzuki. For Whitehead, if desire is the glue of the world, he places it fundamental to sub-atomics where actual entities come together not by mechanistic laws, but by prehended feeling; desire on the most minute, basic level creates events that we perceive as things. This doesn't prevent him, or us, from ending up where we began. How do we get here from there?

But here we are. Given that, let me start with myself. In the days of my illness, when it seemed that I was cascading toward death, my psychotherapist said to me that there was nothing I could do about it, nothing to do but accept it. That might be a good idea in general even now. I imagine I might be peculiar in that I have no memories, no good memories that don't lead to bad ones, no bad ones that don't lead to worse. Inside the labyrinth of my psyche there is no place to hide. If I could but live in the moment of a perfect topspin backhand . . . if the past quickly becomes an abstraction, and the future, however inevitable is yet speculative, then yet the moment cannot be lived in, it moves by too quickly, lost before it is found. So what to do with this suffering of consciousness. Sartre would say there's nothing to be done, nothing that won't make it worse. Who suffers, if the self, the soul, are illusory and time both inevitable and ineffable?

RICK FIRST MET THE WOMAN

IN NEW ORLEANS. Anna Breton. Blonde, wavy hair to her shoulders, her features were both soft and edged, framed delicately by her cheeks and jaw. She wore a full skirt, a blouse with puffed sleeves, her laced boots had sturdy heels and though she was not small, her head came only to the shoulder of the man she stood next to. He wore a civilian's hat, not a riding hat, and his skin was pale brown. She was still young, likely not yet thirty, though she'd already lost a husband before the Yankees took New Orleans. He'd been running escaped slaves to Lafayette's free island off Corpus Christi, then smuggling them north by ship along with cotton and rum. Dangerous stuff. As many Blacks were recaptured and sold back at a profit as there were those who got away to Cuba or beyond. You had to burn that candle at both ends. Apparently his burned out.

Rick met Anna after that. He'd come from New York City where he'd made his money in booze, wholesale distribution, though his parents had wanted him to study law. But the northeast, even New York, was too intimate and too cold. Whatever you did you knew everybody else who did it. New Orleans was quaint and wild. He liked the culture and the sounds, the music, of the free Blacks. He liked the food. He met Shope there and they became friends. And Anna. Anna who he met at a bookshop.

On the other side of a shelf of books. Hatless, an uncommon thing, something a girl might do, not a woman. The sun splintered in shafts through a window blind and ran into the aisle where she stood, shining angelically on her wavy, blonde hair. It was hair you'd want to put your hands in. She looked up. He saw only her clear forehead and pale, crystal blue eyes.

You're in "F," he said. I hope it's not *Madame Bovary*.

It's not, she said. What would it matter.

Or maybe I did hope that.

Do you recommend it? She spoke French, but it was continental French, not local.

He'd been to college. Johns Hopkins. That's where he'd decided against studying law. That's where he decided against studying. So he knew some Latin. French, too. With an accent like that, I'd expect you'd already read it, he said.

I haven't been in France for a while, she said to him. But yes, I baited you. I've read it. I prefer *Salammbo*.

Unreadable, Rick said. Too confusing. And sadomasochistic.

Experimental, you mean, she said. Too difficult? The geography of North Africa is authentic. He'd been there. The woman. The priestess, is strong.

I'm not a fan of strength. Or weakness, he said. Have we reached our borders? This place has a café, you know.

They sat outdoors and had coffee with chicory, beignets. They added cognac to the second round. She'd left Paris with her parents after the madness of 1848. Not that they'd sympathized with the outcome. They would have preferred change. Some form of Socialism, not communism, and not how it ended up, the practical oligarchy, money still ruling, the hands of government lifting cocktails to each other. Her family fled to Algiers. That's where she met her husband. She lifted her left hand and showed him her wedding ring. He'd already noticed, of course. They'd tried to disrupt the slave trade in West Africa. Ended up wanted by both the Dutch and the British. That's how her husband disappeared. She still wore the ring to ward off men.

I see how well it works, he said.

Like anything, she said, it works if I want it to.

She worked as an escort now.

He sat back. Looked around.

No one watches me, she said. I'm my own boss.

In every situation?

In every situation.

Well, he said, it really isn't my business.

It's becoming your business, she said. She had a purse. She opened it and extracted a metal case, then opened that. It held small white sticks filled with tobacco. She offered him one.

We don't have those here yet, he said.

You will, she said. I roll these myself.

And women smoke them?

France, she said. Paris. Women do whatever they want to do.

Not here.

She said, I'm discrete.

He looked to the waiter who nodded to them.

She said, I know him, too.

So he took one and she lit it for him. An intimacy.

Not like a cigar, she said. You inhale the smoke.

I know about it, he said to her. Like opium.

Easier, she said.

Nonetheless, it made him dizzy. Through the smoke, she looked him in the eyes.

He'd been with women. He wouldn't say plenty. If you're attracted to women, to anything, then you never have enough of it, and women, women went beyond anything, your desire for them was beyond instinct, it was Biblical, deeper than Noah or Moses, but when lucky he always had a number of acquaintances, someone on hot nights, or cold nights, or nights too dark to breathe inside, someone who was soft enough, who could share a story or a drink, but he couldn't recall staring into a beautiful woman's eyes through smoke, through mystery, that's what he felt now, a dance with the unconquerable, if not the unknown, because he'd never been in love; at least in this moment, that's how he felt, that he'd never known love before, and suddenly, in an instant, that all had been breached, like touching the moon, that goddess in every culture known to man, her eyes behind the smoke like the moon in the mist, now he didn't know whether to lean forward or lean back, never before had he known an indecisive moment in front of a woman.

Would you like to walk along the river? he said.

She put out her cigarette with the tip of her shoe. Certainly, she said.

The river was broad and green, people, couples, like them, lingered, arm in arm. It was spring, of course, the air sweet, the breeze still cool, it pushed her hair across her face, delicately, she pushed it behind her ear, and turned to him. They kissed.

I don't live far from here, she said to him.

But yet too far, I hope, he said softly.

She stepped back, but he still held her hand.

Let's say we meet again in a week, he said to her.

She took another step back and released his hand. Then let's say we do, she said, and turned and walked away.

Word in the streets said a Yankee fleet was in the Gulf. They'd have to come up the river to get here, New Orleans, and sail between two cement and stone forts, Fort Jackson and St. Phillip, a fusillade from both sides of the river, and stationary torpedoes had been planted underwater in between. From there it was another forty miles to the city. But the South had boats, too, and an army on the shorelines, both the east and west banks. The city wasn't very worried. Up till then, the Union hadn't shown it could win a battle.

Rick had other things to think about. A wagon of rye to move to taverns, French wine to distribute to plantations between New Orleans and Jackson, Mississippi, and Anna Breton, whose visage came to him in any idle moment, her eyes dancing behind gorgeous smoke, her voice sliding like silk. They hadn't said where they would meet, but there were only three possible places, the bookstore, the café, or the river, where he started, tracing his steps backwards, not seeing her. He watched the barges on the river, a paddle steamboat. Late morning, approaching noon, New Orleans, people were already drinking; he chided himself for knowing this exact time a week ago when they met. He walked away from the river into Vieux Carré. On the street, horses and donkeys pulled wagons of sundry that clattered on the cobblestone. As he approached the café, he almost hoped she wouldn't show, relieving him of this obsession. He wouldn't turn this into a haunt, he'd simply walk away from a fond memory, maybe find a bar and a real prostitute. He didn't see her there at the café, but neither did he expect to find her sitting alone. He found her in the stacks, glancing at a novel by Balzac. She looked up, her brow slightly furrowed, then lifted. Those eyes, paler than the sky.

I knew him, she said.

Knew him.

Paris had a lot of parties. She closed the book. Can we go to my place now?

He said, I didn't like *La Tentation de Saint Antoine* either.

Too experimental for you, as well. But I hear the next one will be more realistic, more autobiographical.

You heard that, said Rick.

This isn't a professional transaction, Anna Breton said. I want to sleep with you.

Let's take a carriage, he said. I want to know how you feel next to me.

She said, I'd like that very much.

It was March, fine weather for an open ride along the river. She moved under his arm, kissed his cheek, and rubbed her soft hair under his nose. She was delicate and soft and aromatic. Rick directed them through the Quarter to the St. Louis Cemetery where they disembarked and walked silently among the graves. She took his hand, then his arm. They stopped in front of a family mausoleum where she turned to him.

The water table is so close here, he whispered, that when the river rises you can hear the caskets floating up to knock against the casements.

That would be lovely at night, she said.

This time, they kissed more passionately.

Are we falling in love? said Rick.

It's better if you're in love, she said.

And it was. Even if a little awkward at first. Though the second time his passion was so ardent he gripped himself on the edge of violence, and it felt that she did, too.

I liked that, she said to him. She got up and put on his shirt. Taking possession of him, as if she wore his soul. She poured out two glasses of port, lit two cigarettes and gave one to him in bed. As in France, she said. The smoke was relaxing and romantic, curling in the air as if reiterating the act of lovemaking in the space above them.

So, said Rick, I suppose you knew Flaubert, as well.

I slept with him. *Coitus interruptus.*

Why am I not surprised.

He could be surprising.

Isn't he fat and bald?

And short. But extremely smart.

And I'm?

Handsome and sexy.

You don't write poetry, do you?

I do not, mon cher. I am poetry.

And your husband, he said.

I was faithful, so to speak. In Paris it isn't the same.

As here?

As anywhere else.

She came to him again. Then they dressed. Went into the streets. Ate crepes and drank burgundy at a restaurant nearby. He guessed she'd been in love a dozen times or more, or never been in love, not even now, as she sat across from him exuding love, which made his attraction all the more intense, so he guessed, as well, that she knew that. They parted there, agreeing to meet in a week, again not specifying when or where that would be, that becoming part of her incessant seduction, that he searched for her amidst the flea markets and shops and taverns and bookstores, each time feeling almost as the first, then they'd find a hotel and make love. They ferried on the Mississippi or on Lake Pontchartrain, took carriage rides or went horseback riding across the river in Pecan Grove or a park in St. Charles. She liked the cemeteries, too. In St. Louis again, as they left, the skies opened up and the rain fell in sheets. They ran to a small café where others, like themselves, took respite and laughed joyously at the downpour. She ordered coffee and a pastry filled with yellow cream, he drank red wine. The rain is miraculous and lovely, she said. Let's go back to the cemetery and listen for the coffins.

And they did. They found a spot away from the family mausoleums, where the ground dipped and the singular graves sat like flat boats in the mud. The sky was wet, low and dark, and the city was quiet, the street activity yet to resume. Then the first of the graves knocked. Then another, as the dead rocked in their sleep, answering each other with knocks and rumbles. She took his lapels in her hands and brought herself to him, her face in his chest as they listened to the chorus of the dead. Shortly, it lessened, the knocking fading away as the dead went back to sleep.

Graves made him think about the future, or the end of the future, the only certain future.

Then, in that next quiet moment, they heard the first pounding of cannon fire.

This is some moment, he said.

Maybe, appropriately, our last moment.

That's pretty poetic. Or fatalistic, he said.

Love, destruction, beauty, death, it's been said many times. But most recently, she whispered, Baudelaire.

He didn't want to know who said it.

And seeing that, she said, He was not that kind of man.

Are we thinking at all about our future? he said

The Yankees are in the river, she said. That's the future.

If they take the city I'll be arrested.

For no reason?

They won't need a reason. They'll presume I'm a spy.

You are a spy, of course.

Maybe I am. It won't matter. If the fighting comes here, even if the Confederacy holds the city there'll be soldiers everywhere. What will you do?

When, if ever, she said, has what I wanted had anything to do with what happened?

He said, Maybe this time it will be different. Isn't this different?

How different? she said.

He said, Marry me.

But he'd been prepared for this moment in other ways during this romance, he'd set up his accounts for liquidation and could be ready to evacuate in two days. He'd travel with Shope. He told her this.

There have been free Blacks here since the beginning, she said.

No one's going to care how free anybody thinks they are. I'll get you a train ticket. You can follow us. Pack up. Do you need help?

I do not.

I love you, Anna Breton, Rick said.

RAGE SAMADHI:
CARLA UNPLUGS THE PHONES

AGAIN FOR A DAY. When she plugs them back in, the Jin attacks. The faint ringing was not a ghost, but a Fax machine in the What Books office. Carla unplugs it. She unplugs all the land lines in the house. A visceral calm descends. Lines disappear from under Carla's eyes. She leaves everything unplugged for three weeks. Her life returns, she writes poems. Maybe she'll go mad, says Path. She does. St. Jin goes running through the halls of Prison Village. She's ambulanced to an emergency room, then into a hospital, finally a shrink sees her and puts her in a senior psych facility. And finally, finally Carla exhales, maybe they can do something, put her on something.

Meanwhile, Newsom has shut down the state, every park, every trail, every beach, every fire road; nothing is open but groceries or pharmacies, no restaurants, no bars, not even churches, the religious cannot hold church services, the rednecks can't buy guns, schools close, all sports are cancelled, high school, college, and pro, there is no congregating in groups of any kind, all individuals but family members must maintain a distance from each other of six feet, everyone, in public, must wear a mask covering their nose and mouth, LA County barricades its beaches and beach parking, no one dares use the phrase marshal law, it's all voluntary unless you volunteer not to obey, and protestors hit the streets with Confederate and Nazi flags and rifles, demanding their right to maskless assembly, a heatwave hits and the populations of Ventura and Orange rush to their beaches in crowds; Path, for his part, hopes they all get sick and die; President Rump comes on the television every day to tell the nation things are getting better and better, but they aren't, 50,000 people have died, he suggests that if you can disinfect your hands with bleach, maybe doctors should try injecting it in the lungs; Path's brother in Queens texts to say he and his wife are beginning to recover, Path is counting his drinks, he drops to five, then to four, with a tonic or club soda in between each, his fire insurance wants him to denude his property, he calls his gardener, Gustavo, who will drop by to see what can be done to comply yet save the trees, Carla breaks her phone silence and Jin calls from the senior psych ward, accuses Carla of stripping nude while cheerleading at a high school football game, then, when Jin went to the principal's office to deal with the turmoil, the high school band showed up and played a stripper routine, Big principal's office, says Path, I was never a cheerleader, says Carla, nor a stripper; Jin shrieks, Carla hangs up and pulls the plug, in the grocery they find the last pack of toilet paper; this is how the world ends, says Path, not with a bang, says Carla; beaches are closed, beach parking lots roped off, curb parking near the beaches is blocked off, up in the hills, the State Park is closed, fire roads are closed, hiking trails closed, plastic yellow crime ribbons are strung across the trail heads, red signs with white print say PARK CLOSED UNTIL FURTHER NOTICE, but Path knows his way around up there, he finds a dirt road that is technically in the city and runs along the county line, an access road for the people who have private ranches on Santa Maria, surrounded by a county park, Platero lives on one of those, and they begin walking there in the afternoons, Platero gets a pasture mate half his size and they begin bringing them carrots, the first time the little one acts like he's never seen a carrot before, Carla opens his mouth and puts the carrot piece in it, he chews and swallows, now he knows, in the quietude quails begin to bob about under the oak trees, they spot pheasants, the first Path has seen in thirty years, multi-colored, gorgeous, they strut, tons of crows, hawks swirl in the air, red tailed, red shouldered, a pair swoops in dalliance, it's spring, soon the roadrunners says Path, and snakes, winding trails of their bodies cross the dust, they see a baby rattler, about six inches long, then a big one, maybe five or six feet, curled by the roadside, waiting for a ground squirrel, a girl jogger sees it and screams, what do I do? what do I do? Just leave her alone, says Path, she doesn't want to eat you, What if she moves? She won't move, just leave her alone, the girl runs away, just as well; it's Carla's first rattler, Path's been up here by himself, running or riding his horse, for thirty years, he seldom sees rattlers, maybe a hundred in all that time, but things are different now, Pretty cool, says Carla, Big triangle head, the big ones are female, says Path, like T-Rex, but they can strike twice the length of their body, faster than you can see, like a frog, you can demonstrate in front of a bear or a mountain lion, spread your arms, make yourself big, and they'll likely move off, but a rattle snake will not move off, just in case you find one in front of you on your hike, just stay still; anyway, the next day they find her dead, decapitated, rattle cut off, likely killed with a shovel, that's usually how it's done, the girl ran home, told somebody where to find the snake, you wouldn't have spotted her from your truck cab, you had to be hunting for her, but whoever killed her wasn't hunting, they were killing, it's what we do, but the rattler wasn't a danger to anyone, People hate snakes, Carla says, blamed for the fall of humankind, Snakes and women, says Path, Quetzalcoatl, the winged serpent, the Wind, he put the sun in motion at the beginning of the Fifth Aztec World, Coatlique, the mother of the Gods, had a skirt of snakes, no orifices, that's what Path is reading now, he finished an anthro-archeology of the Maya, now Davies' history of the Aztecs, he's still reading all of Elizabeth Bowen's short stories (on the commode), in the War Years now, Calvino's *Cosmicomics*, lagging there, Bronte's *Wuthering Heights*, dark and bizarre, on the downstairs toilet, Carlos Fuentes' *Nietzsche on his Balcony*, published in 2012, the year he died, but Path doesn't like the late Fuentes, he writes with a kind of bravado posing as bravura, his elitism and narcissism oozing from his syntax, like Kundera, and sexist in an old man's kind of way, pornography and violence, Brett Easton Ellis was only nineteen, violent, misogynist murder writ in clichés, Garcia Marquez got that way at the end, too, and Nabokov's *Lolita*, really? in his office when he's done writing, Path has started Kafka's *The Trial,* and now the biography of Shunryu Suzuki, *Crooked Cucumber*, Path doesn't like cucumbers, all the better, in the biography Suzuki is dying now, Suzuki, who died in December of 1971, has died a thousand times in fifty years, he is dying now, in this time of death it's a sad thing to read of death, there are only pages to go, moments to go, and he shall be gone, though as he himself might say, yes, gone, and not gone, he is alive right now inside Path, Path, now, feeling his mortality in this moment, in this moment feeling momentary immortality, but the next day he finishes the book, he wants to cry but he does not; Suzuki died very near the day that Path quit college basketball and walked away from his mentor and sexual abuser, a man who when Path was thirteen stripped him of his clothes and his religion, Path, the atheist super altar boy, fucking his basketball coach while serving as the Master of Ceremonies to the Archbishop at his own confirmation, talk about stoic ambivalence, (show—don't tell? he wrote a memoir, read that), to this day, in any given situation, he can't tell you how he feels, how do you feel about that, Path? he doesn't know, asked about his feelings Path hits satori, the first principle of Soto Zen being *I don't know*, but in the Taoist, not the Western sense, and right now, having read of Suzuki's death, he has realized that it occurred at the same time he quit his molester and basketball, early December, 1971, as his plumber, Elena of the Pipes once said to him, What's that, some kind of synchronicity? well, maybe, because if you know anything about Buddhism, it's all synchronicity, every damn moment of the cosmos, suddenly Path can feel Shunryu Suzuki, with him, in him, then is now, and now it's gone; two days ago, on their way out for their walk, Path, while unlocking the tall front gate on the steps, tripped; it would have been twelve hard cement steps to the bottom, he saw it in his mind, and as he flew forward his hand reached out and three fingers snagged the gate handle and he swung there, held in the air above the steps until he lightly touched down, he stared up at Carla above him, That was impossible, she said, and it seems that it was, that his flailing arm snatched the swinging gate handle and held all two hundred pounds of him in the air, when he might have, should have fallen and broken his life, his possible injuries unimaginable, even if he recovered they would have had to sell the house of sixty irregular steps, groceries in, groceries out, trash in, trash out; but he hung in the air, that was satori, too, and he landed thrilled and frightened, he's been climbing and descending these stairs for thirty years waiting for this to happen and it finally did, but it didn't happen, though he felt, deeply, that it would happen again, it would inevitably happen, when it happened to his father after a wedding reception in a resort outside Cambridge Springs, Pennsylvania, only two steps, though he landed on his forehead, it was the beginning of his diagnosis for Supra Nuclear Palsy, a fatal form of Parkinson's, a slow, debilitating, horrible death, Path wonders, with his neuropathy, his heavy legs, if this isn't the same, if every time he stares down his steps he's looking at his slow horrible death and, whether or not he's at the onset of Parkinson's, he's looking at it anyways, Suzuki at times said that we must live on the edge of death in each moment, though also the edge of joy, he wonders if he should ask why, this time, it almost happened, and why it didn't happen, and if, in some anthropomorphic ontology, he has been told something or saved for something, if it's in some line of mortality threatening events, motorcycle crashes, falls from towers, his surgery, his cancer that disappeared, now this, that he has been saved for something, by whom? and he looks at his life and speculates as to what that might be, his books? he wrote and published his memoir about his abuse, did it help a few dozen people, it barely turned a head in his hometown, but for the majority of people who hated him, brought no justice to anyone, his eighteenth published book will appear this year to no effect, teaching? really? (it's finals week and the work is piling up on his email), his daughter in Australia, he wasn't saved to save her, she's there and gone, was he saved to see her again, and Carla? would omniscience step in to comfort her now to have him abandon her later, or worse, have him live for her to abandon him and live alone and suffering like St. Jin, or no, the world is accident and wrath, the plague is outside the front door; this moment, this moment, as the nineteenth century philosophers wondered, why existence and not non-existence? he had a nightmare last night, he pushed a button that saved the world, he fell to his knees weeping in front of a military officer who prepared him for court martial and execution, too much Kafka? but he awoke feeling miserable; he reads the newspaper, Rump is pleading with the nation to open up, trade death for dollars, then, checking his Society email account, he's been asked to participate in an all-day Zoom conference on sexual abuse in various institutional religions, Yoga, Buddhism, Mormonism, Catholicism, while back east his lawyer just informed him the Arch Diocese of Erie has suspended its fund to reimburse its abused men, citing Covid-19 as the reason; they had yet to pay anyone a dime.

Prajna Paramita Sutra. The Path to Excellent Wisdom.

71,000 deaths.

Yesterday was Mothers Day.

The day before, Saturday, the landscapers came in and cleared Path's trees away from his house. They didn't have to kill any. Not yet. But this pruning, the contractor argued, would soon make the trees healthier and stronger. The California Oak, which had to be several hundred years old, had grown thickly from the deck and cascaded over the fence to the carport below, if the limb broke it would crush his truck and Carla's car, anyway, things look very different now, Path is preparing the invoice and a description of the work for the fire insurance officials, and he has to find a mason to fix a crack in a brick wall in front of his house that insurance claims is part of his foundation, though it has nothing to do with his foundation and Path wants to make that point but Carla said, don't be a fool, Path, don't engage them, just fix it; on Mothers' Day Path and Carla awaken, Path feeds the cats, takes out the recycling, collects the LA Times and the New York Times, notes the residual damage to his yard, the top of a lamp post knocked off, two plaster angel babies broken, limbs cracked on the beleaguered lime tree, twice it had been dug up and replanted for septic work, this time it looks like it won't make it, crud filling Scotty and Silvio's outdoor food and water bowls; Path comes in and makes bacon and eggs for Carla, he fucks up the bacon and it's too crisp but he adds half and half to the scrambled eggs and they're okay, they read the depressing news, under Rump's encouragement states are opening up their economies as the death toll rises, a prediction of 137,000 deaths, Path retrieves his truck from the lot next door, where he parked the vehicles out of the way of the landscapers, then he and Carla take their walk, the hiking trails have reopened and trucks and cars are piled up at the trailheads, yet Path finds a spot, out in the open air on the wide fire road, they don't need masks, a few vehicles go by, but they conjectured that most everybody would be on the newly opened trails and they were right, here, on the road most traveled, they find the road least traveled by, they mosey for a half mile to their bench on a hill, look out over the western Valley that stretches to the mountains, then walk back and get in the truck, they move slowly on dirt Mulholland Drive, people are out with their children and dogs, the wild animals are back in hiding, a large peregrine falcon has decided to follow them on their walks, she swoops at Path and screes, waits for them on top of telephone poles, Path names her Xenobia, a female, it just makes sense, male birds don't like him, Path says a prayer for a non-lethal snake stretched across the road, when they get back home Carla checks the mail, delivered yesterday, and finds Path's Mothers' Day gift, two pens, a ball point and a roller ball from Levengers, they hold each other and kiss in the driveway, then Path puts his yard back together, sort of, replaces the lamp lid, re-piles the rock tower at the top of the stairs, gathers up the broken angels, Do you want these, Carla? Trash them, Carla says, he takes them down to the trash, he saves the last unbroken angel and leaves it under the leaf of an elephant ear, he prunes the broken branches of the lime tree, why does nothing grow there, says Carla, It's a doomed spot, Path says, he cleans the outdoor cat bowls, puts in kibble and fresh water; on Friday, facing the landscape onslaught, the two of them picked grapefruits from their tree and juiced them, now they have a half gallon of fresh grapefruit juice, Sunday afternoon Carla calls her mother, she's semi-rational but trouble's abrewin', she wants Carla to convince Path to convince her son, Hazlitt, to read her

Wry-Tings, right; as Mothers' Day evening approaches they take Carla's car up to Malibu, but the little restaurant where Carla ordered lobster rolls has a long line and a ton of people in the parking lot waiting for orders, a number of them without masks, too many people, what happened to Carla's advanced order, so Carla takes out her cell and calls a nearby Cuban place and orders Carne Asada, during the half-hour wait they stroll in the ghost town of high-end Malibu shops, looking through the windows, what Path sees, mostly, is his own reflection, things are so expensive here there aren't even any prices on them, as of tomorrow they'll be open for on-line ordering and front door pick-up, figure out how that's going to work, they drive to the La Habana and get their Asada, corn on the cob, and two mojitos to go, suddenly, in this new world, you can get mixed drinks to go, they sip them on the way home, drink champagne, gin and tonic, Path is somber, thinking of his mother who died more than forty years ago on Memorial Day weekend, She would have loved me, says Carla, I would have won her over, even though I'm not Catholic, Her husband wasn't Catholic, says Path, and he sure didn't practice birth control, though she tried, but that's an old story, Frida jumps up next to Carla's thigh, accepts some grooming, then crosses over to Path's shins to stretch out, dropping all four legs like a cat on a limb, a week ago there were lilacs on the breakfast bar, Carla's favorite, When Lilacs Last in the Dooryard Bloomed, Listen to that rhythm, says Carla, fucking Whitman, Carla reads on Face Book that the aliens landed outside Roswell nine months before Rump was born, a patient alien conspiracy, 81,000 people have died, Happy Fuckin' Mothers' Day; the Jin, moved from the senior psych ward to her care facility's nursing section, is crying to be moved back to her apartment, so they move her back, she calls Carla and cries that she wants to go back to the nursing home, they're bringing food to her room but she can't eat it because she can't see it, she can see our phone number, Path says, she doesn't want to be in the nursing facility or her apartment, No, says Carla, she wants to come here, the manager of the home says she sends people to the Jin's room seven times a day, the Jin says no one ever comes to see her, Let's walk, says Path, and on their walk someone has beheaded a baby rattler, it's silver body twisted in curls, belly up, the way a snake dies when beheaded, their body yet writhing. Xenobia picks up the carcass and flies away.

81,000 dead.

THE SELF

WILLIAM JAMES, PRECEDING GEORGE HERBERT MEAD, saw the self as two processes, one socially constructed in the history of social-psychological interaction, the *Me*, a fluid construction of concepts, the other entity, the *I*, was a spontaneous core, moment to moment (alas) springing into the world. He saw neither as ontological, i.e. substantial entities, and in his *Principles of Psychology* launched detailed critiques of numerous theories of the soul and self. In that, simply in terms of narrative weight, James, almost ironically, address the issues of Soul and Self as assiduously as anyone, before or since. His analysis, in the end, is very similar to Buddha's, that in the in the search for a substantial cause of thought, concept, percept, emotion, or will, one shall find nothing but those things and to posit a substance/entity in which those things abide is simply unnecessary, i.e. Self or Soul explain nothing more than the processes of mental life already provide; that they occur somehow conterminous with processes in the brain is mystery enough, our uniqueness is not stamped in our debatable immortality and is not more remarkable than the unique configuration of a snowflake. One might argue that they *feel* a self or soul, but that feeling is illusory, as much of our psychic world is, because, as Buddha said, if you go looking inside for it you won't find it.

When Schopenhauer took this route things turned out a little differently. On the heels of Kant, he accepted that of the objects that can be perceived in the world, including those of the psyche, none could escape the dilemma that perception was ensconced in the phenomenological categories of the mind and that no thing-in-itself, no objective real world could be independently perceived or conceived; that world, that obstinate world, the world, in fact, of science, the world where humans land on the moon, that world, which meets our categorical mind, can never be directly experienced or known, and that would include our thoughts and feelings, as well. We live in and know only a phenomenal world, where the objective world, the noumenal world, meets our minds. Granted all that, states Schopenhauer, upon inspection, there was one thing that could be experienced immediately, from the inside, not through observation or inspection, but felt undeniably as a thing-in-itself: the Will. This raised the Will to the most primary ontological entity, even to go so far as to say that the Will dominates the intellect and creates the world and we as humans do not so much create the world as such as participate in it. This, if unprovable, seems to me quite imaginable, and though the imagination is hardly a critical quotient for the real (unless we trust Wordsworth and Coleridge), some imaginative speculations are more cogent than others, and someone like Bachelard or Baudrillard might venture to say that that's why poetry comes as close as we can get to the truth. That's a lot of weight to put on the back of a metaphor, and would appear to wander perilously between monist idealism (that's what James, a radical empiricist and pluralist would call Schopenhauer's Will) and nihilist nominalism (like Gass or Derrida, though even Gass raised sympathies for ineffable essentialness, unique thought and will that made an author the God of their texts, as he argued against Barthes in "The Death of the Author").

Recently, as recent as spring 2021, in book entitled *Metazoa*, an Australian philosopher and naturalist, Peter Godfrey-Smith, tracing back to the one celled organizations of life as early as 575 million years ago, argued that the first *agency* of motion toward some object, such as food, required a feeling of presence and activity that pervades all sentience to this day, through the animal kingdoms and humanity, and the organization of our complex psycho-social-cultural perceptions and conceptions are accompanied by a *feeling* that finds its roots in the first rudimentary sentience, a feeling of a presence that he calls the Self. Smith is a self-proclaimed monist materialist, postulating this view in order to solve the mind-body problem that persists in philosophical and scientific discussions to this day. He also offers it to explain how some of the higher intellect species, like whales, dolphins, elephants, primates, and octopuses display behaviors of self-recognition. Brains don't create thought, they participate in the process of thought. In my book *How the Animals Around You Think: The Semiotics of Animal Cognition*, I try to demonstrate how, using symbols, indexes, but especially icons, non-human animals demonstrate cognitive behavior. Still, you can't put a thought in a petri dish. The problem isn't solved. Nonetheless, the barriers that have pedestaled and isolated human cognition as qualitatively distinct from, and not evolved from, animal sentience, might be beginning to fall.

FARRAGUT RAN

THE CONFEDERATE MINE FIELD BETWEEN FORTS Jackson and St. Phillip. Now his ships and 15,000 men were less than 70 miles downriver from New Orleans and it didn't look like there was anyone or anything there to stop him, his fleet bombarding the shorelines on both sides of the river.

What few Confederate soldiers there were still in New Orleans fled towards Baton Rouge, abandoning the South's biggest city and port.

Rick sent Anna a note and a train ticket, saying he was liquidating his business and leaving in two days for Jackson, Mississippi. He and Shope would be at the Belle Hotel and he'd be waiting there for her. When he and Shope boarded the train the Yankee's were moving fast, less than a day away. You could hear the guns.

They'll declare Martial Law, said Shope.

I know that.

They'll shut down this line.

She's savvy, Rick said. She'll get out if she wants to.

Should have brought her with us, said Shope.

A white man, a black man, and a French woman, Rick said. No acceptable combination. Let alone her husband. She has to leave him on her own.

It's not a free country?

What country are you talking about? Nothing is free in any country.

As they moved out of New Orleans the train got crowded. Women in long dresses and hats, men in bowlers, children, huge traveling trunks.

Must have relatives in Baton Rouge, said Rick.

Not Jackson?

Mississippi is a different place. You'll see. You'll stick out.

I always stick out. We already talked about that, said Shope. I could play the piano on the moon.

You might have to.

I've got family on the moon, Shope said.

Rick laughed.

Moving slowly toward a bank of blue-black clouds they skirted the south shore of Lake Pontchartrain. Soon the storm brought a thick wall of rain and the lake churned and threw water at the train. It felt like they were traveling inside water. Then it let up. Between the clouds the blue in the sky was miraculous. When they hit the isthmus between Pontchartrain and Lake Maurepas, people exited for the connection to Baton Rouge. It happened again north of the isthmus at Harmond.

That's why we're not getting off, Rick said to Shope. There's nothing between here and Jackson.

Swamp and cotton, said Shope.

And that was right. When they moved through the swamp land there was only an occasional fishing shack, sometimes gator flesh hung from roofs to cure. Rick felt the landscape in his heart and thought of Anna. What a time to fall in love. What a place. He wouldn't go back to wholesale booze. It would be too hard to import large quantities in Jackson, then move it on the limited roads. As well, there would be gangs of road thieves. No law anywhere. He planned to go west, to Vicksburg. They had a port. He could open a club and bring down supplies on the river from Memphis. If Sherman took Memphis it wouldn't stop the booze from flowing. He'd use wagons if he had to, he'd only have to supply his club, not a few dozen of them. If need be, he'd distill his own rye.

The train moved into plantation country. Acres of cotton, brown and white, stretched between mansions. Slave shacks in rows nearby. Blacks working the fields.

Who built those mansions? said Shope.

You're asking?

It's criminal.

Not here it isn't.

A crime against humanity.

As old as humanity itself, Rick said.

Humanity, said Shope. The cotton and the slaves, there's no difference.

Procreation is money in the bank. You heard of communism?

I've heard of it.

Well?

Have you heard of greed? The Cherokee had farms and slaves, and churches, too, what good did it do them. Humanity is rotten everywhere. I've heard the Yankees will have rifles that load in the breach like a long six-shooter, the powder and the bullet are one thing. Load, shoot and load in seconds. They have manufacturing, trains. That'll end slavery, but it won't change much. Why don't you move back to Europe.

Africa is Europe's slave, Shope said.

You're a smart man, Shope, said Rick.

They sat for a while, listening to the train, the click of the rails. Shope wore a suit, like Rick, but he was the only Black in the car.

Shope broke the quiet. Your lady friend has lived in big cities, said Shope.

You, too, said Rick.

I just have to play the piano, Shope said.

And I just have to buy one, said Rick.

Shope laughed.

You won't like Jackson, Shope. We won't stay long.

Just south of downtown, at the Hotel Belle, a block from the train station, they wouldn't let Shope in the door. There were accommodations for Black porters at the back.

He's a free African, Rick said to the doorman.

I'm sorry, sir, he said.

Rick went in by himself and made arrangements to have his mail received, gave them Anna's name, as well, then walked with Shope to the back of the hotel. A woman there told them of an area, Oakland, just northwest of Jackson, where there was a small neighborhood of free Blacks. It doesn't matter if you're free, she said, they can take you anytime.

Back near the entrance it took them a while to find a cab, a covered one where Shope wouldn't be seen. Even so, the driver, an older man wearing a gray cap, was reluctant.

He yours? he said. He had a Mississippi accent, all vowels, almost sonorous; his lips barely moved and there was no space between his words.

He's not mine, said Rick. He's with me. He's a free man.

Might be worse.

I have Federal dollars, said Rick. He showed one.

In French, Shope said, Let me pay him. And brought out his own cash.

Didn't think you were from here, said the cabbie. He took a dollar from Rick.

Expensive, said Rick.

I'll leave you outside, the cab man said, I'm not going in.

He didn't help them with their bags and left them off outside Oakland on a street called Bullard. There was an area of shops and shacks, some small houses, a small brick hotel with a café, table cloths, coffee, beer and food. Opposite the situation on the train, now Rick was the only white, though the clientele was men and women, even some children. They were dressed well, as if they'd come from church or a meeting, so Rick and Shope didn't stand out because of their clothes. The waitress looked to be in her thirties, attractive, she eyed them skeptically. Then she nodded across the crowded café where people lined up at a buffet table. From where they sat, an upright piano stood near the left end.

Food's there, she said.

Can we get beer? said Shope.

She nodded again.

Rick pulled his flask from his jacket and set it on the table without removing his hand. He said, I'll pay to drink this.

You can buy more on the corner, she said, and left them.

The fare was good. Fried catfish, fried chicken, beans, greens, potatoes. Their beer was on the table when they got back. After eating, Shope got up and walked to the piano. Very lightly, he began a ballad, though when no one looked up he played more resolutely. Then he played a song called "The Sad River," then "Swing Low." The room began to hum. Then came the applause. Shope stood and bowed. A man came to him and took his hands and they spoke briefly. Shope found out that they could stay, upstairs. They took a small, clean second floor room with two small beds, a chair and table, candles, an oil lamp, a wash basin, two glasses and a pitcher that they could fill down the hall. They had a window with a view of the street. It was the first of May. The sunset was red. The night warm. They walked down the street to the corner bar. There was a half dozen men inside, all of them Black, in work clothes, overalls, thick boots. They watched the two strangers impassively. Shope got whisky and a pack of cards. Sat down at a table where Rick watched him shuffle and lay out solitaire.

The Yankees are in New Orleans, Shope said.

That was the owner. He told you that?

Shope nodded. Telegraph.

I'll check the Belle in the morning, Rick said. Then we need to buy horses. Vicksburg is a half-day ride.

They chased the whisky with beer, then took the bottle back to their room. Rick lit the lamp and sat on the desk chair, Shope sat on a bed. Rick poured whisky. They didn't know each other intimately, but they were friends, close enough. Rick had run into Shope while doing business at hotels and clubs in New Orleans, Shope at the piano, Rick bought him drinks. They'd hatched this evacuation plan, sans Anna Breton, at the start of the war, when it became apparent that the North would try to choke the South by taking all of the port cities, barricading them from foreign trade, then squeezing in from there, Winnifred Scott's Anaconda Plan. New Orleans was easy prey.

Your lady friend knew Flaubert, said Shope.

Slept with him, she says.

I knew him, Shope said. It was before the *Bovary* noise. I knew the whole crowd.

Du Camp, Balzac, Baudelaire, even George Sands and Chopin. Bourgeoisie who hated the bourgeoisie.

You ran from that, said Rick.

Ran home is all. Europe is upside down. The Second Republic is a dictatorship. Napoleon hated artists, but his brother liked Flaubert. But a free Black man can live in New Orleans.

I was with Brown at Harper's Ferry, Rick said.

Lee, said Shope.

Was a Yankee Colonel. He thought he got everybody, but he didn't. Anyway, either side would hang me now. Rick sipped his whisky. You been in love, Shope?

Shope laughed. Too many times.

Learn anything?

How to shoot someone who just outdrew you?

Now Rick laughed. I wish I had one of those tobacco sticks that Anna smokes.

Paris, said Shope. Cigarettes. Well, maybe tomorrow.

The next morning Rick hailed a cab. It was easier to get a cab in Oakland. He had his cabbie wait for him outside the hotel. There was a letter for him there. From Anna.

Dearest Rick:
I shall not be able to meet you in Jackson. Regretfully, we may never meet again. There are things that I must do. The world is biggerthan the fate of two lovers. We will always have the time we had.
With all my love,
Farewell,
Anna

He tore the note and threw it in the street. Took the carriage back to Oakland. When Shope met him he said, We'll only need two horses now.

Let's face the music, said Schope, and dance.

And now, a year later, she was in his club, with a man. They stood inside the doorway peering across the crowded barroom. His skin was brown. He wore a beige suit, double breasted, and a gray fedora, she wore a fluffy blouse and a long skirt, her head, as always, uncovered, her hair falling to her shoulders. Rick got up and sent Molly to them.

Give them my table, he said.

He turned and went to the bar, retrieved two glasses and a bottle of his best champagne and took it to their table. It's on me, he said. He poured for Anna. Her eyes met his, impassive but soft. He poured for her companion. In French he said, This town will soon be under siege.

Merci beaucoup, the man answered. We know. Would you join us?

Rick waved his arm at the crowded barroom. I'm very busy right now, he said. Maybe another time.

When he returned to the bar Shope came to him. You need me? he said.

Rick grabbed a bottle of rye. I got all I need, he said, then went upstairs to his room, poured, drank, and wept.

THE PROBLEM WITH ANGELS

WHY DOES ANYTHING EXIST AT ALL? Why is there anything and not nothing? And what holds it together?

I have ventured to suggest here that the world did not so much emerge from God as God emerged from the world, that this God is neither fatherly nor motherly, if watchful, then neither conscious nor helpful; Ken Wilber has said that God is the atom bomb as much as God is the daffodil, neither cruel nor kind; we shall die whether we choose to accept Them or deny Them, auspicious or pernicious, that no part of this universe, be it good or evil, could exist without all the other parts (Leibniz, Spinoza, Sankara), God did their best with what they had to work with, or is it so that there are no parts, that parts are an illusion; all is one, all is nothing, nothing but pure emptiness; isn't anybody going to take on some responsibility?

Some time ago my psychiatrist asked me if I believed I had a guardian angel. I wanted to say "no" but I hesitated. Is there a difference between the me who feels a spiritual presence and the me who does not? Would that presence be as tethered to me as the thoughts that accompany me everywhere I go? Do I, Herr Schopenhauer, really perceive, feel, my will?

Let me conduct an experiment and take some time to believe I have a guardian angel. You might find this exercise absurd, but allow me to approach it phenomenologically. Throughout the day I reminded myself to experience a presence near me, disregarding any possible difficulties that the assumption of an immaterial, i.e., spiritual presence, would arouse. I did not, as I think about it even now, feel that presence as something *near* me so much as, as I feel during meditation, feel it *in* me, a kind of mentally stepping away from my stream of consciousness, my "monkey mind." If an entity, I made several attempts to discover their name, and though I thought of many names, mostly angel clichés, Michael, Gabriel, Raphael, none really took. Further, the angel I assumed to believe in made no attempts to intrude on my thoughts; if I stopped thinking about them, they weren't there. Soon, problems followed, like the issue of an immaterial being communicating with a material one, and again, the ontology of my consciousness; do I have a soul, a mind? Is an angel a disembodied mind? I thought then of the portrayal of angels, young men, white robed, sometimes winged, often messengers in the Old Testament and the Koran; the only angel I recall in the gospels is the one who meets the women who approach Christ's empty tomb. More so, as a child I was taught that for every guardian angel there was an accompanying antagonist, a devil. Do I feel both goodness and evil around me, inside me, motivating me, agitating me? Sincerely, I do not. I surmise that people who perform activities that we deem evil, like the murder of innocents, don't feel evil or even bad, or even bad about it. In the laying out of my very existence, if I waste water or electricity, do I perform covert evil acts, or by not accepting Allah as the one and only God, am I evil? When I do something that I think is good, do I feel goodness, do I even feel good about it?

I've wandered from my guardian angel experiment—I think it failed— to the problem of Good and Evil, and it's an old, big problem. Zen would say neither exist; karma is a more prevalent issue than sin and there is the question of whether karma is a psychological phenomenon or an ontic one. The explicitly causal nature of moral causality runs against Buddha's critique of temporal causality, which has led some to speculate that as a religious reformer, he simply followed the Vedic traditions, stepping back from turning over everything. Needless to say, we have gone beyond angels. But the guardian angel is no straw man, nor, in almost all cases, a straw woman; when I read a book on angels some decades ago, written by a Jesuit scholar, the purview was holistically patriarchal, angels, if they ever don an appearance, seem to be young men, likely a cultural overlay or manifestation in human culture of the patriarchy, but we would assume that spiritual beings are really gender neutral, if not, then we're in some troubling territory, God the Father, God is a comforting father figure, as Sigmund Freud might say, but without talking further about the multiple ways that angels fall apart, the problem with angels is that they become typical of any number of proposed ontic entities of which we have no experience, that we generally anthropomorphize them, even so, one must argue from a possibly evident effect to a cause generated in the imagination. I don't mean to throw out the angel with the bath water. William James was both radical empiricist and, spiritually, poly-agnostic, his pluralism leaning him toward polytheism if he had to choose what to be agnostic about. I'll follow him there. But the farther we wander from what is in front of faces, or our math, the closer we move to just making things up to make us feel better about the world's, or our own, frail uncertainties. When I (pretend?) to believe that I'm talking to the plants around me I must acknowledge that I'm not talking *with* the plants, I'm describing a sentient metaphor of our (speculatively so) shared sentience, though how much of that sharing is one-sided falls to my subjective observations. So too with angels, ghosts, and Gods.

THE RIOTINGS ON THE WALL

93,000

Two days later. 100,000. It will be 600,000 soon enough. 80% of the dying are over sixty-five. Path is now sixty-eight. The Sunday before Memorial Day the New York Times published 1,000 short obituaries starting on its front page. Then a policeman in Minneapolis kneels on an unarmed black man's neck for eight minutes and kills him. While he begs "I can't breathe! I can't breathe!" four others watch. The man's name is George Floyd. It's caught on video. The cities erupt in protests, rioting, and looting. At first, the police just watch. Then they go to war and shoot everybody, peaceful and otherwise, with tear gas and rubber bullets. Rump threatens to call out the military. Police chiefs all over the country begin taking a knee like Collin Kaeperrnick. Meanwhile, thousands are still dying of Covid-19. Los Angeles, Santa Monica, Venice Beach, Hollywood, and Beverly Hills are in flames. Trans Kafka calls home and says the looting is justified, it's inevitable class warfare. She posts that on Instagram. Protesting begins in London, Paris, Berlin, Path recalls that in 1993, after the Rodney King incident, four black women attacked him and Carla in Venice Beach, a big woman grabbed Marlena from Carla's arms and threw her on the ground, Path stood between his family and two attackers who bloodied him using pen knives, a fourth woman stood nearby with a video camera, neighbors gathered and Path screamed, Do nothing! Do nothing! They want us on camera hitting them! Anyway, two black policewomen showed up and arrested Path, Path understood, it was sociological, not personal, just like racism. Meanwhile, in D.C., Rump marches from the white house surrounded by an army escort that clears out a peaceful protest with rubber bullets and teargas. He stands in front of a Catholic church and raises a golden Bible with a cross. Dude, when's the last time you were in a church?

140,000

The Fourth of July. Rump travels to South Dakota for a Friday night speech in front of Mount Rushmore. Earlier, in June, he traveled to Tulsa, Oklahoma, for a rally he expected would attract a million people. He spoke to only 6,000. No social distancing, nobody wears masks. He rails against Black Lives Matter, calling them communists and anarchists who want to destroy America. He defends police violence as self-defense against the lawless rioters. A dozen of his CIA operatives there contract Covid-19. Around the nation people are pulling down statues of Confederate generals. In South Dakota, the Oglala Souix, who technically own Mount Rushmore land, say they don't want Rump. He goes anyway. Only 7,500 people show up, jammed together, maskless, in front of their unmasked President. Around the nation, in states that have eased their isolation restrictions, including California, the virus rages back. The USA leads the world in infections and deaths. In Topanga, as Path and Carla drive to their mountain walk, dozens of tourists flock into restaurants and shops, crowding together without masks. It happens all over L.A. The beaches are packed. In no time the virus explodes again. Thousands are dying for their right, their inherent freedom to risk their lives without a thought for those who they are endangering.

On the home front, Carla has tried to step up for her mother again. St. Jin calls and begs to go back to the nursing facility. Carla has her transferred. She calls a day later and demands to go back to her apartment. Carla arranges it. St. Jin weeps and demands to go back to the nursing home, but in two days she wants to go back to her apartment. There, returned, she's found screaming Help me! Help me! She wants to come here, Path says to Carla, I know, Carla says. Path says, There are sixty steps, The nursing home! screams St. Jin. The staff supervisor tells her this will be her last move. For each move Carla has spent hours doing the lengthy paperwork. Your last move says the supervisor, St. Jin says she understands. It lasts a day. While Carla is in a Zoom board meeting with Beyond Baroque, the Jin leaves eight messages. She spits spite. She wants to be in her apartment. She wants her Wry-Tings back. They're her writings, *her* Wry-Tings! Carla is a worthless bitch who has ruined her life. Carla unplugs. She looks at Path. It's over, she says. I'm done. She calls a tech specialist and arranges to get rid of the phone. And while he's at it, the TV. There are giant fireworks across America, the most ever. Fires break out all over L.A. Particles of soot fill the air. The world is murk and fire.

GRANT CROSSES THE MISSISSIPPI

INTO LOUISIANA. After several failed attempts to build canals through the swamps above Vicksburg, he crosses the Mississippi at Lake Providence, but is bogged down in the swamps above Bayou Baxter. He crosses back over and launches an attack east of the river from north of the Yazoo Pass, but is stopped repeatedly at Greenwood and Fort Pemberton. He heads north again and attempts to roll down the Yazoo River, but in the end it's too narrow and shallow. Vicksburg is almost surrounded by Yankees and swamps. Grant telegraphs Farragut to run a fleet from the south past the Confederate batteries at Port Hudson, but only a few ships make it through. He tries to build another canal there, but it floods. Nonetheless, there are enough naval vessels in the river to begin shelling Vicksburg, but they don't have the troops or ships to land there. Union cavalry began raiding the countryside. But Southern swamps and soldiers still held Grant back.

Rick saw Pemberton once during those spring months. Pem had been begging Johnston for troops and cavalry, but Johnston felt Pemberton had been holding Grant off from the north, west, and south; Grant couldn't take Vicksburg. Yet the roar of cannon fire from the river now filled the air around the town like thunder.

What's left? Rick said to him.

East, said Jack Pemberton.

But he's got to get there, Rick said.

He's incorrigible, said Pemberton. We'll have to build redoubts.

Who's going to build them? Slaves?

Pemberton was stoic.

Surrender? said Rick.

A general from Philadelphia cannot surrender the last Confederate stronghold on the Mississippi, said Pem. They were silent for a moment. With the city in peril, the sky rumbling, the frivolity of the club felt impossibly unreal. Rick poured whisky. Why did you come to Vicksburg? Pemberton asked Rick.

Rick laughed. For peace and quiet? He told Pem about John Brown.

Ironic, said Jack Pemberton.

New Orleans seemed like neutral territory, said Rick, but it wasn't.

And Shope?

He should have stayed there. It's my fault. And you?

I believe in the right to secession, Jack Pemberton said. The North invaded the South.

Sumpter?

Was trivial.

And slavery? Rick said.

An anachronism, Pemberton said. Like Lee, I believe that it will come to its own end. Let the South solve it on its own. Lincoln hasn't made this a war about slavery. Grant and Sherman still have them. Washington and Jefferson?

Were Southerners, said Rick. He drank, poured, drank.

Jack Pemberton relit a cigar. I'll pay Black labor to help build our stockades and trenches, he said.

They were both quiet again. Then Rick said, I'm not for anybody, Jack.

Bonded by fate, Pemberton said.

Harassed by malaria and Pemberton's troops, Grant gives up and again ferries his army across the Mississippi at Milliken's Bend. Then he marches south, hopping down the Louisiana side of the river looking for a port to land south of Vicksburg. Sherman was still sitting northeast of the city and repeatedly feigned attacks from the Bluffs, pinning Pemberton's troops in Vicksburg, so he had limited troops to take on Grant to the south. Pemberton sends his best officer, John Bowen, with a few thousand troops and heavy artillery to block Grant's re-crossing the river, stymying him at Warrenton, and again, at Hard Times and Grand Gulf. Having learned flanking from watching Lee, Grant hopped south again, Bowen matching him resolutely until Grant, marching south again, with the help of navy ironclads and barges, manages to cross at Bruinsburg, consolidating his army, and heads for Port

Gibson. Bowen abandons Grand Gulf, heads south to Port Gibson and digs in. But after a protracted battle over rugged terrain, Grant breaks through. To the east he flanks Bowen again by building a fifty-yard pontoon bridge at Bayou Pierre. Bowen, badly outnumbered, can't stop him. Grant contemplates attacking Vicksburg from the south, but Pemberton was entrenching in rugged territory there southeast of Vicksburg. So Grant heads east instead, for Jackson, bivouacking half-way there in Rock Springs.

Pemberton immediately telegraphs Johnston and says that if Johnston can hold Grant outside Jackson, Pemberton will come up behind him and encircle Grant there. Sherman would have to follow him and they could battle it out. Pemberton asks for cavalry and troops. Johnston then asks Pemberton for troops. Jefferson Davis telegraphs Pemberton that his priority should be fortifying Vicksburg. Johnston, technically Pemberton's superior in Mississippi, orders Pemberton to advance and attack Grant's flank. In the east, Lee says he will take the pressure off Vicksburg by invading Pennsylvania while Sherman in fact does leave the Chickasaw Bluffs to join Grant outside Jackson. Trying to compromise between Davis and Johnston, Pemberton leaves a small contingency of defenders around Vicksburg and entrenches in strength just east of the Mississippi River on a bridge over the Big Black River. If Grant would turn for Vicksburg to fight him, he believed he could defeat Grant there and save Jackson. But Grant does not turn back. Fearing that a crucial moment has arrived, Pemberton organizes several Southern corps to converge on Grant and his armies east of Rock Springs at a small town called Raymond, but due to several breakdowns in communication, barely any Confederate commanders, including Johnston, show up. Grant easily sweeps through Raymond and continues toward Jackson. Johnston, claiming that his army was too small to fight Grant off, abandons the capital, heading north, and the Yankees roll into Jackson, burning it to the ground. Then Grant turns west, for Vicksburg.

Rick was in his room on a Thursday evening in early May, going over his accounts when a knock came on his door. A gibbous moon shone through his window and made light and shadows on his floor.

Shope? Rick said.

No, said a woman's voice. Anna.

Just come in, he said. Though he wasn't sure he wanted to see her. She and her friend had been staying downtown in a hotel on the corner of Washington and Clay. They'd come by for an occasional drink, chatted with Shope, but didn't gamble. When she opened the door, he saw she was alone. He turned to her but didn't get up. I hope this isn't romantic, he said.

How could it be anything but? She retrieved her cigarette case from her purse. May I smoke? She opened the case toward him but he shook his head.

I don't want to look for those eyes of yours through smoke, he said. Memories live in smoke.

She lit for herself. The man I'm with, Henri, is my husband, Anna said. I found out about his escape after you left New Orleans. So I stayed.

I'm happy for you both, said Rick. Where's he now?

Grant is on his way, said Anna.

That's not news to anybody, said Rick

Pemberton wants to employ slaves to help build defenses. Henri is organizing them to negotiate wage demands.

Paid slaves, Rick said.

It's a step, she said.

Unlike me, your husband is a do-gooder, Rick said. He got up, retrieved a bottle of sherry and poured for the two of them. Am I supposed to hope he gets killed out there?

One should never hope for anything, Anna said. She extinguished her cigarette in a glass ash tray, sipped her drink. Don't you think that all virtue is self-serving, and self-destructive?

If you mean it's foolish to think about your feelings, or feel your feelings. But it's all we've got, isn't it?

Her expression exhibited demure. They come and go, she said.

Love? said Rick

She looked down and away from him, then quickly looked up and met his eyes.

What are you reading? Anna asked.

He remembered this dance, but he didn't want to dance it anymore. I gave up reading, he said. I watch the moon. I think about the moon.

It comes and goes, too, she said.

That's it, like my feelings. But you can count on the moon coming back.

I'm back, she said. She put down her glass, came close and kissed his lips. If he made love to her again, what would it matter?

WHEN MY MOTHER DIED OF A BRAIN TUMOR I was, by chance, living and working near her in my hometown. Watching her vitality, her life, ebb, was very sad. When she fell into her final coma I yet whispered in her ear that I loved her, but her retreat from consciousness devastated the last remnants of my faith in mind.

When I was a boy I had an intimate, if one-sided, relationship with God. I spoke to God, He was a Him back then, consulted Him, felt His presence in and around me; that constant presence filled me with a deep sense of morality. Even then, so dependent and innocent, I didn't pray for home runs or touchdowns, for victory, or the love of an impossible, beautiful infatuation, but for the grace to be good, to be a better person. That was called Actual Grace. The reward for actually doing good was called Sanctifying Grace, the grace you accumulated to get into heaven. But very early in adolescence a couple things got between me and God. One was religion. I didn't feel God in those rituals, not even in taking holy communion, the prayers of religion were not my prayers. Both the praise and humility seemed false. I found Genesis unsatisfying, Original Sin didn't make sense; I found Eve to be a scapegoat. I couldn't feel or understand the concepts of grace or God's justice. Nonetheless, I didn't find religion oppressive until my basketball coach, then mentor, and then sexual abuser, began a systematic attack on the cruelty in the Old Testament and the miracles of the New. Noah's Ark! he'd say, and belly laugh. On Sundays, when I skipped mass and sneaked off to a drugstore to read comic books, I felt tremendous unburdening and liberation. I was young. Death was impossible. Later, philosophy graduate school didn't mend that rupture and my mother's deterioration ended my flirtation with the mind-body problem. I became a thoroughgoing materialist. Still feeling a religious impulse, I satisfied it with yoga, meditation, Advita Vedanta, and eventually Madhyamika Buddhism, sometimes intensely, sometimes not. This brief digress explains the fifty-five year trek to this essay.

With the onset of my own cancer I began to live my inner, reflective life in duplicity. After surgery and radiation failed, without conviction or belief, I began to meditate, my shrink called it prayer, on individuals in the religious pantheons, Christian, Hindu, Buddhist, Islamic, with open acknowledgment that they were likely and simply icons in my imagination, if I could picture them at all, admitting, I suppose, more to the power of prayer than to any entity that I prayed to. I didn't get much beyond that. I didn't pray for a cure. I prayed for help in dealing with my illness. Anyway, inexplicably, my cancer went away and is currently still gone. My surgeon said there was no medical explanation. I don't know what to think about that. Sometimes I thank the pantheon. Sometimes I just say thank you to the Void. I never asked the question 'Why me?' when I got sick, though I began to think about it when I mysteriously got better.

If my survival is somewhat miraculous, it is yet difficult to describe it as a miracle. If the cosmos and the world that we inhabit are miracles of the laws that ensued upon creation, then a miracle is an occurrence that defies those laws, albeit that my doctors said there was no medical explanation for what happened to me, in fact the same surgeon, during my chagrin at the failing of the cure procedures, turned to me and said, "This is biology, pure and simple." Yet the horrible suffering, both natural and inflicted by humanity, witness the 2020 Covid-19 pandemic, make it difficult to rationalize providence. Buddha did not perform miracles. Purportedly Jesus did.

For William James, a self-proclaimed radical empiricist, a subjective truth is as real as any other; in *Varieties* he cites dozens of examples of people who have experienced the ecstasy of God, an experience that can be neither demonstrated nor denied. I have, in meditation, though it has come upon me spontaneously as well, experienced something like that ecstasy, but I can only relate that I *feel* it; I can't tell whether it comes from somewhere or arises from within. Maybe that doesn't matter, maybe it does. Admittedly, the more I practice, the more it happens, though equally I might be overcome by panic or groundless fear and depression, and I don't look for an outside source or entity who visits it upon me, unless it happens between dream and consciousness in the night, then it might feel personal, I might feel something, someone, envelop me with caring. I awaken longing for it. If, in Freudian fashion, it arises from my unconscious, then it is less a thing than a wish. And my unconscious can be as close or distant from my consciousness as, say, God.

Let me take some time to play in this space. Buddhists like the Vajrayana (Tibetan Buddhism) believe in a forty-nine day afterlife space called the Bardo where the no-soul that one has perpetuated by desire and karma, migrates in transition toward rebirth. There are a number of stages, but the beings one encounters in the Bardo, some benevolent and some horrible and threatening, arise like the entities in this life, from our own mind, whatever that might be. The forms they take are cultural, i.e., if I've been raised in a Christian culture, they will appear as saints, angels, and devils, if Vajrayana, divine beings and demons (which happen to have been lifted, or transformed, from the pre-Buddhist Tibetan native religion, the Bon); if we haven't learned in our previous life that everything is unreal, then these beings will appear as real as anything else. So now, in this life, if I choose to meditate on someone who is both kind and brave, I am more likely to come upon the image of St. George than of Rama, and that what St. George slays is the dragon of my ambition, the dragon being as equally metaphoric or real as the saint himself, but the meditative act may indeed help me to quell my nagging ambition and, so too, meditating on the Buddha or Jesus might help me calm my fear and panic, or on St. Theresa of Avila (not Cita?) allow me to feel the vast serenity of God; the issues of existence or non-existence, inner or outer, proof or disproof, become irrelevant, or as Shunryu Suzuki would say, when I sit with my legs crossed and my back straight, my hands folded in the mudra, then true and false don't matter. This is frail territory. St. George would not protect me from a speeding bullet. Nor would God. No one, no saint or angel, would even tell me it was coming. Whose counsel but my own could keep me from any occasion, including the line of fire?

VISION OF A SAINT

141,000 AMERICANS DEAD FROM COVID-19

The United States has more infections and deaths than any other country. California, especially LA, continues to light up and Newsom shuts down gyms, bars, restaurants, hair and nail salons, again; the first case infiltrates the Prison Village Nursing Home where St. Jin is staying; Carla and her brother, Hazlitt, supervise the removal of Jin's possessions from her Village apartment, some to consignment, some to charity thrifts, a few things to her new room, Carla keeps only a couple photo albums, but her older brother, Burt, in Columbus, goes berserk over a vague glass statue of the Virgin and Child that he wants sent to him, during the cleanup Carla discovers that the Jin has trashed every last vestige and image of Carla, Path calls the phone company to have his and Carla's land line shut down; St. Jin calls Hazlitt and wants to know when she's moving back to her apartment, her supervisor tells Hazlitt that they all think they're going back, then St. Jin's old supervisor leaves a message for Carla that says, You mother wants you to call her, Carla does not call. St. Jin turns 89.

The Rump praises the sentiments and heroism of the Confederacy, says the virus situation is improving and the disease will soon disappear and that wearing a face mask is not community protection but an individual choice; he refuses to rename ten army bases named after Confederate generals, he calls Black Lives Matter and Covid-19 reporting the tip of a conspiracy between leftist communists and the liberal media to ruin the economy and destroy America and American history, he sends Federal troops in unmarked vans to arrest protesters in Portland and Chicago, holding them in secret locations (it's legal; Obama instituted it in 2008 to corral terrorism). Now the California Latinx and American Indians want the statues of Junipero Serra removed from public spaces, the Society had one in front of the university library but moved it, somewhere, the LA Times publishes an article about John Muir's anti-Indian racism, though they offer no specifics, of course, if you were keeping up, Muir's racism is not news.

On the toilet Path finishes the 782 pp. of Elizabeth Bowen's *Collected Stories*, he picks up Proust's *La Recherche du Temps Perdu*, which he has started twice before and put down, in his office he's reading a page or two a day of Kafka's *The Trial*, on his reading chair, he finished Davies' *The Incas* (after finishing *The Maya* and *The Aztecs*) now zipping through Yuri Herrera's *The Immigration of Bodies*, its cover blurbs compare it to Shakespeare, Raymond Chandler, Bolaño, Cormac McCarthy, but they're all from bookstore owners, and really it's pretty much straight up hard boiled noir, the setting, in a huge Mexican city during an epidemic, two warring Italian families feud, a son, Romeo, and a young woman, Baby Girl, are found dead in the opposite family's basements, the epidemic and city are mostly irrelevant, the detective, the focalizer, is named The Redeemer, fast on its feet, its violence doesn't rise from the page or resonate, can noir resonate? Path's glancing at Volodine's *Minor Angels*, but maybe *Radiant Terminus* has killed Volodine for him, he reads Alberto Salvinio's *The Lives of the Gods*, and re-reads Nāgārjuna's *Mūlamadhyamakakārikā*, he re-read *The Diamond Sutra*, and just re-read Samuel W. Mitcham Jr.'s *Vicksburg*, a pro-confederate history of the siege; he put down Carlos Fuentes *Nietzsche on his Balcony*, sadistic porn bores him.

Last night Path had an ecstatic dream. He has returned from a long trip, returned from an unnamable place, possibly India, maybe from death, maybe from the Bardo, before bed he and Carla remembered Varanasi, a charred dead baby floating in the Ganges, but now, in the dream, he walks into a familiar but unspecifiable ranch. Jackie O is there, standing outside a row of stables. She is calm, and excited. He places a green, cloth headstall over her head and buckles the headstall on, hops on her bareback from the left and hugs her neck. Then he turns her and begins to walk her into the woods. Jackie O hates the woods, but now she is miraculously calm. Then he remembers from a dream the night before that he's left his wallet at the ranch. Last night he spent the whole dream looking for his wallet, but he knew when he put it down he'd never be able to find it, it was one of those dreams, where you leave your car or your suitcase somewhere and know, as soon as you walk away, that you'll be unable to get back to where you left it, but tonight he walks back with Jackie and when he dismounts a man he doesn't know hands him the wallet. Grateful, Path pockets the brown leather wallet, he doesn't even look inside, then he mounts Jackie O again; he remembers the days standing with her on the trail in the sun thinking *I am a man on the back of my horse, I am the luckiest man in the world*, now they walk, casually enjoying each other, and then, Path hears an orchestra in the distance. Jackie O hates sounds in the distance, particularly shouting men, but now he feels a peculiar singular confidence, in both man and horse, and they begin walking toward the orchestra, are they playing a waltz? maybe, and Jackie and Path come to a clearing with a bandstand where a red-coated military band plays to an open field, no audience at all, and Path pets Jackie's neck and says, Let's dance, and the two of them trot onto the field, Jackie dancing in her high Spanish step, they stop in front of the band and Path spins her, back feet planted, forelegs prancing, 360 degrees, first right, then left, then she plants her front feet, and her back legs spin, he side passes with her at a trot, left then right, then circles her and she side passes at a lope, all the training, all the tricks, he lifts and so does she, pawing the air facing the band, and as the band plays he spins her again and they lope into the woods; now she's sweating and he's sweating and their bodies are one, they hit an incline and Jackie breaks into her smooth gallop, he feels her with his thighs, her long, smooth stride, they are one body of happiness and confidence and Path is feeling so intensely overjoyed, nothing is like this, nothings as perfect, a man and horse together one, together running. He awakens bathed in gift. He has, in his life, spawned a thousand nightmares, and then, now, this; he yet viscerally feels the dream around him, he touches Carla, then gets up, puts on robe and goes to his reading chair and sits there surrounded by the feeling and his soul, oh god, his self, tries to hold onto it, if only it were real and yet it is, he's conscious and awake and it's still around him, he returns to bed, enraptured, he snuggles to Carla and lies on the edge of sleep in ecstasy, now full of the warmth of his lover's love; yet in the morning the ecstasy it is gone. But the dream, he remembers.

One day, a little while ago, Carla didn't walk with Path. She was meeting a friend, another poet, Karen K, for a secret walk along the Montana Avenue area of Santa Monica, which is re-opening for curb side pick-ups since being boarded up during the late May, Black Lives Matter riots. They can window shop in masks. Bandits have lost their identity. Sometimes Carla meets other women poets there, too. They call it bad girls walks.

Path drives his truck alone up the canyon, north to Santa Maria Trail. He drives slowly. Rabbits, squirrels, and flocks of quail crisscross the one lane road. In a clearing near the horse trail where he once rode Jackie O, five deer, two doe, two fawns, and a buck, graze. He stops to watch them. The deer lift their heads. A man and deer, watching each other. Now he drives to the top of the road and parks his truck. He carries a mask in the front pocket of his hoodie, but out here in the open, alone, he won't need to put it on. He begins his walk along the dirt road. The west Valley stretches out before him. A hawk dives. A scrub jay. Ground squirrels squirt back and forth. On the hills around him, Monkey Flowers, Mustard Plant, Arizona Blue Eyes, Jimson Weed, Tree Tobacco, Cow Parsnip, Snake Weed. In the sky, a giant winged bird glides above him, circles, and like the vulture on the trail, dives at him, wings spread, she screes, rises up. Her wings are pale, chest mottled. She's not a red tail or red shouldered hawk, but a huge falcon, a peregrine; she rises up, circles, and dives to him again, dropping a feather from her chest that floats to his feet. He stoops, picks up the feather, and puts it under the rim of his hat; he once collected feathers when he rode Jackie or Nikki on the trail; he'd dismount and put the feather in his straw cowboy hat, though now those days are gone; his hat is felt and the feathers acquired while walking. The bird perches atop a telephone pole. He stands beneath her watching. He names her, Xenobia. What more could anyone ask?

Down the road, a runner approaches, a young woman in a gray, sleeveless T, black tights, pink running shoes, her long hair is tied back. She stops. It's St. Veronica. She drops her hands to her sides. Well Path, she says, you should have expected me. I don't have the virus, she says, I'm not even material. She turns away, then turns to him again. She looks exactly like Carla now, pink lipstick, blonde hair layered over black. Would this make it easier? she says. No, says Path. Have you never been unfaithful? That's a long story, says Path, Not even in a dream? Veronica asks, This would be like that, like a dream, she reaches for him, but he's keeping his social distance, You move like an animal, she says, he says, We're all animals, and she says, I'm not, I'm a dream, like a dream, a dream of a dream, your dream, where do I come from? from you, where would I be without you, Path?

Is it time for me to step in? I say to Path, This is a story, Path, it's not your life, and Path says, I fail to comprehend the distinction. Who's writing whom here?

I'm stepping into you now Path, says Veronica. I'm in your dream now. There's nothing you can do.

IT BEGAN

AGAIN. ANNA CAME TO HIM, in her way, inexplicably and unexpectedly, in the morning or the night or day. Under the roar of the gunboats in the river, she slipped from her clothes, took him in her hands, her mouth, placed him inside her, on his back or hers, sitting on his lap, or lying feet to head, he licked her sex while she blew him, afterwards, a cigarette, a drink. She did not spend the night. He'd watch her dress. She moved so gently and assertively, slipping into her clothes as if it were one continual motion, without self-consciousness or care, but yet with meticulous precision. All her motion was that way. The way she held a glass, the way she smoked, exhaling sensuality and mystery, wordless suggestion floating into the air. Out the window, a crescent moon set. He could imagine it reflecting in the river between the gunboats. What did he offer her? What had he ever offered to anyone?

There was something there. They were drawn to each other in ways that couldn't be explained and he knew to not try to explain it, not to talk about the future, not to talk about the sex, no talk of love this time, not from him, for all he knew, for all he might want to know, she could stop showing up tomorrow, a letter would arrive, Henri is back, goodbye, until some other tomorrow. She read his thoughts. We are bonded in unrepeatable moments, she said. Such a time this is.

At the time it was evening. He should be in the club, he should be minding the casino. He sat up in the bed.

Your work, she said to him, but you are always there, even when you are here. This is there. Your people are loyal. Is there anything Shope cannot handle? Molly?

The war on our doorstep? he said.

You will handle that, M. Rick. Your people, they have lovers, too, you know.

That's not my business, said Rick. Things are going to change. There will be considerations, he said.

She pulled him back down to her. Do you ever consider moving? she asked.

Now?

You could. You could any time.

And be a coward or a traitor or both.

She touched his cheek, ran her fingers along his chest. Then when it's over. You could meet me in Paris.

I don't know anyone in Paris.

You'll know me.

And Henri?

You might get along with him. You'd be surprised.

Rick laughed. You'd cheat on me with him.

Anna laughed, too.

Let's not talk in bed, said Rick. Bed is for sleeping or sex.

She slid away from him then, stood, took possession of his shirt, a ritual, like donning his soul, laying a ghost over a ghost, her smallness a reminder of her possession. Now we can talk? she said.

Now we can drink, he said, and then I go back to work.

This isn't your work? She gazed out the window. The moonlight dimly poured upon her, turning the curves of her body into a shadow underneath his shirt. We loved each other, once, she said softly. Or I would not be here now.

He sat up again and got up from the bed. He put on his robe, not his clothes, and stood facing her, the tussled bed between them like a symbol or a scar.

She turned to him then. Now talk?

Whisky or sherry, said Rick.

I fell in love with you, said Anna.

He poured two whiskies. Brought hers, which she accepted, cupped in both hands, the glass, glistening, balanced between her fingertips. She smelled it. Her nose twitched over it, then she looked up and offered him a wry smile. He turned, placing the width of the bed between them again. She said, You don't serve this in the bar.

We aren't in the bar.

Exactly, said Anna. And you are yet in love with me. Men seldom know what they're really feeling.

Well maybe just as well. What good would that do, feeling that? he said to her. Where do we go from there?

New Orleans? she said. She sipped her whisky. Paris? New York? Rome?

Dear Anna, said Rick, the world doesn't open into possibilities. It closes in circumstance. Then a web of circumstance. You're married. A refugee.

What does that matter? You're here with me now, she said. That is the circumstance. And we would not have this, this quarrel, if we were not in love.

In an interval of silence, a shell whistled overhead. It didn't land with a crash or an explosion, but a resonant thud.

What if a child were underneath that, said Rick, or a mother.

Your friend, Pemberton, will have to close this place, M. Rick.

I have a cave, he said, like everyone else. People will still need whisky.

Everyone who is white? she said.

Anyone who still has money.

Some caves were better than others. He knew that she wasn't staying in a cave. He knew she went back to the hotel, back to Henri. There were things the Yankees bombed, things they didn't. Most of the shells from the river flew over the town. Some landed amidst the caves, but most didn't. They were lobbed to hit the rear of the works and trenches. So too, with the cannon fire on the front. The infantry took the brunt. The Yankees could blow up Vicksburg, but they weren't doing that kind of thing yet. They'd starve Vicksburg out, march into the city with much of it still intact. Who knew why? Grant had burned down Jackson. Maybe, in Jackson, he'd let the citizenry walk out first. There was no sense burning down homes, there were warehouses, storehouses, ammunitions to burn. Save the cotton, drink the booze. When Pemberton closed him, he'd take most of the booze with him.

Do you have escape plans? he asked her.

I think I'm going to get back in the bed and then won't have to talk. She drank some whisky again, moved her mouth around it.

You don't worry about money, he said.

No, she said, I don't have to.

So you could go anywhere.

In the world, she said. Not the moon. Or I would, so you would stare at me. Mark my phases.

Does Henri know about me?

Implicitly.

My phases? he said.

My phases, M. Rick. It's about me. There will be plenty to do here, before and after the Yankees.

You can't survive here. There's nothing here for you. You need to think about getting out, Rick said to her.

She sat on the bed and shook her hair onto her shoulders. She said, We're done talking, N'est ce pas?

MEDITATION AND DELUSION

MY LIFE PARTNER, GALA, HAS AN AGING MOTHER who hears voices, though she has done so all her life. She calls them "they," (though she doesn't know what non-binary means) and says they come from above. She alludes to levels and spheres, similar, I assume, to Edgar Cayce's, and simultaneously she believes in the conventional Christian vision of the world, a muscled and bearded great deity, directing his creation. Early on, before Gala's adolescence, her mother took her to psychic conventions where Gala's mother was repeatedly told that she was special, a psychic-mystic herself. Psychics, can tell the future, often as poorly as most of us recall the past.

Currently the mother receives messages from a prophet named Zacharia. I looked him up; he wasn't a prophet, but briefly a king of Judea, vaguely in the 800's BCE, and he died mysteriously or possibly when he launched an unsuccessful invasion into Egypt. Zacharia has predicted an immanent world apocalypse that she calls "The Happening." In fact, we might be on the cusp of one right now. A lot of scientists might agree. For sixty years or more she has written down what the voices have told her, mostly in doggerel, that goes on for thousands of pages; Gala is to transcribe it, I am to publish it, and when the apocalypse hits her youngest son will become a world leader and disseminate the Wry-Tings, issuing in a new age of universal love, at least among the few survivors.

At her worst, or best, the mother hallucinates graphically (like a shaman?): children run around raucously in her apartment, men, she calls them gremlins, float outside her second story windows, choirs of children sing nonsense songs, random, blond, blue-eyed babies appear on Gala's lap. On one frightening visit she related to us that she'd died; attendants dressed her in a beautiful gown, placed her in a coffin and put it on a train that went to heaven where passing through the lower spheres she waved at friends and relatives as she passed by, because she was moving on, upward, to the highest sphere. That episode got her hospitalized whereupon she clammed up mid-sentence and told the doctors that she'd never heard voices or seen anything unusual, i.e., she has some operable internal censor. This back and forth has gotten worse over time and is an ongoing story that needn't be followed further.

What I'd like to instigate here is an investigation of the difference, if there is any, between belief and delusion. In any number of religious ontologies, the world, as it is present to us every day, is not truly real. Asian perspectives, both Hindu and Buddhist, often argue for the insubstantial nature of phenomena, material reality, that is that everything is in constant flux, starting with the sub-atomic, so there is no substantial reality in our perceived reality, but it is sustained by some absolute, say God or Brahma for Advaita Vedanta Hinduism, Emptiness or Nothingness for Buddhists from Nāgārjuna to Zen. In the West it starts before Plato (Pythagoras, Heraclitus, Parminedes, the Atomists following Democritus and Lucretius and others) and doesn't end with Plato, abiding in various Idealist positions and still extant in Christian Science. For Plato what's holding this all together is the Good. Not that difficulty should be part of the criteria for finding the real, in whatever variety or unity we find in our phenomenal world, it is immersed with cruelty, tragedy, catastrophe, suffering, and death—certainly the world that Buddha saw—and it's hard to imagine it lying on the back or the belly, let alone the mind, of Goodness, unless those things are the product of an equal and powerful evil demiurge as in Manicheanism, the religion St. Augustine fled and fought. Of course, anything is possible and there are those, like the Stoics, who believed that we developed, or were given, minds to figure it out; a form of providence, or that it's a calculated, if not evil, trick played on us by God, as proposed and rejected by Descartes, though he's often seen as more rhetorical than cynical in proposing it. Yet belief, belief in *something*, seems difficult if not impossible to avoid.

The other evening, over wine, I proposed to my lover that the difference between delusion and belief was that belief arose from self-conscious choice. That didn't last long against analytic scrutiny, but little does, witness the poles between James' "Will to Believe" and Santayana's "Skepticism and Animal Faith," one of the problems being, as Peirce pointed out, that so much belief arises from unselfconscious, unquestioned roots like tradition and authority. But for the sake of discussion, let's briefly take my casual suggestion as a plausible episto-metaphor. In the case of hallucination, there is one obvious test of truth—corroboration. When my mother-in-law saw and heard little children running and singing in her apartment, my lover and I did not. But corroboration isn't always so simple.

Some years ago my younger brother (though not my youngest) experienced what came to be termed *alien abduction*. He didn't call it that, in fact, at the time he was unaware of the phenomenon. Though he did take a Polaroid photo of three equidistant puncture wounds—if connected they formed an equilateral triangle—below his right hip. Both Gala and I saw the actual punctures, as well. It looked like he'd been, well, plugged into something? This is not (yet) a discussion, per se, of alien abduction, so I'll not discuss his other symptoms here, at least not for now. Some weeks later, when I related what had happened to my brother to a close friend, he told me of another friend's wife who experienced the same things, almost precisely. My friend was the first person to use the term alien abduction in front of me. He suggested a book. I read it, skeptically, because the author seemed narcissistically invested in the importance of why the aliens contacted him to help save the world from immanent disaster (sound familiar?). As I did more research, I found that this, as well as fear and paranoia, were not uncommon responses to the abduction scenario. But more importantly, my research found a consistent reiteration of the initial (and sometimes repeated) experience: an inexplicable loss of time, nose bleeds, scars like my brother's, paranoia, false memories or "memory screens"—in my brother's case, when he tried to remember what might have happened to him, he instead remembered a book case that he, in fact, didn't own. Later my brother recalled lying on his back on a metal table and being shown apocalyptic imagery, as if they wanted to test his reaction to it, and, possibly, some sexual manipulation. Among men this implied sperm gathering, for women, insemination and later removal of a fetus in a second abduction.

Some abductees felt they were especially chosen to warn the world of impending environmental disaster if humans didn't clean up the earth (nuclear destruction and pandemics aside). My brother did not think this. Does a tagged zebra or wildebeest, he said, feel it was especially chosen, and wouldn't it be wiser to abduct someone important, like a movie star or a First

Lady? In any case, does this repeated corroboration of shared details confirm the experience as real, or at least, if believed, constitute legitimate belief?

In the end my brother just tried to forget about it. He didn't have a recurrence. Though even now, as I recall what happened, I realize he didn't know anything about alien abduction; real things happened to him that were the *same* things that happened to many other people, these things happened to him, to them, without them knowing what those things were. I am less arguing here for alien intervention than I'm doubting the argument for mass hysteria, that the victims of the abduction phenomenon were, as well, earlier victims of some other kind of abuse and living in the denial of that resulted in the arousal of alien abuse; there's still the problem of previously uncommunicated corroborated details, a kind of social collective unconscious hysteria.

I was sexually abused by the same man as my brother, and though I was honest with myself and others that I'd had sex with him for six years, ages 13 to 19, I didn't come to terms with the fact that it was painful sexual, psychological, and sadistic abuse until the period of 45-50 years old. Nor was I later abducted by aliens, though there were nights during my brother's breakdown, when he moved in with us for fifteen months, when we worried about the possibility of them coming for him again, or my family. It felt that real.

Thirty years ago, I had a college student, a Catholic girl, who, upon realizing that she had been sexually abused by her uncle, developed a stigmata. The psychological symptoms of abuse aside, and I have many of them, as well as my research on sexual abuse, has made it clear to me that these symptoms are shared by many abuse victims, physical, behavioral, and deep psychological repercussions, whether explained by Freudian, Jungian, or Bardo-like analysis, i.e. that our culture creates the form of our illusions, these symptoms themselves are quite real. Though my brother can decide to be agnostic about his abduction, he cannot be agnostic about his hip wound and nose bleeds. If something takes hold of me with profound and visceral subtilty, and I feel and think a calm and transcendental insight that the world, despite its cruelty and suffering, sickness, old age, horrible death, that there is a One-ness to this world, whether it comes to me from within or without, by training or accident, is it as real as the scar on my brother's hip? Does it arise from context like the spirituality of a Catholic ritual or a Baptist ecstasy?

SHERMAN

IT WASN'T LIKE NEW ORLEANS where bars and saloons stayed constantly open. Vicksburg shut down at night and so did Rick's. If you wanted to keep drinking you could take a bottle with you. Rick noticed one night that Shope stayed on after closing and went back down to the bar to meet him. He poured whisky for them at the piano.

You could just come get me, he said to Shope.

I have power in this spot, said Shope, and I'm going to need it.

You have some truth to tell me, Rick said.

Shope closed the keyboard cover, sipped his whisky and put it down on top the cover. You're sleeping with Anna again, he said.

You don't approve.

Her husband is a good man, Rick.

He's French, said Rick. It's not the same for them

She's French. He's Algerian. I've lived in Paris. You're not French.

Rick threw back his shot. He said, I'm not in love with her anymore.

He's working with the Blacks.

I know. Getting them paid.

Maybe I should be out there with him, Shope said.

Grant's on his way, Shope. There won't be slavery for much longer. Rick filled their glasses.

The North is tired. Maybe Lee wins in Pennsylvania. The French step in. Lincoln loses the election, said Shope.

What would you do, Shope? Teach fencing?

Reading and writing? Shope said.

That could get you hung, said Rick. Davis told Pem to fortify Vicksburg.

Johnston told him to attack Grant. He's compromising. Building redans here, advancing to Champion Hill. He's smart enough to beat Grant, but he's outmanned and outgunned. He can't trust his best general.

Loring is a bastard, said Shope. He backbites.

Pem knows that, said Rick. That stockade construction is why your friend Henri Coutre is still alive. But even if Jack beats him on the hill, Grant will just regroup and attack again.

You know about the caves, said Shope.

When Grant gets here, I'll be living in one, Rick said. Pem will have to shut me down. You want to join me?

I think you should stop sleeping with Anna Breton, my friend.

It takes two, said Rick.

That's right, said Shope, she can't do it by herself.

Champion Hill was a hard-fought Yankee victory. Pemberton might have won it, but insubordination and miscommunication doomed him. He retreated and entrenched again east of the Black River Railroad Bridge, but when the Yankees came on in force, the Confederates broke and ran. They were routed in thirty minutes. Sherman swept north and took Hanes Bluff, then dug in, again, above the Bayou. Pemberton retreated to Vicksburg and entrenched, but in a few days Grant had him surrounded. Grant met with his generals and on the next afternoon, May 19, launched his attack on the Stockade Redans on all fronts. But the rebels who ran away on the Black River, now under Jack Pemberton's fiery urging, this time turned and fought. Grant was repulsed on all fronts. By the way, that's where I died. With hundreds of canons and mortars, the Yankees began to pound the city. The citizens of Vicksburg began moving their belongings to the hill caves between the city and the trenches. On May 22, Grant attacked again, this time on both flanks, but after horrific fighting, Pemberton held again. Rick sent him a bottle of champagne and he and Shope began packing up in the quiet, empty casino and the booming air.

His saloon was on the river in western Vicksburg and the navy's shells flew over his roof. From the other direction, the ground artillery from Grant's lines sometimes hit the city, but didn't reach him. He was waiting for Pem to show up and officially shut him down, but the general who showed up at his door wasn't a Confederate. It was William Tecumseh Sherman.

A PROFOUND VISIT

RECENTLY, JUST BEFORE THE PANDEMIC HIT, Gala and I were visited by an ex-student, Rosiland, who we met in our first year, and her first year, at our university in1986, now thirty-four years ago. Over that time we had stayed in touch, through her first marriage and the raising of two sons, and after her divorce. Her father was from Iran and her mother from Peru. Farsi and Spanish were her first languages. Her first husband was Argentinian. Though not prolific, she is a writer of complexity and imagination. She stayed in touch with another person from the U, a Jesuit theologian, Father R. I don't know too many people who I'd describe as a mystic, but by demeanor, joy, outlook, and perseverance, I'd say that Rosiland is. About five years ago she met and married a prolific and bright journalist, Anthony V, some twenty years her senior, at 74 years old now. He's an Italian from Brooklyn. The two of them are truly in love, as are Gala and I.

There is much to say about this visit, though it was brief, but significant to this essay; as Rosiland drove the four of us to a reading I was giving in Beverly Hills, from the front seat, their backs to us, they divulged that they had reconverted to Catholicism and talked of the pleasure that they now took in the rituals of it.

Anthony, who had lived both on the edge of fame and the fringe of culture, had just been through two threatening medical issues, a stroke and severe prostate cancer. He wasn't specific about either, but expressed that both were ongoing. In the car he spoke of the joy he felt when, after decades of alienation from Catholicism, he went to confession and took Communion. He'd left Catholicism at age ten when he went homeless to escape his psychotic and alcoholic mother. Rosiland, I think, was always spiritually devout, beyond doctrine, and addressed this renewal of faith as a renewal of commitment, not to the facts or beliefs that the vision offered, but to the metaphors, sorrow and expiation, the truth of the metaphors. Later that night, as the four of us sat drinking, getting drunk in fact, under a placard of the First Soviet International that I'd found in a cul de sac in Prague, Anthony V pointed to it and said, "See, that's the same thing." "The dream," I said. Yes, whatever the horrors of the Inquisition, be it Catholic or Communist, there is yet the dream, of heaven, or if not heaven, the *desire* for a knowable ontology, for Plato's *Good*, be it everywhere or nowhere, and evil is its absence.

On the verge of ending this essay here, let's return to its beginning and the image of plucking our memories, whether they are ours or not, from the electronic air around us, not gifts of mind, nor the mind of God, or Gods, but the coming together of the pluralisms lying on the back of Nothingness. I think someone like Rosiland would plop that down next to her Catholicism and say, "Some things just are." Or philosopher poets like Calvino or Bachelard to say it's all noumena and metaphor , that's all we got, metaphors all the way down, Gass would say it, too, the Post-modern era is an era of sophism, an inclination that's at least 2,500 years old, when societies become sophisticated, when science reaches out to touch nothingness, when cultures turn from democracy to tyranny because of the fear that there is only the self and the self is not enough; send your prayers into space, where there is no oxygen to breathe, that's where the Gods reside, the difference between us and them, they need neither food nor air, what is the image there? the likeness? for a mere thirty-three years out of infinity Jesus had to eat and breathe, and maybe bleed; what, at our core, drives us to desire more than mortality?

If every particle and every star is composed of a plurality of desires to perpetuate itself as long as possible against its inevitable non-existence, well, we can't ask why, *why* is the endless cavern that leads to nihilism, yet here we are, here I am, fact without purpose?

THE WRONG PATH?

BOTH PATH AND CARLA WERE PREVIOUSLY MARRIED. As for Carla's first marriage, Path already wrote a book about Carla's life before Path appeared on the scene in Salt Lake City, he'd included more than forty pages about his life before he met her, but cut them; the book was about Carla, not him, so we began this section thinking we'd write about Path's first marriage, but Path doesn't want to go there; oddly he was spurred by a photo that his ex, Kara P, placed on Facebook to celebrate her thirtieth wedding anniversary to the historian, Donald, the two of them holding hands at arm's length, grinning wildly, facing the camera and spreading out their other arms, fingers splade, joyous; if you recall, Path drove his truck to San Luis Obispo to see Kara P's one-woman photography exhibit, anyway, Path's not going to let me narrate his first marriage, doesn't want to explain that romance, the fights, the infidelity, the wedding, that he now remembers he wrote about near the end of his second Loop novel; right now, he wishes me to notice that Camus' *The Plague*, has first person, retrospective, omniscience-capable narrator who doesn't participate in the story, ironically implying that he survived the Plague, and implicating the survival of the story's main character, Dr. Rieux, as well; Path just finished reading a passage where the doctor and his idiosyncratic friend, Arnoux, discuss death, the plague, and God, in whom the doctor, living on the edge of witnessing hundreds of painful deaths, does not believe; on the throne, Path has fallen into *Swann's Way* successfully for the first time; Proust is self-conscious and smart, his images fly; Carla read Volodine's *Bardo or not Bardo* and found it repetitious and tedious, she put down *In the Time of the Blue Ball*, she thinks Volodine is a failed poet, narcissistic and sophomoric, a careless and vague world builder, not one interesting woman character, all true, admits Path, though sometimes he's imaginative; on their walks they've seen a lot of rabbits, many of them babies, blue birds, finches, woodpeckers, scrub jays, vultures, and large hawks, red shouldered and red tailed, a huge peregrine falcon high above them on a wire, it plucks a feather from its chest and drops it, it floats to the road and lands at Path's feet, Carla picks it up and says, put it in your hat, and he does, it's the most beautiful one, she says; at the Society, the U has cut back their health benefits and ended contributing to their retirement; as they prepare for their first semester of teaching online, they've yet to receive contracts, Carla is convinced it means there will be cuts in pay, as well, we must unite in facing the lethal virus and pitch in, the Provost declares; as of August 9, 2020, 161,000 Americans have died, yet Rump, who denied that the disease is serious, wants to postpone the presidential election in November because of it; here, in California, the landscapes ignites and a month later half of California is on fire.

THE FLIPSIDE OF DESIRE

IS FEAR. IF ONE IS THERE, THE OTHER IS ITS SHADOW. I hesitate there because I hesitate before dualisms, though it seems to be one of the fundamental ways we humans feel impelled to categorize our world: life—death, good—evil, body—soul. Derrida, not unlike Nāgārjuna, liked to flip them back and forth until they fell apart leaving, well, nothing, though the method is Hegelian, as well (the master—slave dialectic is a classic example), though the thesis—antithesis—synthesis movement is triadic—we can go back to Saṅkara's replacing Nágárjuna's Nothingness with Brahma, the Absolute—C.S. Peirce agreed, the fundamental principles were not dualistic, but triadic, thus his phenomenological categories: Firstness, Secondness, Thirdness; his semiotics: sign—object—interpretant, agreeing with Hegel's rejection of Kant's failure to resolve dualistic dilemmas, his notorious unresolvable antinomies, such as free will vs. determinism, God vs. no God, with phenomena—noumena at the top, that notorious noumena, that unknowable and thus only posited, reality, upon which knowable phenomena rests (and the antinomies are among the problems of phenomena); Kant, in a magnificent attempt to pull it all together, blew everything up, and Hegel, trying desperately to put it all back together again, ended it, at least in Europe, until the second incarnation of Wittgenstein, where we circle back to language, language games, and metaphor; across the Channel, Ayer, Austin, Russell and the early Whitehead, and then Einstein; across the Atlantic Ocean, William James and the ignored Charles Sanders Peirce, but I've traveled this digression to find out, once again, where I am, here contemplating Peirce's cosmic reckoning, the triad of cosmic forces: Love—Necessity—Chaos.

Because I can't live in metaphor (can I?) I must live in reality. This impossible reality.

Nonetheless, much of the world we live in seems quite predictable, in fact, if we fall too far in that direction we could, or even must, conclude that if we knew enough, it would all be predictable. This is Old Hat Determinism, a world of a billion-billion-trillion efficient, univocal causes. William James went so far as to admit that if he accepted his radical empiricism, he must accept determinism. But he could not accept it morally and, later in life, subjectively, even, by the time of *Varieties*, his last lectures before his death, willing (pun intended) to accept subjective experience as true. Earlier in this essay I spent some time discussing, or at least trying to investigate, the difference between individual and corroborated hallucinations. Are there hard realities and soft ones?

Let's argue, as George Herbert Mead did, that the human self is an emergent characteristic, arising from the combination of genetic factors and the capacity of the human brain for language, and the social, i.e. societal contexts that allow us to develop, emerge, as human selves: play, games, dressing, grooming (the person in the mirror); we begin to learn roles in familiar, intra-family and inter-family social interactions, and build a concept of self, based on objectifying and internalizing the person who fills those relationships. Mead calls that part of the psychic self the *Me*, borrowing the concept from William James and, as well, borrows the accompanying concept, the *I*, the spontaneous core in the constant present, the present stream of conscious life. For James, the *I* is not ontological, it isn't a thing or an object, but a node in the constantly thinking stream of thought, the subject to which all else, including the *Me*, is object. Basically, Mead would agree in principle, though his *Me* is a more sociological, and he would say social-psychologically constructed concept. Both would deny this Self ontological, i.e., pre-empirical, status, if we're looking for a more elemental thingness, or essence, something like the Cartesian mind or soul. As Sartre says, existence before essence. Yet how permanent or immutable must something be to be ontologically essential? Is not the moment essential? For Parmenides, all change is inessential. For Heraclitus, and Gautama Buddha, there is only change.

I'm writing now amidst one of the greatest disasters in world history. A plague, a virus, is sweeping the planet. Hundreds of thousands are dying. No medicine mitigates it or fights it, there is no cure, a potential vaccine is at least eighteen months away. What is essential? What is inessential. All is vital now.

Now, all seems trivial.

From my depleted book shelves (last summer I threw away hundreds of books—no one anywhere wanted them) I picked up Kafka's *The Trial*, read the last page where K, the main character, is executed at knifepoint. I now read the novel when I'm in my office, after I write, at about two pages a sitting. I ordered Camus' *The Plague* online and did an unusual thing, I read it; I usually take months to read a book, but I read *The Plague* in a week. It's a chilling and remarkable novel. I woke up at 5 a.m. this morning and finished it. Written between 1941 and 1947, it's often read as an allegory of the German occupation of France (Camus, an Algerian, fought for the French resistance). Hannah Arendt and Simone de Beauvoir both thought that Camus avoided the politics, the evil of the Nazis, by using the plague as allegory. But politics narrows the focus of *The Plague* too constrictively. The story is about an absurd threat and the absurd fight against it. Camus did not believe in heroism, nor evil. The plague just is, and it will come again. It has.

I suppose I have, day and night, over-contemplated death, but, of course, from the outside, not from within, where it shall be experienced, and even so, it will be dying that I see, not death itself. With death all around, let's turn again. What is the Self? What is it that so inimically does not want to die. That's what originally inspired this essay, the examination of all the world's desire to persist, from the smallest of things, to the giant, ancient oak outside my office, to me, to the people in the flowing traffic outside my office, I could go on and on, like Whitman; what is the nature of desire? Freud said Death. The nature of desire is to seek the cessation of desire. That's why we are all mad. If I were a poet, I'd stop there and find an image on the brink of madness.

> Like a meteor, like darkness
>   as a flickering lamp
> An illusion like hoarfrost or a bubble,
> Like clouds, a flash of lightning or a
>   dream:
> So is all conditioned existence to be seen.
> —*The Diamond Sutra*

Yet we want it so much. Every cell, every atom. Every lightning flash. Desires to persist.

SHERMAN

WAS NOT IN UNIFORM, but wore a gray overcoat over dark pants, dusty riding boots; his beard, graying and spotty, looked several days old. Hatless, his hair, mottled as well, was close cropped. He handed Molly his pistol when she greeted him at the door. After hours, she said. He said, I understand, and nodded toward Rick. The bombardment had suddenly stopped. Shope went to the piano and tinkled lightly as Rick faced the doorway.

I'm alone, Sherman said to him.

Fine line between brave and crazy, said Rick.

No line at all, said Sherman. May I come in?

Rick motioned to the closest table with his hand. Rye, I assume, he said.

To be courteous, Sherman said. He came forward, almost light-footed and sat down as Rick did.

Molly brought two glasses and the bottle. Old friend? she said.

Of mine, said Shope. He and Sherman looked at each other briefly

He knows everybody, said Rick.

He taught me how to draw, the general said.

Sherman sipped his whisky, as did Rick. The general took a deep breath through his nose. He seemed, for a moment, to almost relax. Smoke and booze, he said. Your place smells like a bar. A good smell. I miss it.

Molly by now had recognized that this was an unusual event. You drinking, Shope? said Molly. I am. She walked to the piano and poured for herself and Shope.

Am I under arrest? said Rick. He chuckled and Sherman did, too.

Be patient, said Sherman. And they both laughed again.

Do we need a secret meeting?

This is secret enough, the general said. We can't break through. Vicksburg is impregnable. That's no secret.

So a siege, Rick said.

It's not how I like to fight. This city voted against secession. Now it's the key in the door of war. There are brothers, cousins, staring at each other across the lines.

You've got Johnston behind you, Rick said. He could be at your back.

Johnston is a coward. Like McClelland.

Pemberton is no coward, said Rick

Pemberton is no coward, Sherman said.

Have you offered civilian evacuation?

No takers. The sky will be on fire. Vicksburg will starve.

Rick put down his glass. He wished he had one of Anna's cigarettes so he could put up a wall of smoke. What do you want from me? he said.

My sister lives here, said Sherman. On upper Clay.

You want to get her out.

That's right.

What makes you think I can do it?

You're the only one who can do it. We have relations in Cairo.

Illinois, said Rick. Little Egypt.

Across the river from Kentucky, said Sherman. You get bourbon from Kentucky.

It's expensive, said Rick. Takes longer to age. It has to be shipped.

Through both Union and Confederate lines, Sherman said. But you do it.

Rick looked at Molly and pointed to the bar. She put down her glass and went behind the bar, came out with a fifth of bourbon, walking it to Rick who placed it in front of Sherman. Sherman picked up the bottle and nodded once to each of his audience. You can take it with you, Rick said. Husband? he asked. Kids?

They're estranged. No kids. Katrina Atterlee. I don't want her in a cave.

With the rest of us, Rick said. Why don't you just take her?

Because it's impossible. I don't want her in a cave.

Pemberton?

We're not really on speaking terms. He pulled the cork on the bourbon, offered it to Rick. It's only polite, he said.

It's good, too, said Rick.

We know everything about you, said Sherman.

John Brown?

Yes. The navy won't target this structure.

They target?

Sherman smirked. After a pause he said, She'll need a letter from Pemberton, to clear Mississippi and Arkansas, my signature will clear Tennessee and Kentucky because we technically occupy them.

I'll need a favor, too, Rick said. A personal one. Breton and Coutre are here.

We know that, too.

Can they travel with your sister?

I'm not fighting to free the slaves, Sherman said.

I'm not fighting anybody, Rick said. It's personal.

Sherman downed his drink. They sat quietly. All right, he said. It's not a great distance, but it's a lot of jurisdiction hopping. I can do the paperwork, but we'll need a guide. A civilian.

I can do that, said Shope.

I know you. I can trust you, Sherman said. Cairo is across the Ohio and Mississippi junction. You'll need horses, not a carriage.

I know how to do this, Shope said.

It has to happen fast, said the general. Now. During this lull, while the siege settles in. You'll have the papers tomorrow. He stood. He nodded to Shope, then Molly. Then, finally, to Rick. Thank you, he said. Good luck. He took the bourbon, fetched his pistol and left, alone, on horseback.

Rick turned to Molly. Tell Mrs. Atterlee tonight, he said to her. She'll have to travel light. One soft pack. Day after tomorrow, at dawn. Daylight. No sneaking. Then tell Pem. Tell him why. He lives across from the convent.

I know the house, said Molly. The nuns are turning the convent into a hospital.

Well, said Rick, they're nuns. Take the small carriage.

For a man on the outside, you sure end up in the middle a lot, Shope said.

You're the one in the middle, Rick said.

Anna and Henri? Molly said.

Tell them tonight, Rick said to Molly. They're downtown at the hotel. I can meet with them in the morning after I'm done with Pemberton tonight.

Tonight? said Molly.

Yes.

Will he come with me?

He has a wife, Rick said. And you have to stop at the hotel.

You're taking a lot for granted, Shope said to Rick.

Nobody has a choice here, said Rick. Really. Except you.

Shope held his right hand over the piano keyboard. He held it there, suspended. It was a gesture Rick knew well. He could touch the keys or not. An allusion to Schopenhauer the philosopher, and Chopin, too. Shope had known them both. He could touch the keys or not. Was that choice free or ultimately determined?

Pemberton did arrive that night in full regalia. You almost missed me, he said to Rick. I'm going to the front tomorrow.

Your wife has support? A cave?

She has a staff, said Pem. A paid staff. I think our house is safe. Given what we've seen of the shell trajectory. As safe as a cave.

You'll let me know if she needs me.

Pemberton nodded. So you met William Tecumseh.

Now Rick nodded.

Anybody can get out of here, Rick. Soldier or civilian. All they have to do is leave.

And go where? The plantations are pummeled, sacked.

Pemberton rubbed his forehead with his thumb and forefinger. He brought down his hand and put it on the table. Not across the river. Not from here. Illinois, I assume.

Cairo.

Pemberton pointed to the rye. Rick handed him the bottle. Offered a cigar. Pemberton turned down the cigar but swigged the rye from the bottle.

In France they roll their own tobacco in paper. Cigarettes, Rick said.

I know about them. The plantation owners imported it with their wine, said Pem.

At least they used to.

Things can get in and out of here, Pemberton said. If anybody knows that, you do. Grant has us surrounded, but he's not everywhere.

Food, Rick said.

Food will be a problem. He paused. I know about Coutre. And Breton. I'm all right with it. But when things get worse, I'd prefer to have them out of here. Atterlee, too. I'm not inhumane.

Maybe too humane.

If I were humane I'd surrender now.

You'd never be forgiven.

Eventually, I won't be anyways. But for now they can't break through. We can hold out a long time. With bayonets, if it comes to that.

Until we starve, said Rick.

Until we starve. Johnston must attack. I telegraph him every day.

Sherman is confident he won't.

Pem took another long swig. Guess you two had a pretty good talk.

If Lee wins in Pennsylvania, Grant will have to pull back. That will sink Lincoln, said Rick.

If we can hold out that long, Pemberton said. Are you getting out too? You'll have to shut down regardless.

As you say, there's nowhere to go. I can sell booze from a cave.

If anyone has money. Molly?

Has family here, Rick said.

And Shope?

Shope will take them to Cairo.

He might never get back in, said Pem.

One man on a horse. Sherman did it, said Rick.

Pemberton got up, as did Rick. They shook hands.

Till the end, Pem said. You'll have the documents in the morning.

Sherman's and Pemberton's documents arrived the next day, just before Anna. She wore a hat today, brown with a short brim rolled on both sides, a thick, black velvet hat band with a single purple feather, a double-breasted coat that reached to her ankles. She held her purse upright on the table.

No Henri? said Rick.

What if I don't want to go? she said.

Does he want to?

In fact, said Anna, he does.

This would have to end anyways, Rick said to her, regardless. We'll be under siege. Close quarters. People are already talking. He didn't, for a fact, know that they were. But they would be, soon enough. When they win, the Federals won't want you here either. They've got their own plans. You'd just be in the way.

We've always been in the way. We live in the way.

You said 'we,' it's good to hear.

But Henri could go without me.

Do you have a cave picked out?

Your cave, my dear Rick? She removed her gloves and took her rolled cigarettes from her purse, offered him one.

Okay, said Rick, one, for old time's sake.

She lit for him, then for herself. They smoked, quietly. He watched her, gorgeous in smoke. When they finished he said, This is impossible.

I've lived for the impossible, Anna said. Champagne?

Rick shook his head. You need a city. You would suffocate here, then what? You need Henri, not me. I have no ideals.

When it's over we could move back to New Orleans, said Anna.

We'll always have New Orleans, but it's the past. And you always get what you want, Rick said to her. But I'm not what you want.

And you always think you know, but you don't always know.

The perfect mismatch, he said. I'll pour you a sherry, then you have to leave.

He retrieved two sherry glasses from the bar, filled them. He toasted her, touching the back of his fingers to hers.

You'll have to do it on horseback, he said. I'll have the horses. One soft bag. In the morning, Shope will get Mrs. Atterlee then pick you up at the hotel.

She drank the sherry in a few quick sips, then put out her hand. He kissed it. She was a proud woman. She'd make this her own decision. She said, Monsieur Rick. Au revoir.

It's a big cave, Rick said to Shope, but I don't know if I can get the piano down there.

The sun was coming up and pushed a red glare through the windows of the casino.

Pem's shutting you down? Shope said.

I should be moved by the time you're back, said Rick.

This time Shope fetched the sherry. It's summer light, he said, we could make it by evening. Still, I'm bringing blankets.

Make sure everyone has water. I've packed eggs and bread. And a canteen of whisky for you.

Shope offered him a tight smile. He rubbed his forehead. He said, You're doing the right thing. For Breton, too. Why don't you just come along?

And say good-bye in Cairo in front of Coutre?

No, for good, said Shope. You could make a go of it up there.

Rick let Shope pour. This is simpler, he said.

Shope said, What I'd give for simple.

The horses should be ready. I tacked them in the stable, said Rick. Take Brownie, she's small but smart and fearless.

And unobtrusive, said Shope. Rick didn't have to spell it out for him, Coutre was dark, too. Documentation aside, let the casual observer assume that he and Shope were owned by the women.

Rick just nodded. They'd known each other for some time now, travelled together. They can keep the horses, he said. You have a gun?

Yes, said Shope. I'll conceal it. He drank. Poured more and threw it back, sighing a deep, deep sigh, deeper than the pre-dawn dark. I'm going over, Rick, he said. I'm not coming back.

Now Rick paused. He knew this was a possibility, that's why he asked Shope to do it. But he'd hoped, he'd hoped his friend would return. Unless you're wearing blue? he said.

Blacks aren't treated much better over there, Shope said. But, well, I'll fight if they let me.

You have papers, Rick said. Find Sherman. He took Shope by the arm. They walked to the stable where they silently loaded the horses. They hugged.

Leg up? Rick said.

Sure.

Rick cupped his hands. Shope stepped into them and Rick hoisted him into the saddle, then retrieved the other three horses on lead lines and handed them to Shope. The naval bombardment from the river had begun. And now, to the north and east, Federal ground artillery poured missiles into the sky, every minute, a roar, a screaming shell, a thud or explosion or both. The ground shook. Rick held Shope's shin. They looked each other in the eyes. Rick took Shope's left hand in his right. Squeezed it. Well Shope, Rick said, you never know. You never know. Shope prodded his brown mare and moved out of the stable. Rick watched. He'd be alone now. He watched Shope's back as he rode out, his best friend leaving to take the woman he loved north, under the fiery shrapnel, beneath the screaming rainbow of hell.

LAST NEXILE

LABOR DAY: 200,000 DEAD (650,000 BY NEXT MEMORIAL DAY)

He couldn't have predicted it would end so quickly. The Persian business man showed up with his eight-year-old daughter, Sky. Path fetched Nikki from her corral. The little girl did cart wheels. Path saddled Nikki, let the girl mount, and led them to the riding ring. On tether, Nikki walked gently, then trotted. He could feel her accepting the girl. She liked her, and the girl knew how to ride. He released the lead line and Nikki loped out gently. The father, Sayeed, turned to him. I want the horse, he said. Path said, Are you sure? The father picked up his cell phone and watched his daughter on the gorgeous golden horse with a black mane and tail. In ten minutes, a pick-up with a horse trailer arrived. The driver emerged from the cab with an envelope that he gave to Path. A cashier's check. Can we have the saddle? Sayeed said. Path just nodded. What use would he have for a saddle? Sky dismounted and Path helped the driver load Nikki into the trailer. He reached into his pocket and gave her the last of his carrots that she mouthed ravenously. Good-bye Nikki, he said. Sayeed shook his hand he and his daughter got in their Lexus and followed the trailer out of the ranch. Path watched till they were gone, then removed his black, straw hat. He took all of the feathers from the band and tossed them to the wind. But they didn't sail off. He'd pictured them scattering in the air, a symbolic, feathery farewell. But instead they fell in a clump on the dirt. Path dropped to his knees in front of the meaningless pile, put his hands over his eyes, and wept.

Years passed. Maybe decades. Friends fell away. His brothers and sisters fell ill, got better, or died. The sea rose. Island nations flooded. The plague took another half-million American lives, around the world, millions more.

Ended. Returned. Mobs attacked, entered, and sacked governments. Tyrants arose. Tyrants fell. Rockets carried the rich to Mars. But when it came to the end, it felt like it happened in a blink. It seemed like only yesterday when he returned home red-eyed to find Carla packing. She looks up. She's gone? she says. Path nods. Pretty unceremonious, Carla says. What's left, he says, nothing's left. You're packing. Are you going to see your mother? She's dead to me, Carla says, I'm never going to see her again. I know this is bad timing, but I'm leaving. Your mother? My family, everything. Me? he says. You. I'm suffocating, Path. I'm leaving. We can work it out later. We can't talk now? he asks. She shuts her bag, lifts it, and rolls it to the door, then lugs it out and down the steps to her car. He knows she doesn't want help, but he follows her. She puts the luggage in the trunk and turns to him. We've been talking for years, she says to him. He tries to look her in the eyes. A red shouldered hawk lands on a wire above them. She says, You've been crying. You owe me nothing, he says to her. Don't forget your masks. I have them, she says. That's when they hear the first fire engine. They pause, listening. Another engine screams up the road. Then another. More engines, and now helicopters. In minutes, ten more firetrucks blaze past their house. Her chest heaves. She turns away. A black cloud rises from down the road. On the hill across the way, smoke and ash fill the air. The canyon is on fire.

www.ingramcontent.com/pod-product-compliance
Lightning Source LLC
Chambersburg PA
CBHW021138190726
48288CB00008B/2711